1 - 2

The Rainbow Recipe

PSYCHIC SOLUTIONS MYSTERY #4

PATRICIA RICE

One: Pris

HALLOWEEN PARTY

AFTERTHOUGHT, SOUTH CAROLINA

"BEAUTIFUL PEOPLE ARE BRAINLESS." PRISCILLA MALCOLM BROADHURST ADDED THE last smear of crab and caviar to a potato crisp and garnished the lot with dill. *"Brainless people have no minds to block."*

Repeating that mental refrain, she checked her blurry reflection in the stainless steel refrigerator door to make certain no strands of wiry hair escaped its thick layer of gel. No one could call *her* beautiful. But in honor of the occasion, she'd aimed for *colorful* and added orange dye to the natural white streaks.

Normally, she enjoyed Halloween. Normally, she would be thrilled to cater to such a prestigious crowd. Normally, she wasn't down three staff members with flu and could stay in the kitchen, where she belonged.

She needed a kitchen of her own. This catering business was growing old.

Counting the dollars that tonight would add to her savings account, she heaved the heavy tray to her shoulder and practiced mental blocking. "Hate this, hate it, hate it," she chanted under her breath as she shoved through the door from the ginormous company kitchen into the crowded lobby of Larraine Fashions.

The noise of a few hundred guests high on champagne and excitement inundated her senses. Mechanical witches cackled. Paper ghosts flashed before her

1

eyes. How the Samhain had the nerds created those? Shouldn't men with PhDs and engineering degrees have better things to do?

More earth-bound creatures in creative costumes milled and laughed and snatched glasses and appetizers from passing trays. The party was just warming up.

Larraine Ward, mayoral candidate and owner of this high-end clothing company, had invited every voter in Afterthought, South Carolina to her Halloween fundraiser, plus out-of-town sponsors and media.

The potential for impressing clients who could finally take Pris's catering business to the next level didn't unnerve her as much as the rising tensions and mental vibrations of a few hundred people jammed all in one place.

Wearing spectacles and a floppy witch's black hat, her prescient Aunt Mavis lurked outside the door. "Block them, child," she ordered. "You know most of the braying asses, and there's trouble afoot tonight. You'll need your wits about you."

Pris had lived in Afterthought all her life, so yeah, she knew how to mentally block the braying asses. But so many people at once, combined with the unfamiliar fancy-schmancy gathering over by Larraine's platform. . . She really didn't need to know about trouble afoot. "Halloween brings the freak out. Should I avoid the Barbie dolls occupying center front?"

Most of the local attendees were sporting their favorite homemade costumes. Pris and her staff wore formal black and white. The Beautiful People by the podium flaunted clothing so elegant that they might as well be costumes in this crowd of farmers and small merchants.

"They're my competition," Mavis replied grimly. "If they represent the changes Larraine means to introduce to town, I may vote for Hank."

Mavis adored Larraine and had encouraged the flamboyant designer to run for office. If her aunt was resisting change—her psychic vibrations must be almost as painful as Pris's mental terror. And it wasn't officially Halloween yet.

Cousin Evie arrived in time to catch the discouraging words. "La Bella Gente is not your competition, Mom. You sell herbal remedies. They sell olive oil lotion and soap. A high end boutique like theirs will draw shoppers from the city. They're good for business."

Financial advice from an orange-haired genie in purple diaphanous drapery was a little hard to swallow, but Pris added her reassurances. "I'll wager the Beautiful People don't own a single crystal ball or tarot deck. You're safe, Aunt Mavis. And if I'm to stay employed, I should probably take this tray over to them."

Jaw clamped hard, mentally blocking braying asses as instructed, Pris wove through the costumed crowd carrying her tray of gourmet appetizers, and focusing on Larraine's VIPs. The men ranged in age and height, but they were all dark-haired and wearing expensive suits. The younger two had the rugged, square-jawed facial structure and poise of male models.

Oddly, for a boutique selling lotions, only one woman accompanied them. Tall, Hollywood-thin, the long-haired blonde in designer black wearing a fortune in ancient-looking gold around her neck appeared to be suffering from dyspepsia. Or maybe she was just drunk, since she kept clutching the arm of a shorter, older man. She occasionally smiled tightly at her entourage but didn't appear to be enjoying herself. One of the men had apparently snatched a bowl of almonds from the buffet to offer her. If that was her supper, no wonder she was thin.

Pris frowned as the blonde took a large swig from a shot glass. For many reasons, her catering budget had deliberately allowed only champagne—a few expensive cases followed by increasingly cheaper sparkling wines.

She had not provided shot glasses or hard liquor.

Holding the tray over her head, Pris edged through the animated crowd while dodging dinosaur tails and vampire capes. Perhaps, if she learned the strangers' wavelengths, she could block them. Did they speak Italian? That would help. She didn't.

In testing her theory, she sought the newcomers' vibrations. The first few intense spikes she received were basically incomprehensible except in terms of emotion. Despite their promotional material about their Italian origins, though, she caught a few distinctly Angle-Saxon curses.

The whole crew came off as anxious, when they should be relaxing and celebrating their introduction to their new neighbors. And maybe the woman was actually in pain. Someone seemed to be anyway.

Maybe she should sympathize instead of scorning them for their pretty faces. After all, it hadn't been easy for these outsiders to set up a European boutique in a rural town like Afterthought. Half the town's inhabitants considered all Italians —and most Yankees—to be fascists. The town council had been opposed to the newcomers on the general principle that *all* strangers were suspect—and like Aunt Mavis, they feared competition.

Out of sheer mule-headedness, Larraine Ward had bought a building for the boutique and rented it to the new company. That had been a risky move for a mayoral candidate, but Larraine was more invested in her agenda than winning elections.

It would be a shame if the strangers really were Mafia. They were emanating a lot of unhealthy vibes.

As Pris approached the newcomers, she decided the blonde's smile had more to do with Botox than strained relations. Was this the one the newspapers were calling Lady Katherine?

A sharp-nosed woman she recognized as a Charleston reporter approached the group at the same time as Pris. The mental tension escalated. The blond lady grabbed a handful of almonds.

"Lady Katherine," the reporter gushed. "I'm so glad you've finally agreed to an interview. Your lotions. . ."

Pris blocked out the rest of the sycophantic speech. Lowering her tray to offer her appetizer creations, she suffered an intense flash of panic, followed by a familiar image. *Dante!* What the. . .

Pulse pounding, Pris shot a quick glance over her shoulder.

Dante couldn't be here. She'd have known it instantly. The uptight Indiana Jones wannabe gave off masculine vibes so substantial it was a wonder he didn't cut a swathe through any room he entered. He'd returned to Italy weeks ago.

All she saw was her cousin Evie's partner, Jax, in a stupid Sherlock Holmes deerstalker hat. Related to Dante, he had similar features but not enough to confuse anyone who knew them well. Taller and more suave than his American relation, Dante was an English-Italian archeologist who flew around academic circles. She didn't think it possible for a fashion model to know him.

Lady Katherine seemed to be gasping for breath, as if in shock from what she was seeing? Still, she released her grip on the pendant and managed to help herself to Pris's caviar.

Pris realized she should have asked Evie about the strangers' auras. Out of sheer curiosity, she warily lowered her mental barriers a little more. Someone had very murky vibrations, but she couldn't differentiate them enough to tell if they were male or female.

Cut it out, Pris, she warned herself. *Concentrate.* Her future kitchen depended on good reviews.

While the reporter nattered, Lady Katherine took another swig from her shot glass, then bit into her appetizer, practically inhaling the whole thing as if starved. Nothing delicate about this lady.

Pris passed the platter to the gentleman hovering next to the lady.

A rush of excruciating pain—followed by strong bolt of triumph—pierced her mental block. Pris staggered, the agony so intense as to be almost physical. Her tray tilted, releasing all her carefully created confections onto polished shoes.

To her horror, the blonde slumped to the floor, her shot glass rolling to Pris's feet amid the caviar.

Two: Evie

HALLOWEEN PARTY

AFTERTHOUGHT, SOUTH CAROLINA

"I LIKE THE HAT," EVIE WHISPERED SEDUCTIVELY, TUGGING ON THE SHERLOCK Holmes flap-eared cap Jax wore as his version of a costume. "Where did Loretta find it?"

Their eleven-year-old ward had more money than should be legally allowed and still haunted the local thrift store.

"I think Dante found it for her when he stopped in England. It smells of mothballs. Am I mistaken, or does your cousin Pris look as if she swallowed a prune pit?" In a tailored black suit that molded to his brawny shoulders, Damon Ives-Jackson would fit in nicely with the Beautiful People Pris approached.

That Jax hung out with *her*, Evangeline Malcolm Carstairs, the town dog walker, instead of the seductive newcomers, proved his rare intelligence. More probably, he was hooked on her nearly transparent genie costume. He had a healthy appreciation of their sex life. She followed his gaze.

Right before their startled eyes, Lady Katherine collapsed in a writhing heap at Pris's feet.

They both reacted automatically, following their own dissimilar instincts. Evie aimed for her cousin, waving her arm in the family signal for circling the wagons. Jax whipped out his phone while barking orders into his mic to Larraine's security team. She left him calling Sheriff Troy and an ambulance.

5

Evie narrowed her eyes as her cousin surreptitiously used a linen napkin to scoop up a small glass rolling on the floor, hiding it on her tray. Pris might look like a gel-haired punk ditz, but she was scary smart in ways no one understood.

While people hysterically shouted for doctors and to give the lady space, Evie's family angled through the crowd, forming a circle around La Bella Gente's staff and the pale blonde twitching spasmodically on the polished floor.

"Kit-Kat!" The anguished cry was distinctly British, from one of the shorter, but no less stylish, gentlemen. He fell to his knees at the woman's side and attempted crude CPR.

CPR didn't work well with convulsions. Mavis shoved her way in and knelt beside the victim, taking her pulse. Lady Katherine's eyes rolled back in her head and her twitches of agony halted. Evie didn't need to see the almost imperceptible shake of her mother's head to know the lady's life had just ended with a final shudder.

Evie had never watched a person die. Molars locked and shaking, she waited to see if a spirit rose, but in her experience, it took time for a life essence to coalesce into visibility. Trying to focus on ghosts did not stop tears from running down her cheeks. She didn't even know the woman, but she'd been alive and seemingly healthy just a few minutes ago. How was this possible?

A slightly paunchy older gentleman hauled the weeping young man back, whispering in his ear. The younger one shook his head frantically and tried to pull away. A taller, darkly handsome man took his other arm and murmured what sounded like reassurances. Evie couldn't hear what he was saying but she understood auras.

The frantic young man displayed clear red in his root chakra, passionate if not entirely affectionate.

The taller man exhibited a muddy green in his heart chakra—he was jealous or resentful of someone in this scenario. He didn't strike Evie as caring about the woman on the floor at all. His gaze was fixed on the gaudy necklace around the victim's throat—but Evie's family forced everyone back.

Black hovered around the older man. That could mean any number of things, none of them healthy or showing compassion for the dead woman or her lover.

The auras of the two male model types were murky with gray and brown, concealing their better selves in guardedness and distrust. That poor woman chose her friends badly.

Six-feet tall in sky-high heels, Larraine Ward sailed into the melee wearing a Cher-length black wig and a costume with more beads and spangles than the performer ever wore. For Halloween, the mayoral candidate had apparently foregone her usual sophisticated elegance, flying her rainbow flag, and letting her inner drag queen shine. Anyone attending tonight would have no doubt of Larraine's gender identity. That was one of the reasons Evie adored her—she was bluntly honest and so very not a politician.

With the authority she'd developed fighting her way to the top tier of the fashion world, Larraine ushered the crowd toward the buffet. With their departure, Jax and the security team set up a dressing screen to block off this portion of the lobby.

In her wake, Larraine left the local GP, who stooped down to examine the body.

Pris caught Evie's elbow and whispered, "Any ghost?"

Evie shook her head. "I've never been on the scene when someone dies. I don't know if their spirit immediately departs or what happens, sorry. What did you sense?"

"Triumph," her cousin replied grimly. "Someone in the vicinity felt triumph just before she collapsed. We need to find out who gave her the limoncello."

"The what?" Evie asked before sensing someone listening in. She turned and frowned at the nondescript frump she recognized as the Charleston columnist covering the party.

Jax stepped behind Evie to firmly direct the sharp-nosed journalist toward Larraine at the other end of the room. She protested, but security moved in, and the reporter fled.

Security consisted of Evie's partners, Jax's former military intelligence team. Reuben and Roark were even taller and broader than Jax and far scarier looking, even though they'd attempted to dress up. That meant removing nose rings and bones in top knots and wearing long sleeves to hide the tats—although Rube was also wearing a vampire cape. Muscled Roark's shirt clung to his chest and bore a bat signal.

With her usual disregard of this blatant display of masculinity, Pris answered Evie's question. "Limoncello, basically lemon juice with 40% alcohol. I'd die if I drank it too, but I'm guessing the taste would disguise anything short of a nuclear bomb." Pris surreptitiously passed her the shot glass wrapped in linen. "I don't want to be involved. Give this to Troy."

Evie could hear the sheriff's booming voice approaching. He would have been patrolling close by for a shindig this large. She took the glass and hid it in the arms of her gauzy genie sleeves.

Jax returned and held out his hand. "Let's give whatever you and Pris are hiding to Troy, then try to direct the journalists to better topics."

Evie stood on tiptoe and kissed his tense jaw. "I do love you even when you're being an obnoxious lawyer. I need to talk to Troy first."

Jax's protective streak practically glowed luminescent, but he reluctantly waited at her side until Troy arrived. The sheriff consulted with the physician, nodded at Mavis, and warily noted the rest of Evie's family circling the scene. "All right, folks, there's nothing further we can do here. Who is the lady's next of kin?"

The lady's entourage remained silent.

Jax all but growled under his breath. Looking as if he'd swallowed acid, he stepped forward. "Vincent, give the sheriff the lady's information. He's a good man, just trying to help."

Evie's uptight lawyer lover had been working with La Bella Gente to establish the proper legal papers for running an American company. He didn't say it, but Evie could tell he didn't like them. He wasn't really a corporate lawyer and had only taken the job as a favor to Larraine.

Hoping Larraine wouldn't be caught in the backwash of this nasty incident, Evie lurked while the sheriff set his men to taking notes from the newcomers, with Jax's aid. Judging by accents, they were apparently British. Interesting. She'd thought it an Italian company.

She waited until the medics arrived, and Troy stepped away, before cornering him.

"You're all but humming loud enough to be an alarm," Troy said in disgruntlement when Evie approached. "What do you have to make my life more difficult?"

She handed him the linen-wrapped shot glass. "She was drinking from this when she dropped. She was surrounded by bad vibes. We don't think this was natural."

Troy sighed and slid the napkin-wrapped glass into an evidence bag. "Doc says she had a heart attack. She may have been surrounded by Mafia for all I know, but that doesn't mean she was murdered."

"You want to wait until I start seeing ghosts? Any evidence will be gone by then. You're the only man we can trust to take a deeper look." Evie batted her lashes at him, knowing full well they had no effect. Sheriff Troy was old enough to be her father and knew Evie's ploys too well. She just kept it up for practice.

"I can't imagine what evidence we can find with a party this size trashing the place, but I'll keep my eyes open. Larraine was just asking for trouble bringing in these strangers." Troy walked off to talk with one of his men.

Evie saw the vague formation of a murky pink glow above the body as medics lifted Lady Katherine to the gurney.

She hoped Jax was telling Troy that the lady wasn't a lady but a tramp.

Three: Pris

ELECTION NIGHT

Afterthought, South Carolina

"They say it was poison, not a heart attack," a voice whispered in the crowd behind Pris.

Pris knew better than to let down her mental barriers on election night, more so after the fiasco at the Halloween fundraiser. She gritted her teeth and attempted to edge away from the scandal monger, but city hall was jam-packed.

If she'd had a choice, she wouldn't be here at all, but in this fraught election, she had to support her family and their candidate as they watched the committee count paper ballots. Her family had been mostly responsible for supporting the gender-bending, racially diverse candidate, Larraine Ward.

On top of that, Jax and his team had worked hard to have the city's fraudulent voting machines thrown out so Ward had a chance against the establishment, several of whom were now in jail for federal crimes.

"Who is *they*?" a voice Pris recognized replied—the school principal and one of Larraine's staunch supporters. "The sheriff has said nothing about murder."

"Only because he doesn't want to rock the boat," the gossip insisted. "Everyone knows what that coven of witches would do if the sheriff charged one of their own. If Larraine Ward loses the election, Troy could be out of a job."

One of their own: meaning Pris. How anyone could envision her eccentric,

9

frumpy family as a coven strained the imagination. Sure, Pris knew she was weird. She worked at it. But *witches*? If only she knew a magic spell or two. . .

Thanks to Jane Lawson, the scandal-mongering columnist, paranoid rumors had run rampant this past week. Lawson theorized the Bella Gente owner had been murdered by a conspiracy of Blacks, meaning Larraine and half the town's voters, and *witches*, Pris and her family. While Jane's audience numbers grew with her hate-imbued idiocy, Pris's catering business had dropped off.

Maybe she ought to listen and figure out what motive she had for killing off a potential customer, but crazies were seldom rational. The awful part was that Pris was convinced half of the conspiracy theory was right—Katherine Gladwell, Bella Gente CEO, had not died of a heart attack.

"We'll be a laughingstock if that. . . *creature* is elected." A familiar nasal voice repeated the refrain she had pounded on all summer. "No decent business will move here. And if a mayoral candidate is accused of murdering the one upscale business owner who dared locate in Afterthought. . ."

Pris rolled her eyes and bit her tongue. She could point out that Larraine was standing right there with the CFO of La Bella Gente and some of his employees. They didn't seem particularly wary of being murdered. She resisted, not needing to agitate the troll into badmouthing her even more.

Just as someone else countered Lawson's stupidity, the crowd parted. Not waiting to hear the blogger's response, Pris pushed toward her family. Tonight, they needed to stick together. Fraught wasn't even the beginning of the election-night mood.

Afterthought, South Carolina barely had a thousand registered voters, but half of them seemed to be in city hall tonight. Ballot checkers hovered as the votes were tallied. This was a special election to fill a vacant position, so the count was simple. The room grew tense as they reached the bottom of the ballot stack.

Hank Williams, the hardware store owner and Larraine's opposition, stood with a group of men Pris recognized as a majority of the town council. They looked grim at the tight tally. Even Jane Lawson's conspiracy theories hadn't completely ruined Larraine's chances.

Dressed in one of her sophisticated fashions, the designer nonchalantly talked on her phone. She seemed unconcerned by the drama and more interested in her business call. Pris admired her for that. Business first. Drama, pfft.

Except Pris knew it was an act. Larraine had to put on a performance every time she appeared in public. With tension escalating, she had to be aware that the tally had finished and the committee was consulting before making the announcement.

Bill Wright, the shy bank president chosen by both candidates to head the election committee, tapped a water glass to ask for attention. He didn't have to tap hard. The room quieted. He squirmed nervously. Mrs. Thomas, the elementary school principal and also a committee member, handed him a small white board with large numbers to hold up.

"Ladies and gentlemen, I am proud to announce that Miss Larraine Ward has won the mayoral position by a count of 489 to Mr. Hank Williams' vote of 477. Congratulations to both candidates for a fair and honest race."

A roar erupted. Pris noticed with interest that she didn't have to work at shutting out minds when everyone was mentally screaming. It didn't seem to matter if it was joy or outrage, the psychic cacophony provided its own barrier. Learn something new every day.

She didn't bother joining the crowd surrounding the new mayor to congratulate her but began elbowing her way to the exit.

Jane Lawson, part-time newspaper blogger and full-time bigot, approached as if armed and dangerous. Her narrow eyes squinted, her sharp nose sniffed, and her thin lips wore a permanent sneer. Or maybe Pris just didn't like her. The woman didn't have enough brains to send strong vibrations and was easily blocked.

"How do you believe Miss Ward's win will affect your business?" she asked into a microphone, as if she were a TV reporter.

The woman's snide slurs about Larraine, added to her insults about Pris poisoning the appetizers, had encouraged a following of haters, a business model that worked surprisingly well on social media. But Jane's candidate had lost, and she was simply a sore loser.

Despite her earlier refusal to rise to the bait, Pris was riding high on triumph and wasn't much inclined to impartiality. "Electing the candidate with the most financial and business expertise works for me. Hasn't sneering like that hurt your eyesight?"

Any sensible person would have let her walk away, but the hate-monger grabbed her arm. "Most businesses prefer that their mayor represent their customers and people like themselves. What kind of freaks will you be serving now?"

After suffering weeks of insults, fury reined, and Pris yanked her arm free. "Afterthought is half Black, half white, half male, half female. Looks to me like Miss Ward represents *my* clientele. Or are you saying I can only market my business to white females because I'm white and female? Do you only want white females reading your byline? Or perhaps you should expand your narrow point of view and consider we're all *human beings*?"

As she walked away, she heard the bigot call, "You'd better be careful! The coroner is asking for a full autopsy on that poor woman the two of you murdered. We'll see how well your Miss Ward fares."

If Pris meant to commit murder, it wouldn't be of a stranger.

Four: Dante

ARCHEOLOGICAL DIG

ITALY

"Duck, Leo," Dante Ives Rossi told his truculent neighbor for the fiftieth time. "That tuff will crumble back to ash before your hard head does. The Etruscans didn't dig these tunnels because the ground is hard."

Younger and more compact than Dante, Leo flattened and slowed to a crawl over the uneven sandstone, shining his headlamp deep into the cavern. "They're caves, Rossi. Caves won't stop them from running a highway through my vineyards."

Leo's *cousin's* vineyards, but after swearing she'd never leave the farm, Lucia had left for an easier city life. Not that Dante was resentful or anything. Leo had benefited from her defection, at least, depending on whether or not one considered a life of farming ancient grape vines a benefit.

"I've had some of the artifacts we've found analyzed. They're not Roman. You may be sitting on *Etruscan* tunnels. Archeologists and universities are slavering over any evidence we can produce on their life and times. That gold cuff you found at the entrance is a work of art." Dante knew the cuff had been stolen, but he couldn't explain to a disbeliever the mysterious means by which he knew. Only his weird ancestors could relate.

What he couldn't tell and *needed* to know was if the stolen goods had come from here or elsewhere.

When Leo had first told him of the find, Dante had hoped and prayed that his neighbor had found a site that would allow him to stay home and work and help a neighbor while he was at it. But this cuff. . . Would pay an awful lot of Leo's bills if sold on the black market.

And quite possibly destroy Dante's career if his name were associated with it.

"A trove of gold would be fine if I could sell it." Leo let his bitterness show. "Why do we have to tell the authorities?"

"Because if you try to sell that cuff, you'd be in jail faster than you could spend the money. The laws change regularly, but reporting the find first is always best. Artifacts like this advance our knowledge of history and reporting the find provides you some protection." He squeezed his broad shoulders though a passage meant for a much smaller man. "You need to turn it in."

Leo beamed his headlamp ahead and wriggled faster. "History won't plant more olive trees or buy new vines. I need cash."

Dante understood that dilemma as well as anyone. His love of knowledge fed his family and little more. But the law was the law for a reason. He waved a metaphorical carrot. "The Etruscans possessed a wealth of expertise even beyond that of the Romans at the time. You might have a historical landmark as big as Vulci, only easier to access. It could be visited by thousands of tourists a year."

"They'll want to build a highway through the vineyards to reach it. I need to get back to the harvest. This is a waste of time."

"Head down, Leo!" Dante shouted as Leo's hard hat struck an outcropping.

Leo ducked—too late for Dante. The ceiling cracked and caved.

Five: Pris

DANTE'S VILLA

ITALY

PRIS DAMNED WELL HADN'T POISONED ANYONE. YET. NEITHER HAD LARRAINE. THE idea was blatantly ridiculous to anyone with half a brain, but apparently half the population was brainless. Or Evil Lawson's Faux News followers were. Or both.

The petition for a mayoral recount was ridiculous enough, but now the council wanted *licensing* laws to prevent Pris from operating her catering service so she couldn't poison anyone. Not that anyone had officially been declared poisoned. That was just Lawson's rumor-mongering and the council's bigotry at work.

Only—Pris was as convinced as Lawson that Lady Kat's death had not been a heart attack.

So, if the cops weren't looking for the reason for Lady Kat's death, she'd damned well search for it herself—before a killer got away with murder. La Bella Gente had an Italian owner who sold olive oil products originating in this area. Would that owner want to kill their CEO? Or know who would? Any good research had to start by covering the basics.

Having had the eternal plane trip to learn the Euro coins the bank had ordered for her, she stood on the villa's stairs and counted out the fare for her loquacious taxi driver. She added the tip recommended by the guidebooks. He smiled hugely, so she'd probably calculated wrong. Oh well. Money had never been her forte, probably because she'd never had any.

She had never been in an airplane *or* out of the country in her life either. Exhausted from lack of sleep in cramped economy seats, drained from struggling with unfamiliar languages and customs, she wearily studied the crumbling stone where the driver had left her luggage. Stairs like that were dangerous and probably condemned in forty-eight states but apparently not in Italy.

She longed to turn around and go back, but after this past hectic week of her entire family learning how to obtain an emergency passport and scraping up the money to send her, she couldn't quit now.

She finally lifted her head to study the imposing stone edifice presumably belonging to Dante Ives Rossi, Conte Armeno—Jax's distant Italian relation. Everyone thought she was crazy to come here.

Only she knew she was plain certifiable.

She should have given up catering, found a sous chef job in the city where rumors wouldn't touch her. She didn't *have* to live in Afterthought. She didn't *need* her own business.

She just hated being trampled by a yellow-dog journalist and her small-minded readers. Well, she hated being trampled, period. She had spiteful dreams of blowing up Jane Lawson's theory and Jane with it.

With no other clue, Pris was left relying on her gift for *knowing*. She knew something was off about La Bella Gente. Evie's geeky Sensible Solutions team had determined the boutique's origin was in Umbria. The company's London base might have been a better place to start, but she didn't know anyone there.

She had at least met Dante. He possessed a hardheaded mental block she couldn't penetrate and was probably the most irritating, uptight man on the planet, but it gave her some small pleasure to annoy the arrogant Italian Indiana Jones by showing up on his doorstep as unexpectedly as he'd appeared in her life.

He hadn't told her he was a damned *count*. He'd left it up to Evie's team to learn that. She'd known he was hiding secrets but dang. . . Way to intimidate a girl.

She looked for a bell to push or pull but only found a heavy metal knocker on an ancient wooden door painted in peeling turquoise. She'd been briefed on Dante's background and knew, despite his ancient title, he wasn't wealthy. He was simply the all-knowing prick who had passed through Afterthought one week and left without a word.

Well, it was possible she'd driven him into fleeing. She often had that effect.

But it couldn't be coincidence that La Bella Gente had shown up in town after he left, not when the boutique's owners were related to the landowners near Dante's home and purchased their olive oil from this region. And then someone in the group had mentally thought his name in panic. Nope, he knew something, and she meant to find out what.

No one answered her knock. She heard childish shouts through the open window so someone was home. Children? She'd thought Dante unmarried. One more secret he kept from her?

She knocked a little louder, then winced at the frantic vibrations emanating from within. Since she had no means of running back to town, she threw up the mental shields that made her look like an automaton and tested the iron door handle. The door swung inward. She stepped into a cavernous hall with marble floors in need of polishing and a gilded ceiling with peeling plaster. Impressive.

"*Ciao?*" she asked tentatively. She'd been listening to internet tutorials, but they didn't tell her how words were used in normal conversation.

Voluble Italian exclamations poured from a back room, followed by a matronly figure in black wiping her hands on a towel hurrying into the entry hall. The stream of Italian aimed in Pris's direction passed right over her head. Was she being welcomed or thrown out? Did she dare lower her mental shield and let in the onslaught?

Tentatively, she took another step into the gloom. "Hello, I'm Priscilla Broad-hurst. I sent word that I'd be arriving today?"

The woman threw up her hands in what appeared to be welcome—or maybe relief, given her next words, in perfect British English. "You're here, thank all the heavens. I'm sorry. It's an emergency. I don't have time to introduce you to the children. They're in the nursery. There's been a dreadful accident. I must run. Make yourself at home and I'll be back as soon as I can."

"Um, children?" She'd asked if she could rent a room while she took a cooking class. No one had mentioned children.

"Alessandro and Arianna. They eat at six. Bless Dante for sending you!"

Before Pris could question more, the woman grabbed an enormous black purse and rushed out the open front door. A moment later, a car engine roared and gravel rattled.

Um. . .

Well, at least she must have the right house. Taking a deep breath, she opened her mind again and studied her surroundings.

The villa had probably once been spectacular. The marble entry led to an impressive—dusty—marble staircase. A fading fresco adorned one wall, an aging wooden cabinet with painted figures filled the opposite wall. Peering in, she found an old overcoat and a modern nylon downy jacket.

Deciding she probably ought to be certain the children weren't murdering each other or someone else, she stepped deeper into the huge foyer, glancing into the spectacular front room with windows overlooking a valley dotted with distinctive Tuscan cypress.

She didn't have a great deal of experience with children, except for avoiding them when she had to work in private homes. Her cousin had a six-year old who was mildly competent. Evie had an eleven-year-old ward who was too old for her age. But they had Malcolm heritage, and Pris acknowledged that made a difference. As a Malcolm herself, she knew weird when she saw it. She couldn't count on these children having anywhere near the understanding of her psychic family.

No one interfered with her progress. She'd expected servants in a place this size. Shouldn't a busy man with a title and a fabulous house have a few servants scattered about? But no one emerged to ask what she was doing as she checked out the downstairs.

Not hearing any more shouts and rather enjoying the freedom of exploring without interference, she took her time. The library was all dark wood shelves, velvet draperies, parquet flooring, and better tended than elsewhere. Someone spent time here. An electric fire burned in the grate, keeping the books dry against the early November damp.

She stumbled into an immense kitchen of modern appliances and fell in love. Running her hand over the gleaming six-burner stainless steel stove and admiring the colorfully tiled walls and counters, she studied the amazing view out the aging French doors. A stone veranda with ancient urns filled with topiary led down to a terraced garden still green with herbs and late autumn vegetables. Chickens pecked in the fading sunlight.

Here was the heart of the villa.

Why play hide-and-seek with invisible children when she knew how to lure them out?

With satisfaction, she opened the enormous stainless-steel refrigerator and gathered her ingredients.

Six: Dante

Italy

PAINKILLERS WEARING OFF, DANTE GRIMACED AND SWUNG HIS CRUTCH UP THE crumbling stone stairs. His mother worriedly followed, chattering about suing Leo, fretting over the dinner she hadn't cooked, and the nanny he'd supposedly sent. His mother was one of the many reasons he traveled for a living. She was a non-stop worrier. And talker.

The moldering villa he hadn't the funds to repair was another reason. He hated the reminder of his incompetency at repairs and inability to earn fortunes in his chosen profession. But right now, opening the aging front door to air redolent of garlic and tomatoes, he almost—almost—appreciated his crumbling home.

Catching the scent at the same time he did, his mother exclaimed and bustled down the hall, leaving him to fend for himself. He smothered a grin at that familiar impression of abandonment. Being an only child in an empty villa led to strange fantasies.

And then he remembered the job he was supposed to leave for in the morning, and he growled in irritation. How the hell could he climb a mountain on a crutch?

He didn't think he could even climb the stairs to his room. Maybe he'd sleep on the enormous kitchen counter he'd spent a year's wages on to pacify his mother. That had been the year the twins had arrived. She'd needed a lot of pacifying.

The twins were another reason he never came home.

Clumping along on his crutch, he couldn't expect to catch the fake nanny by surprise. If she was cooking, he hoped it wasn't poison. There were plenty of people who wouldn't mind finding him dead.

The scene in the kitchen froze him without need of imaginary toxins. *What the friggin' Hades?*

Sitting on tall counter stools, the twins bent their dark curls over a pastry board. At age five, their hands were still pudgy and inept, but they earnestly rolled out rounds of dough with tiny wooden rolling pins. But it wasn't the twins causing him to blink twice.

The she-devil in wiry, striped hair was expertly slicing up the pasta dough his mother had probably left standing before rushing out to pick him up at the hospital. The intruder wielded a wicked knife and an expert arm, flinging the noodles into the boiling water with the ease of experience.

The last time Dante had seen her, she'd been wearing ominous red stripes in gelled hair. Today, the stripes were silver and the hair was a puff ball of mouse-brown frizz. He recognized the intense focus on her usually impassive features—she was ready to kill. He'd last seen that expression after he'd told her she was insane if she thought he wanted anything more to do with her eccentric family—after she'd nearly got him killed and/or arrested in a potentially career-destroying escapade.

That she was here now. . . gave him cold shudders. Insulting witches was probably a bad idea.

She glanced up, shot him a look that should have shed blood, and flung the remainder of the noodles into the pot. Ignoring him, she helped the twins press down on their dough until it was flat enough, then sliced it into noodles and added them to the pot.

Dante figured they'd all die of food poisoning from the twins' dirty fingers. He swore they could wash their hands all day and still be dirty.

"Sit, sit," his mother cried, gesturing at the centuries-old trestle table she'd insisted on keeping. "I will bring the salad." She plopped a bottle of wine on the table with an opener and glasses.

"If he's on painkillers, he shouldn't be drinking." The demon woman spoke for the first time—not a greeting but her usual dire warning.

"Do you even know how to say *hello* or *how are you feeling* or any of the normal things one would say after taking over a person's home?" Spitefully, Dante popped the cork and poured himself a glass.

"Waste of time." She nodded at the children. "Go wash your hands again. Soap and water make everything taste better."

The twins obediently climbed down from their tall seats and ran to the sink to climb up on a stepstool. They never went anywhere without running.

They never followed orders.

After splashing about in the water, Alex jumped down, hands still dripping, and loped over to wipe them on Dante's trousers, causing him to wince at the assault on his cracked shin. The boy dashed off, giggling at his boldness. Nan politely dried her hands on a towel and ignored him, much as the fake nanny did.

Well, he probably deserved that. They hardly ever saw him, after all.

Politeness was a waste of time? Fine nanny she'd make. But he already knew that the nanny masquerade was rubbish. Taking another fortifying sip, sitting on the high-backed bench his mother shooed him onto, Dante swung his injured leg up on a side chair and debated the reality of stepping through the Looking Glass. If the demon-woman shouted *Off with his head,* she was out of here.

"I'm sorry I didn't have time to properly introduce myself earlier," his mother chattered, filling the tense silence. "I'm Emma Malcolm Rossi, Dante's mother. I assume you've already met my son."

"Malcolm?" The she-devil's mousy eyebrows shot straight up. She glared at Dante instead of his mother, as if it were all his fault they might have a seventeenth-century ancestor in common.

"I'm from Scotland," his mother continued, happily setting the table with her favorite colorful chicken-decorated plates. "Dante's father was Italian, but he has family in Edinburgh and went to school there. It was kismet."

Dante sipped his wine and waited. As long as his mother was around, he didn't have to speak, which was probably for the best. He wasn't exactly in a conversational humor.

"Malcolm-Ives attraction," the fake nanny declared. "I understand Dante is related to a friend of mine who just discovered he's an Ives."

"Oh, is that how you met! How delightful. Are you a professional nanny? Or just wanting to spend some time here? I assume from your accent that you're American. Let me finish up, and you take a seat and tell me all about yourself." His mother grabbed the pot of boiling pasta from the stove and nudged their guest aside.

"Shouldn't the children be sitting at the table? Where did they run off to?" The impostor peered into the other room rather than take a seat near Dante.

"They'll come when they're ready. They don't see their father often, so they're probably up to mischief. I've given up trying to reason with them." Emma tasted the sauce simmering on the stove, added a few herbs, and tossed it in with the pasta. "I'm sorry, I left in such a hurry, I didn't catch your name."

Dante normally would have stood up to help his mother with the heavy pots and bowls, but his leg wasn't allowing it today. He'd need twice the painkiller later, but he was too caught up in this scene to leave just yet.

"Priscilla Broadhurst but call me Pris." She grabbed the heavy bowl and carried it to the table.

He noticed she didn't use her entire name, Priscilla *Malcolm* Broadhurst. He appreciated that. His mother would be off and swinging up and down the family tree.

Intrigued by her family tale of fleeing New England witch hunts in colonial America, he'd already ascertained that any connection to his mother's family had to date back to the 1600s.

"Well, Pris, have a seat and tell me all about yourself. You obviously know how to cook." Emma took the chair on Dante's right.

Prissy Pris all but glowered and reluctantly settled at the far end of the table. "I own a catering business. I want to take it to the next level, so I enrolled in a cooking school near here. I asked Dante if I might rent a room rather than pay the exorbitant price the school is charging."

Why did he find that hard to believe? Maybe because he'd never received the message to start with.

"Oh." His mother looked vaguely puzzled as she dug into her salad. "I thought Dante said he was sending a nanny to help out. I'm sorry I left you on the doorstep."

He grimaced and dug into his food rather than answer that. He had vaguely, and in quiet desperation, made that promise eons ago. But who had time to hunt for nannies? Affordable ones.

"My message must have gone astray," demon lady said without blinking a lash. "I'm the one who should apologize. The school's hours are limited, so I could help out in lieu of rent, if that would suit. I have to return home when the session ends in two weeks, but maybe that will give you time to find someone more suitable."

Dante studied his salad bowl. What had she dressed it with? Liquid gold? Oil and vinegar had never tasted so good. His mother must have been experimenting with herbs again.

"I don't even know where to begin," Emma said with a sigh. "We're too far out of town for anyone in the village to be interested. And the twins. . ."

As if they'd been listening, the little brats popped out of the cellar. He would have to buy a better lock for the outside door or they'd never be found again.

Once used for wine and olive oil storage, the villa had cellars more confusing than Etruscan ones.

The she-devil motioned his mother to stay sitting. Without a word, she pushed salad bowls to the twins' bench side of the table and got up to produce bread sticks. Why hadn't he been offered a bread stick? Dante reached over and grabbed one. Damn, the thing was fresh. And *sweet*?

"The children baked this afternoon. They must have their grandmother's talent." She munched a stick, apparently savoring it for the benefit of the twins.

Witch. He had to remember her family was known as witches for good reason.

The twins giggled and dug into their food. They were growing up fast. The last time he'd been here, they'd thrown food at each other and him. His mother had said that was how they communicated. They weren't much into talking —like him.

Except he talked. That was half his job. He just didn't talk at home because he had nothing to say.

Or he had so much to say, he didn't know where to start. And no one wanted to hear what needed to be said. His mother filled in the silence quite well.

"If your thoughts get any louder, I'll hear them," the demon woman said, forking up her pasta without even looking at him. As if she'd actually heard him thinking.

His mother looked confused, rightfully so. The twins picked up lettuce in their fingers and shoved it into their mouths.

"My mother is an excellent cook. She could probably teach you more than the school." There, he'd said something pleasant.

"It's a class on appetizers. That's what I serve most. I believe an acquaintance of yours accused me of poisoning his daughter with my crab and caviar crisps. I thought I'd up my game on his home ground."

Emma gasped. Dante reached for the pasta bowl. "I assume no one else died and that's why you're not in jail. Does the acquaintance have a name?"

"Vincent Gladwell, owns a farm around here, ring any bells?"

Dante almost dropped the bowl.

Seven: Evie

KK'S GHOST

AFTERTHOUGHT, SOUTH CAROLINA

ROAMING LARRAINE FASHIONS, SURROUNDED BY PEOPLE IN TAILORED SUITS AND HIGH heels—even the men in some cases—Evie felt like a rat catcher in her T-shirt, corduroys, and sneakers. Maybe she ought to buy more fashionable ghost-hunting duds. Maybe Larraine had a closet of spare clothes somewhere. . . Except Evie was only five-two and couldn't come close to model thin.

Trying to imagine herself in a tailored suit, deciding she might rock heels, she wandered the echoing reception hall in search of a misplaced aura.

After taking an urgent phone call, the newly-elected mayor of Afterthought rejoined her. A worried frown marred her usually complacent expression. "Nothing yet?"

"She's here. I've seen her." With Larraine as guide, Evie started down the complex corridors of the sprawling fashion factory. "Ghosts normally attach themselves to people or places, but Lady Katherine didn't belong here, so she's not rooted to anyone or anything."

"Maybe she went home with her family. Should I hire a European private detective? Reuben is having difficulty cracking databases in Italian." Larraine frowned worriedly and rubbed at her rings, a sure sign of anxiety.

Evie didn't just read auras. She read people. Generous, genial Larraine Ward was more than anxious. Evie feared she'd done this to her by encouraging her controversial run for mayor. "Her friends and family left *before* I saw her aura. She may be looking for them, but she's still here. I assume she must have unfinished business. Give Reuben a chance to connect with Italian hackers. Everyone knows the accusations against you are political. Jax will spit in their faces."

Well, Jax's specialty was fraud, but he was local and knew the howling jackals accusing Larraine and Pris of murder on no evidence—especially since the coroner said Lady Kat died of a heart attack. Jane the Lawless, the sensationalist columnist and blogger, kept the snake pit stirred, trying to reverse the election results. If it got worse, Jax knew how to threaten lawsuits.

Of course, Larraine's supporters were blaming Pris, except Pris had taken herself out of the line of fire. That meant the heat was turning up under Afterthought's first transgender, non-white mayor. Evie would blame small town minds, but part of the howling came from state-level politicians and that stunk of politics playing to the lowest common denominator.

She wanted to be the kind of witch who hexed idiots. Unfortunately, a ghost-buster who stood between earth and the spirit veil needed to be non-judgmental. Maybe frustration made her ADHD.

Larraine all but washed her hands compulsively. "I've had to pester the sheriff for days for an autopsy. And they're still not certain. Last I heard, they're just saying they found something weird about her stomach."

"Facts won't faze conspiracy theorists. The state lab tests should be back shortly, so we'll know whether we have anything to worry about." After Pris's warning, Evie was already worried, which was why she was hunting Katherine's ghost.

Inconclusive autopsy or not, she had to stomp out the rumors about Pris and Larraine.

Larraine's phone beeped and she glanced at it. "Sorry, hon, but it's city hall. Hank won the case for a recount, and I have to look happy to see it done. You just wander anywhere you will."

Hank had lost to Larraine by a dozen votes. In a town of less than a thousand voters, that was a fair margin. A recount meant that more trouble brewed.

Or as Evie's mother would say, a black cloud loomed over city hall.

Evie really didn't need the hassle. Her Sensible Solutions Agency had its hands full these days. Admittedly, their cases hadn't yet generated sufficient cash to move Reuben out of the cellar or Roark out of Ariel's cottage. Not that she thought Roark would leave Jax's sister even if he won the lottery. Still, if Evie could find the ghost of Lady Katherine Gladwell, it would let Larraine and Pris breathe easier and cement their little agency's reputation.

"Kit-Kat, where are you?" she whispered, heading into the gender neutral lounge. The victim had worn designer clothing and fistfuls of cosmetics, so the lounge full of mirrors should be a familiar comfort zone.

Evie grinned in triumph at the flash of an aura near the full-length mirror. "Hello, Lady Katherine! Or should I call you Kit-Kat? That's what your boyfriend called you."

The aura rippled in a muddy orange with streaks of red. Why did no one ever have a lovely blue, communicative color? Or even a nice friendly earth color? Shadows of black indicated an unhappy, possibly even unhealthy person, but it was hard to focus on chakras when there was no body.

Evie could sense the spirit's discontent, but communication didn't seem to be happening. Her ADHD went into hyper-focus, calling up the names of the men who'd been around the boutique owner that night. "Vincent, he's your father, right? He's distraught over losing you."

The ghost uttered a rude noise, mostly inside Evie's mind. Then anger seemed to rise. Still, no communication.

"And Nick is devastated. I assume he's your lover? He stayed behind to make funeral arrangements. You don't happen to know who gave you the limoncello, do you?" It wasn't that anything was found in the shot glass, but Evie wanted to pin the spirit to the moment she died.

Matt was the word that floated across Evie's brain. "Matt? The male model? What did he have to do with the boutique?"

Brother. Stupid gay. The angry red darkened.

Evie tried to piece together being gay with stupid and brother with what the spirit was feeling, but she simply didn't know the people involved well enough to bridge the gap.

To her annoyance, her phone shrilled with a fire alarm—Loretta's idea of a joke. Evie switched off the ringer—too late. The aura evaporated. With a sigh, she called Jax back. "I had her, darn it, and the phone spooked her."

"I spooked the spook, new record for me." Jax sounded more amused than concerned. He was starting to accept that Evie could do weird things, but his pragmatic lawyer mind didn't fully comprehend the supernatural. "Roark's been digging around in the sheriff's files."

"I thought the state cops took over? And that's why they're trying to pin motive on Larraine, because the governor hates her rainbow image tarnishing his true-blue state?" Evie checked behind stall doors but the lounge was empty.

"You still haven't learned politics, have you? Anyway, Sheriff Troy has his own informers, it seems. You'd better hope nothing ever happens to him. That man has your back, whether you know it or not."

Evie wandered out of the lounge and down the hall, looking for inspiration. "He has the hots for my mother, but she won't give him a second look."

"That's what happens when one has her head in the clouds instead of right down here on earth. Let that be a warning to you."

Evie laughed. "After last night, you think I'm not right down here on earth with you? Tell me what the sheriff found out."

Jax might be a pragmatic lawyer, but he was a creative lover. She didn't know how she'd ever done without him—and that wasn't just in bed. He was the side of her brain that went missing at birth.

"Lady Katherine was a mere Katherine Gladwell without a hint of Italian in her."

"Not a lady, gee, who woulda guessed?" Evie mentally smacked herself for being judgmental. Aristocrats might have suspicious auras too. But frauds. . . yeah, that almost made sense. *Not Italian?* Her mind spun into overtime.

Accustomed to her spinning wheels, Jax ignored the commentary. "She used to sell cosmetics in one of London's department stores. Vincent, her father, is a dealer, always looking for investments for his next big thing. He's been bankrupt a time or two. Their big break came when Lucia Ugazio, Katherine's half-sister, came to stay with her a few years back. Lucia is the actual Italian in the family."

"Half-sister, huh. Kit-Kat and Lucia shared a mother, who presumably was not Italian?" Evie tried to form a picture puzzle in her head as she searched for the fraudulent Lady Katherine's elusive aura.

"Yes, but the mother died. The problem is, no one can find Lucia. Her father was the Italian in the family. He left her the estate where La Bella Gente obtains its olive oil. She's supposed to be the brains behind the manufacture and sales of their products, but no one ever sees her except in commercials."

"Do they know when she was last seen? Maybe she lives in Italy."

"They're working on tracking her. Her passport hasn't been used since she went to Italy a few years ago. Her passport address is the house she shared with Katherine. Katherine may have been the last person to see her."

"Well, if Lucia's passport hasn't been used, unless she's traveling with a fake, she couldn't have been here to kill her sister. Pris went to Italy because of the olive oil connection. She can check out Lucia's farm." Not that her cousin did anything she didn't want to do, but Pris wasn't stupid. It was her career being jeopardized by vicious rumor. "Do we know how the other guys are connected?"

"Matthew Gladwell is Katherine's brother and CFO. Rube hasn't traced the male models except to learn they were hired in London. The boutique's products are made in the UK by a company run by Vincent and his investors. Nicolas

Gladwell is in charge of marketing, another relation to our victim, a distant cousin from her father's side."

Evie frowned. "The man who wept over her? I thought they were lovers."

"The family tree looks like a banyan, so many divorces that it's hard to say who's related to whom. He might only be a cousin-in-law or a step-cousin. Whatever, they're keeping it all in the family."

"And Katherine is dead while Lucia is missing. Hiding, maybe? And Lucia and Katherine's mother is dead also? Not a lucky family."

"The mother was English, apparently didn't like Italy, abandoned Lucia to her father and returned to marry Gladwell as far as we're able to tell. But she died not long after Lucia left Italy for London."

"Huh, not liking this family. How many more boutiques does the company have or are we the first?" Evie decided she might be more productive if she visited La Bella Gente to see who was in charge.

"They're opening shops up and down the east coast. They have several in London. Roark and Ariel are looking into their finances. At least those are in English."

"Any nearby besides the one here?" Keeping her eyes open for flitting colors, Evie aimed for the side door of the plant.

"On this side of the pond, their business model seems to be tourist towns. Myrtle Beach and Hilton Head, I think. I don't know why they didn't try Beaufort instead of Afterthought."

"They had Larraine to back them here. Our new mayor loves their product. I have to go home and fix an after-school snack for Loretta and catch up on the gossip. Will you be home for dinner?" Evie stepped into the parking lot and aimed for her Subaru.

"Unless the brouhaha at city hall gets any worse, I'll be there. Tell Loretta I'll help her with her project this evening." He signed off.

Evie gave a sigh of happiness. She had feared guardianship of a millionaire child would be beyond her abilities, but it was turning out to be the best thing that had ever happened to her. And to Jax. His uptight aura was starting to unfurl in cheerful hues that might actually reflect happiness for a change. And Loretta said Evie's bubble was bubblier instead of sharp these days.

And a souped-up, cherry-red station wagon was far better than the Miata she'd once dreamed of owning. She settled behind the wheel, turned the ignition. . . and almost jumped out of her skin.

In the passenger seat glowed a very confused lemon-yellow aura marred by angry tinges of red with hints of muddy blue fear.

Well, she'd wanted to see blue in a ghost for a change.

Eight: Pris

ITALY

PRIS STUDIED THE ENORMOUS, DRAPED POSTER BED IN THE ROOM TO WHICH EMMA Rossi led her. The room itself was probably larger than her studio apartment. The bed might be the size of her kitchen. But the draperies were worn chintz and brown water spots stained the fading pink walls.

Still, from the double French doors, the view of the hill bathed in moonlight was spectacular. Once upon a time, she supposed, there had been gardens and terraces. Now, only the kitchen garden remained. Palaces were difficult to maintain without servants. Or very large families.

She'd seen olive trees on her way up here, so she assumed Gladwell's farm and production plant were nearby. She had no notion of how to approach it. She just resented the heck out of being accused of murder by bigots like Jane Lawson.

Pris hadn't had a new call for her services since the poisonous lie had hit Lawless Jane's faux news column. Maybe she shouldn't have insulted the columnist on election night, but it had been too irresistible. Who knew people actually listened to idiots if they shouted loud enough?

When she'd set her sights on Italy, she'd rather counted on Dante being on an archeological dig elsewhere, though. She already knew that she couldn't use her gift to influence his thoughts, drat the man. He'd seen right through her head games—or he was thick as a brick.

The area did have cooking schools, and she'd love to attend one, but she didn't have that kind of cash. It had taken her entire savings account and everything the family could scrape together to send her here.

Thinking on minimal sleep and a six hour time difference wasn't productive. She should hit the sack, but childish giggles in the hall meant trouble. The dolt didn't know what he had in those kids. Their open minds were quite brilliant.

Wondering who and where their mother was, she eased open the heavy door and studied the hall. There, in the shadows, wearing thin nightshirts, the twins crouched on the marble stairs, peering down between the stone railings.

Growing up in a family as weird as hers, Pris imagined all sorts of possibilities, but accepting that most families were normal, she joined them. She could hear Dante muttering below and caught flashes of the denim shirt he'd been wearing at dinner. What was the man doing?

She'd been accused of reacting without thinking, but what was there to think about?

Pris took the stairs down, the twins on her heels. They caught the giant imbecile in the act of balancing the quilted coat from the wardrobe and what appeared to be a stack of table linen while maneuvering his crutch into the immense front room. What did one call a room like that? It was big enough to be a ballroom. Or a grand hotel lobby.

He glared at them and continued on his appointed path.

Her nemesis was a large man, as tall and muscled as her cousin Evie's team of demented military rejects. Worse yet, he was even more good looking than the male models who'd been escorting Lady Katherine. Dark hair with a slight curl—check. Square jaw—check. Rugged cheekbones—check. . . Oozing testosterone —lethal.

Unfortunately, he had a poor opinion of women who took matters into their own hands, which was great. She'd irritate him as he did her.

"You are seriously strange." She usurped the stack of table linen.

Hanging on to the coat, he lurched on his intended path toward a sofa with gilded, delicately curved legs that would never hold him.

"You don't have sleeping bags or air mattresses or cots or anything in this gothic palace?" Pris refused to lay the linens like sheets on the delicate antique.

The twins dashed over to bounce on the upholstered sofa, raising clouds of dust in the dim light of a single lamp.

"If I were in my flat in Rome, I'd have all the above. Those things weren't invented in the 1800s and thus do not occupy this hellhole." Finally speaking, he glared at the twins, who didn't seem to notice.

"This is where communication matters. Don't expect me to read your mind." She gestured at the twins. "Upstairs. Show me the blankets."

Amazingly, they took off in the direction of the stairs. She followed. At least they understood English.

Dante had stacked his weird bedding on a chair and fixed himself a drink by the time she returned with arms full. Behind her, the twins dragged a narrow foam mattress. "On the floor or on that antique? Will it even hold you?"

He glanced at the narrow sofa with distaste. "Probably not, but I don't think I can manage the floor."

Forming a simple image of a lounge chair, she projected it to the kids. "Any big chairs down here?"

They screwed up their little foreheads in thought, then dashed off again. She didn't normally intrude on other minds like that, but children were delightfully simple. The resulting headache was almost worth the attempt.

"Shouldn't they be exhausted and sleeping?" Dante asked irritably, setting down his drink and attempting to arrange the foam on the narrow sofa.

"I suspect they're night owls, accustomed to prowling while your exhausted mother sleeps. They really do need a nanny. How bad is the leg?" Pris talked while watching the twins to see their direction.

"Bruised tibia, maybe cracked, minor damage. It will heal on its own if I keep it iced and stay off of it for a while. Staying off is the problem. Why are you really here?"

The twins shouted from the rear of the house. Ignoring his question, she followed the noise to the open kitchen doors. They were wrestling with an old—rusted—iron lounge chair on wheels. Pris assumed it once had a cushion. It was now no more than uncomfortable mesh, but it might work.

It might work better with a little oil, but she managed to get the corroded wheels rolling the short distance into the kitchen so she could shut the doors. By that time, Dante had lurched his way back to join them.

He snorted, lifted the thing in one hand, and moved it against a wall out of the traffic pattern of the kitchen.

"Tell them they did good," Pris whispered as the twins puttered around the chair, probably stirring the spiders.

"Thank you, Alex, Nan, you are geniuses," he said in a gravelly voice that could indicate disuse as much as it might show emotion.

"Can we have a dog?" Nan asked instantly, proving they could talk when interested.

"I'm afraid that's up to your grandmother," he said with what sounded like genuine regret. "How about a cookie and milk before you go to bed?"

For a very brief moment, Pris almost liked the man.

That wore off fast. Once the twins had consumed their treat and Pris attempted to usher them upstairs, Dante caught her arm.

"If you're not their nanny, then you can stay down here and explain what the hell you're up to."

~

DANTE DISLIKED SITTING STILL. HE WAS ACCUSTOMED TO STAYING BUSY FROM THE moment he rose to the moment he hit the bed, which could be twenty-four or thirty-six hours later, depending on travel schedules. Alcohol and painkillers had slowed him down tonight, but he still wanted to pace while the she-devil debated running away.

To her credit, she chose to make up his bed instead. He probably shouldn't call her a she-devil, but the irritating female had a way of looking at him as if she could see straight through his skull. Her eyes were almost amber in this light, like cat eyes, with great long lashes that concealed shadows beneath them. Beneath those witchy streaks of silver hair. . . *Si*, she worked at that image.

He grabbed one end of the bedding and helped arrange it, then collapsed on a tall kitchen stool. "I'm not the one refusing to communicate now."

"You're not supposed to be here. You're supposed to be running around the world, too busy to help others." She opened the refrigerator and began removing items.

He winced, remembering how they'd parted. But he really was busy, and she had plenty of family more than ready to go off on insane trajectories and wild rides. They hadn't needed him—and he didn't have time to be needed. "So you thought you'd just pop in and make yourself at home? How do you even know where I live?" He found one of the leftover breadsticks and chomped down on it.

Her eyebrows raised in perfect brown arches. He wouldn't have been surprised if they formed a diabolical curl. She fished a ceramic bowl out of a cabinet and smashed eggs into it before she answered.

"You do remember my cousin Evie and her team of hacker geeks? Do you really think you popped into town, then disappeared again, without anyone checking you out? Jax might take you at your word, but friends don't let friends get taken for a ride." She whisked the eggs, then began flinging in other ingredients without measuring.

"Ives have their own genealogical genies to prove my identity. Jax didn't need help. And I only came to give him a warning. It wasn't as if I asked to borrow money. So don't bullshit me. Why are you here?"

Damon Ives-Jackson, his newly discovered distant cousin, had explained some of his significant other's witchy family history. Dante had heard weirder. His mother's side of his family kept entire libraries of their eccentricities. The fact that this particular American branch of Malcolms had developed a reputation for fraud. . . Probably didn't hold water. Still, Dante had seen them in action and remained wary of their anarchy that had almost got him arrested.

"Well, since Vincent Gladwell and his daughter entered town on the heels of your departure, resulting in the destruction of my reputation and business, I think I have every reason to check them out. It seemed overly coincidental that he's a neighbor of yours." She filled a second bowl with flour and began adding handfuls of this and that.

Dante processed this, but it made little sense. "Gladwell doesn't own the land. Lucia Ugazio does. She's his stepdaughter. Her cousin is running the farm these days. I've never spoken to Gladwell. I'm not certain he's ever been here."

He had ten tons of resentment he could dump on the subject of Lucia Ugazio, but that was none of her damned business.

"That's not what he leads everyone to believe. According to the La Bella Gente website, Vincent developed a special variety of olive tree that flourished on this particular type of soil, generating top quality oil. Using old family recipes, they've been producing an extraordinary lotion that will make everyone who uses it rich and famous. Or something like that." She threw handfuls of the flour mix into the eggs.

Dante snorted. "That's a bunch of marketing rot. Those trees have been there since the beginning of time, along with the grape vines. Leo is slowly replacing the oldest of both with new varieties and testing the results, and the family did once sell creams and lotions in the local market, but wine and olive oil are more lucrative. What's La Bella Gente?"

"Boutique selling olive-oil-based cosmetics. They're also opening small Italian bistros where they sell gourmet olive oil, among other things. Their dried pasta cooks up like leather." She pounded her fist into the dough, sending up clouds of flour.

Oddly, when she was beating up dough, she looked almost angelic, wrapped in bliss and peaceful. Her halo of silver-streaked brown frizz fell innocently on her forehead and bounced to her own strange music.

He'd look lower but she'd donned one of his mother's massive aprons over her turtleneck. "Huh, first I've heard of it. Leo tells me the farm is barely breaking even. So, how are they destroying your business?"

"His daughter Katherine, the company's glamorous figurehead, dropped dead while eating my crab-caviar crisps. Coroner says it was a heart attack, but

Gladwell started nasty rumors about my cooking." She flung the dough on a floured pastry board and began beating it up some more. "My crisps weren't any more poisonous than the limoncello she was drinking. He's muddying the waters for his own purposes, an old con trick. I want to know why."

Dante finished the bread stick but still couldn't process this. If memory served, Katherine Gladwell was Lucia's half-sister, the one she'd run off to help half a dozen years ago. This was the first he'd heard of La Bella Gente. "Katherine and Vincent aren't Italian. Lucia inherited the land and the olive oil operations from her Italian father. She left her cousin Leo to run them while she fled to London for the glamorous easy life with her English mother. You're barking up the wrong tree."

"*You* are the last person Katherine Gladwell thought of before she died." She grabbed a rolling pin and smashed it into the pile of dough.

Dante paused in reaching for the last breadstick. "And you know this how?"

"I was there, remember? Serving her poisoned caviar to go with her limoncello. Really nasty combination. She was supposed to be drinking champagne and celebrating the boutique's grand opening."

He was knackered and in pain, and he still saw through this obvious ploy. "You said I was her last thought. How? Was she cursing me? As far as I'm aware, I never met Katherine Gladwell."

The she-devil plopped the round of dough into the bowl, covered it, and glared at him. "You wouldn't believe me if I told you. Just accept that unless there was another Dante in her life, she practically died with your name on her lips."

"Since I don't know the woman, it had to be another Dante. I'm not the only one in existence." Except Lucia had gone to stay with her mother, who had married a Gladwell. "You're saying this Katherine Gladwell was *murdered*?"

"The autopsy isn't complete and the sheriff isn't talking, but how often does a healthy thirty-year-old woman die of a heart attack?"

"You came all the way here and don't even know for certain that the death wasn't natural? Not buying it."

She washed her hands, then eyed him skeptically. "You're talking. Do you only do that when interrogating people?"

He crossed his arms, glared, and waited.

She glared back. Unlike her impish cousin Evie, Priscilla did glares very well. He still wasn't impressed.

A malevolent gleam lit her cat eyes. "She thought about you while terrified and just before she keeled over. Someone else, quite possibly male, shouted in mental triumph. Someone killed her, no matter what the coroner says."

Even through his pain, he caught that. *Mental* triumph? "You read minds?" he asked in incredulity.

Nine: Jax

Jax took the stairs down from settling Loretta into her attic eyrie, rubbing his hand over his over-long hair. In his carefree bachelor days, he'd always made time for haircuts.

He had to face it—despite his single status, he was no longer a carefree bachelor.

He encountered the second reason for that in the cluttered Victorian parlor. Looking like a particularly scrumptious sunset-haired genie, Evie sat cross-legged on the hearth, examining a Ouija board. Given her difficulty focusing, she'd be calling in her family next, except it was a school night, and her sister was a teacher with a kid to put to bed.

He was even starting to think like a parent. With Evie's aid, he didn't mind. Evie soothed his often rebellious soul, allowing him to reason clearly instead of punching something.

"All right, go over this again." He dropped in the recliner he'd added to the décor. No more balancing on hippy papa-san chairs or Victorian horse hair for him.

That he had bought his own chair for Evie's home warned him he was on a precipice.

"I'm being followed by a moon shadow?" she suggested in wan amusement.

36

"A very confused one who alternates between fear, anger, and worry. Communication is still iffy. I'm used to ancient spirits. I'm still learning about fresh ghosts."

"You're assuming this is Kit-Kat?" He'd reach for a beer, but he needed a clear head to deal with Evie's weird problems. He hoped it was progress that he now accepted she had problems odder than most.

"She's the only person I know who died recently, and she seems to respond to names Kit-Kat knows." She leaned over the Ouija board to touch the planchette.

"OK, I have to get this out of the way—will she be coming to bed with us?"

Evie shot him a look he couldn't interpret. "Want to try taking her back to London?"

"Pricey, but if that's what it takes. . . ?"

"I think if we give her a little time. . ." Evie shrugged when the planchette didn't move. "I wish Pris was here. She's a better sensitive than Grace or Iddy."

Evie's cousins were far weirder than her sister Grace. Together. . . Jax shifted uncomfortably. "So we play this one by ear until you can bring your family together?"

"It's frustrating, but realistically—in my experience, ghosts don't remember names or even how they died. Maybe if it had been prolonged torture. . . She really doesn't know any more than we do."

"Can you ask her where Lucia is?" That seemed like a dangerously missing piece.

Evie rubbed her temple and searched the room. "I don't even know if she's here."

That couldn't be good. Jax shuddered at the idea of a ghostly rainbow appearing over their bed at an inconvenient moment. "If I touch that Ouija thing, would that help?"

She shrugged. "We can try. If there's any clue in Pris hearing Dante's name before Katherine died, then maybe another Ives will help form a connection."

"You realize family names are artificial, and that genetic links to any distant ancestor are ephemeral, don't you?" Jax sat on the floor across from her.

"You can look at my family and call our genes ephemeral?" she scoffed. "Now hush, clear your mind, seek outside yourself."

Feeling like three kinds of fool, but accepting that for a woman as rare as Evie, he'd play clown if necessary, Jax set his big hands on the bamboo planchette. Evie had an old board, of course, no plastic for her family. The triangle didn't move.

He shivered. The big old house had bad central heating.

Evie muttered under her breath, glanced up in exasperation, then widened her eyes. "Oh, that's not good. Take your hands off."

Jax lifted his hands and thought about finding a sweater.

Evie glared at him. "Kit-Kat, he's taken. You're dead. Cut it out."

Okay, not going there. Jax retreated to his recliner. Evie continued to glare at where he'd been sitting. Nice to know that she wasn't glaring at him. He tried to see what she did, but he simply lacked anything close to super abilities.

"If you want his attention, tell us who wanted you dead."

Jax winced at being offered as bait for a ghost. Maybe he'd join Reuben in the cellar and hunt suspicious characters on the internet.

As if called, Reuben slammed into the kitchen. The cold dissipated. Evie shook her head in disappointment and flung a pillow at their houseguest when he entered the parlor, carrying a beer and a sandwich.

"What?" With the reflexes of an athlete, the top-knotted nerd lifted his grub out of the line of fire. The pillow bounced harmlessly off his muscled chest.

"I had Kit-Kat right here. You scared her. Or maybe I scared her by asking questions. I think I'm calling for a sage cleanse. She's the most useless ghost ever." In disgust, Evie stood, dusted off her shorts, and plopped down on the rickety bamboo papa-san chair. "So, what exciting news do you have for us?"

Professor Nerd shrugged and dropped to the aging sofa. Since falling into Larraine's clutches, Rube's wardrobe had gone from ripped T-shirts and cutoffs to fitted khakis and the fanciest pullovers Jax had ever seen. This one even had a collar. But it was still the anarchist hacker with a PhD beneath the designer apparel.

"Nothing exciting. We already know Vincent Gladwell is a fraud. His famous farm in Tuscany doesn't exist. He does buy high-quality from the Ugazio farm—in Umbria. But he also buys a lot of low-quality junk from anywhere he can get it cheapest. I'm not a chemist and can't figure out how oil is used in production, so I've sent a bunch of crap to someone who might understand. And I still have no idea what this has to do with anything."

"Because Pris says Kit-Kat was scared, and someone was happy when she dropped dead. It stands to reason one of the men around her wanted her out of the way, and what other reason would there be except the business?" Evie hugged a pillow and went into one of her third-eye blank faces.

"Without any evidence of a crime, the sheriff didn't have any reason to hold non-US citizens on limited visas. Vincent has gone back to the UK. The half-brother and some middle managers are staying to take over the boutique chain. We don't have a lot to work with on this case—not that anyone has actually hired you," Jax reminded them. "Pris and Larraine will come out fine eventually. You should put your energy into something more profitable."

Reuben bit into his sandwich and waited for Evie to return to this plane. It wasn't as if Jax's former intelligence officer had ever paid attention to orders anyway. Evie had offered Rube the acceptance his family and the military couldn't provide. She had an uncanny way of drawing people to her.

She popped back and regarded them blankly for a second. "Our lady of the olive oil hates the boutique's lotions. Maybe we should check them out."

She stood and wandered up the stairs, leaving Jax and Reuben to work that one out.

"I'm not going to bed with a ghost," Jax shouted after her.

"Neither am I," she called back. "She likes you better than me."

Rube snorted beer and headed for his hideaway. "Better you than me, man. Sometimes it pays to be Black and gay."

Deciding Evie could damned well keep him warm if her apparition put in another chilly appearance, Jax grabbed an extra blanket and followed her upstairs.

What he couldn't see or hear couldn't hurt, could it?

Ten: Pris

IN THE EARLY MORNING HOURS, PRIS LOCATED THE VILLA'S LIMITED WI-FI, ascertained it had no passcode, and checked her email and messages. She didn't have a European chip for her phone and wasn't paying a daily ransom to use her data roaming if she could avoid it—not after burning through her savings with no future income on the horizon.

She caught up on family emails and confirmed that Gladwell didn't own the olive oil farm. Well, heck, where did that leave her? There had to be *some* connection to Dante.

Could she possibly have imagined that terrified cry? She wasn't very imaginative except when it came to food.

Since it was still dark outside, she glanced at the online news. Jane the Lawless gossip monger had no new scandal to add to the murder investigation. That didn't stop the columnist from drumming up an audience by speculating that Larraine had been jealous of the attention Kit-Kat was receiving and had somehow persuaded Pris to do the dirty deed with poisonous blowfish.

That was a particularly creative addition. Did blowfish cause heart attacks? Could she feed them to scurrilous reporters? In sushi, maybe. Probably not caviar.

Sensing the rest of the house stirring, she shut down her phone. She'd hoped to play tourist today, poke around the village, learn more about Katherine and her family. . . But Dante had cut her off at the pass. The knowledge that the Gladwells didn't even own the farm—*dang*. Recalculating. She'd spent a fortune just to be harassed by a man who hated her?

After pulling on brown corduroys and turtle neck, Pris glanced in a mirror, and snarled at her hair. If any of the frizz fell in Dante's food, he could deal with it. She wasn't putting on gel for him.

By the time she got downstairs, his mother had already dumped bowls of sugary cereal in front of the twins. Dante had made up his make-shift cot and disappeared. Comfortable with kitchen routine, Pris took her dough from the refrigerator and flattened it on the pastry board.

The twins instantly climbed up on the stools to watch. She handed them each a dough ball to roll.

Emma bustled around, making coffee, emanating worried vibes. Accustomed to silence, Pris worked without speaking. She sprinkled the flattened dough with brown sugar, cinnamon, nutmeg, and some chopped nuts she'd found in the freezer, then rolled it up.

The twins waited expectantly. She gestured for them to flatten their dough balls a little more, then covered them with the filling. She just had them fold the dough and pinch the edges.

She'd sliced the rolled dough into rounds and set them in baking pans by the time she sensed Dante approaching. Even if she didn't feel his strong vibrations, she'd smell his fresh shower scent and aftershave. There must be a downstairs shower. The man was a walking tower of sensory bombardment.

He wielded his crutch with more grace this morning, but he still took a seat before accepting a mug of coffee. "I've postponed the lake country job. We'll go down to the Ugazio farm this morning."

"*We* will?" Pris put the buns in the oven to rise and helped herself to coffee.

"You are supposed to rest!" Emma protested.

The twins climbed down, aiming for their father. Pris diverted them to the sink and soap, handing them a sponge to play with.

"Miss Broadhurst can drive." He gave her a slant-eyed glance, reminding her that their last car ride together had been death-defying. "Leo has a golf cart. I'll be fine."

Pris gritted her molars. Normally, she could ignore men and follow her own path. Unfortunately, she couldn't ignore his injury, not while sensing the pain he hid beneath obnoxiousness. Besides, she wanted to see the origin of La Bella Gente's products. Cogitating, she made an ice pack and dropped it on his propped up leg.

"To keep down swelling, you should keep the injury elevated and iced," she said, looking for a path to leave him behind. "I can take myself wherever I need to go."

He snorted rudely. "You don't speak Italian. You won't even find the farm. I want to send some men to clear that ancient tunnel we uncovered. You can ask questions while I work."

He was being entirely too agreeable. Still, she couldn't ignore his offer just to be *dis*agreeable. The sooner she could investigate, the faster she could leave and go back to work. If she could find any.

Pris baked the buns while Dante consumed the omelet Emma fixed. As she ate, Dante's mother recounted all the local gossip. In between anecdotes, she slipped in minor repairs that maybe Dante could look into since he was home. He grimaced at each request and Pris hid an impolite grin. That was the trouble with linear thinkers—they couldn't look *around* the problem to a solution. They thought all obstacles should be tackled head-on.

Problem-solving required ingenuity, and she had a lot of practice in getting what she wanted.

As the kitchen filled with the aroma of cinnamon, the twins scattered cereal and bounced up and down in anticipation. They watched Pris while she made the icing using two forks, instead of a whisk, so they each had one to lick.

Emma prepared more coffee and the chilly morning air gradually dissipated, helped by the warmth escaping the oven as Pris removed the buns. She didn't know what sick urge had driven her to bake, but mixing the dough had been satisfying at the time. And knowing she had an appreciative audience helped her past the unexpected awkwardness of dealing with Dante. She probably shouldn't wave red flags at injured bulls.

After she added icing, she plopped the pan of hot buns on the table and let them fight over their selection while she cleaned up her mess. Savoring her coffee and cinnamon roll, even Emma didn't jump up to claim the sink.

"My Gerard loved his sweets in the morning," Dante's mother reminisced. "I had to teach him to eat a proper breakfast."

"Oatmeal. She made us eat oatmeal," Dante scoffed.

"Porridge is good for you. It sticks to the stomach." Emma licked her fingers, then took napkins to the twins. "But it isn't easy to find here. Everywhere, they have pastries!"

"Whole wheat pastry with scrambled egg inside, maybe." Thinking about how protein and fiber could be added, Pris returned to the table to finish her breakfast. "Sausage would be easier than eggs."

"Not Italian sausage." Dante used his crutch to stand. "Outside in half an hour."

"Not Italian?" Pris inquired, forgetting she didn't want to speak to him.

Emma gestured at the refrigerator. "Salami. Maybe you could grind it."

Dante stomped out while Pris investigated the refrigerator.

≈

"I DON'T HAVE AN ITALIAN DRIVER'S LICENSE," THE OBSTINATE FEMALE DECLARED when she finally deigned to join Dante outside.

"Given how you drive, you're fortunate to have any license." He shouldn't be insulting the woman. He needed transportation.

"Right." She headed back up the steps.

With a sigh of exasperation, he pointed down the long hilly lane. "That drive is private land. The drive back to Leo's place is all private. You only need to go a mile on public roads. Surely you can manage that without attracting the attention of the *polizia*. There isn't time to bring the Fiat up to sixty." He angled the crutch and himself into the front seat of the midget car his mother used for running around town. It was never an easy fit.

"For all I know, they're waiting at the bottom of the hill to extradite me for murder." Looking like a disgruntled brown mouse in her all brown attire, she slid behind the wheel without effort.

"Did you think you'd hide by blending in with the dirt?" He cast her outfit a disparaging glance. Mistake. It fit all her curves much too well.

Intent on learning the gears, she didn't even waste a glance to glare at him.

That unsettled him. Since childhood, as the only son and heir, he'd been treated like a prince. Since adolescence, women fawned over him. He was unaccustomed to being ignored. "They wouldn't have let you out of the country if they thought Katherine was murdered. I can read. Rumors are not indictable offenses."

"The police aren't publicly admitting that she was murdered. The newspapers know nothing. But *I* know there is a killer on the loose, and he's smart or experienced enough to get away with it. That is *not* a good feeling. My family could be next. How many others may he have killed?" She checked the car's instruments, then turned on the ignition and pushed all the buttons and gears.

Dante had had time to think about her declaration of reading minds. His family had its fair share of known eccentrics. None of them read minds, although some possessed freaky knowledge that was almost as good. But reading minds. . . would drive any sane person insane. Whatever it was she thought she knew, it couldn't be the mind of a murderer.

"Just because you think Katherine was afraid, doesn't lessen the chance of heart attack. Stress can kill. Or she had some underlying condition." He buckled in and pushed the seat back as far as it would go as the car jerked into motion.

"Believe whatever you like. I'm not waiting for our abysmally slow law enforcement system to find out she was killed by her limoncello. That stuff could be used as paint stripper and would eat any signs of poison as far as I'm concerned. I can't imagine why it doesn't strip taste buds."

Dante thought limoncello too sweet, but to each their own. "Be that as it may, Lucia's farm has nothing to do with her half-sister's death. Leo is hanging on by the skin of his teeth. We can check to see if he's heard from Lucia recently, but I don't see anywhere else you can take your strange investigation."

Although if she actually read minds. . . No, that was still ridiculous and useless in this case. Leo was a farmer, nothing more.

"Lucia doesn't live here?" she asked with a frown.

"Not for years."

She pondered that while waiting for directions once they reached the bottom of the hill. Despite the hellish ride she'd submitted him to the last time he'd been in her company, this one was uneventful. It was almost restful not having his mother nattering a mile a minute. He adored his mother and owed her more than he could repay, but he was not accustomed to idle prattle. On a dig, he gave orders. When seeking funds and giving presentations, he lectured and talked business. Time mattered.

Which presented a problem if he wanted to chat up a woman.

He directed her down the rutted lane to Leo's sprawling farmhouse. Like the villa, it was well past its glory days. Leo had no more funds than Dante did to restore his home. The stucco peeled. The roof drooped. And chickens occupied the dirt yard.

"Not the glamorous image La Bella Gente portrays," his companion said dryly.

"I looked up their website last night. Those are stock photos from Tuscany. This is Umbria. I don't think they paid a photographer for original images. The ones of Vincent and his family are photo-shopped onto the background." He opened the car door after she parked where he indicated. Prying himself out of this rolling tin can was going to hurt.

It didn't hurt as much as seeing those photos of a smiling Lucia. She'd looked happy against the pristine background of a farm Dante couldn't give her.

Priscilla came around and offered her shoulder so he could stand. Her head barely reached past his shoulder, but she was sturdier than she looked. With her aid and the crutch, he managed not to jar his leg too badly.

"Thanks," he offered grudgingly as Leo emerged from the shed.

Dante's neighbor wasn't much taller than Priscilla, but he was muscular and good looking enough to attract his share of women. Dante waited for his guest to gravitate to Leo's side, but the witchy female had already taken off to examine the olive trees. This late in the season, the olives had already been harvested.

"What's going on?" Leo whispered. "I got your message but didn't expect you back here anytime soon. How's the leg?"

"I'll need your cart for getting around, but it's fine. Did you hire those men I recommended for cleaning out the tunnel?" Dante swung the crutch and ambled in Priscilla's direction.

Out here in the morning sun, he couldn't call her a she-devil anymore. The silver accents in her dark frizz were real, not an affectation. Without the punk gel, she almost looked approachable. And she hadn't said anything obnoxious in twenty-four hours or more. In fact, she'd actually been helpful a time or two. He'd remain wary, but that was second nature for him.

"I'd rather have the crew planting and pruning," Leo grumbled, loping towards the shed where he kept his cart. "Back in a moment."

Priscilla turned, her face its usual impassive. "He speaks English."

Dante shrugged. "Lucia's father was Italian but spoke English. Her mother was English. Leo spent a lot of time here growing up, helping out. He had to learn. Many Italians speak English. It's Americans who are ignorant of other languages."

She nodded, whether in acceptance, agreement, or just to say she heard, he couldn't say.

"He's very unhappy and a little annoyed at us. He has better things to do with his time." She walked toward the golf cart bouncing down the drive.

Dante could have told her that without reading minds or auras or whatever in heck she thought she was proving. He crutched his way after her.

The irritating female stuck out her hand to Leo after he drove up and climbed out of the cart. "Hi, I'm Priscilla Broadhurst. I'm a chef learning about olive oil production."

Leo brightened considerably. "Leo Ugazio. My friend here spends too much time in the wilds of nowhere and forgets his manners."

"It happens." She shrugged. "While he plays in the dirt, perhaps you could just follow your usual schedule, let me go along, and fill me in as we go?"

Oh, si, the she-devil was plotting. He just didn't know what. "*Allora*, I can follow you about in the cart while the tunnel is being cleared." Dante swung onto the bench seat, gritting his teeth.

"It's really not necessary," she said with a toplofty glance. "I'll be fine with Signor Ugazio."

"Leo, call me Leo, *per favore.*" He offered his arm. "We'll start with the press.

She didn't take his arm but stuck her hands in the back pockets of her corduroys. Dante had never seen such heavy fabric filled out so—artfully. She had one hell of a posterior. He kept the cart on their heels as they strolled toward the sheds, just so he could study the cut of those trousers.

He didn't follow them into the press room. He'd wasted too much of his life tracking Lucia in there or in the orchards or anywhere but the house. He wasn't following another fool woman around. He pulled out his phone and caught up on business while his guest toured the facilities.

Blessedly, she emerged in record time, nodding her head at whatever Leo was telling her. As she approached his cart, he heard her ask, "I understand you used to produce creams and lotions. Was that an old family recipe?"

"Lucia and her grandmother." Leo threw up her hands in disgust. "They had some fool notion we could make our fortunes with beauty products. We haven't the equipment, of course. And ingredients on a small scale are much too expensive. People don't want to buy expensive grease."

Americans do, Dante thought.

Witchy woman cast him a glance. "Americans will," she said, almost tauntingly. "But I imagine the manufacture would require chemists and health inspections and so forth. I can see why you would prefer a simple production. Lucia is your cousin?"

"She inherited the place." Leo gestured at the fields. "But she likes city life better. That has its advantages. She found us a good sales outlet for our oil in the UK that paid top dollar, until Brexit happened, anyway."

"The UK leaving the EU raised tariffs? I can't get good Italian wine or olive oil without paying a premium, but I assumed that was the cost of shipping."

Dante shifted restlessly. He had no interest in market talk, but for some reason, he stayed attune to this conversation.

"The cost of everything went up, including shipping. I've been trying to tell Lucia that we'll have to negotiate a substantial price increase with our next contract, or I'll have to return to selling local, but she's been ignoring me." Leo started toward the bottling shed.

"Her half-sister just died. I imagine that leaves her buried in obligations." The devil woman didn't sound concerned.

Dante was pretty damned certain that was an act.

"Katherine is dead?" Leo asked in surprise and shock. "How?"

"They're saying a heart attack. She was opening a line of boutiques in the U.S. It was in all the papers." She strolled along, allowing Leo to open the shed door for her.

This time, Dante maneuvered himself out of the cart and followed.

"I don't have time for news. Lucia must be devastated." Leo hunched his shoulders in thought. "She and Kat were polar opposites, but they were there for each other after their mother died. I'd send flowers, but the last address I have is old. I wonder if I could call the warehouse and ask where to send them."

"That's a thought, although a personal note might be better. It's hard to say when they'll hold the funeral."

Leo didn't know where his own cousin lived? The one who owned his livelihood?

As if Dante had screamed his thoughts, Priscilla turned to study him. "Since you were neighbors, I assume you know Lucia?"

Leo answered for him. "Lucia dumped Dante when she left for London. She only returned once to leave the twins. No one said my cousin is an angel."

Dante knew a lot about devils in disguise.

Eleven: Evie

WEARING THE KITTEN HEEL PUMPS LORETTA AND REUBEN HAD INSISTED SHE BUY TO look business-like, Evie nearly stumbled over the La Bella Gente Boutique threshold into the glossy interior of glass, chrome, and discreet lighting. Cursing inwardly, she plastered a smile on her face and tugged her ghostly companion inside.

Kit-Kat still wasn't communicative, but her aura brightened perceptibly at familiar surroundings.

"May I help you?" the impeccably groomed saleswoman behind the counter asked in a plummy British accent.

Where's the bloody git? The specter in her head demanded.

Oops, talking to a ghost and a salesclerk at the same time could be problematic. And the ever-present problem of ghosts not remembering names. . . She really couldn't ask after a *bloody git*.

"I'm looking for gifts. Do you have sample boxes, perhaps?" Evie had no credit card other than Loretta's, and she was disinclined to use that. She prayed her tiny bank balance was sufficient if she ended up buying anything.

Jax had insisted that she open a business account for Sensible Solutions, but it was a struggle to keep a minimum balance.

As distracted by Evie's ADD meanderings as much as Evie was, Kit-Kat tugged loose and vanished.

The salesperson gestured at a neat stack of beautifully beribboned boxes on a center table. "These contain trial sizes of our face and hand lotions, plus a bonus gift card for our extra-virgin olive oil that can be redeemed at our bistro when it opens next week."

The display had no price. Evie knew if she had to ask, she couldn't afford it. "The bistro is still opening? That's fabulous. I feared with the loss of Lady Katherine, expansion would come to a standstill."

The clerk shrugged with a slight moue of distaste. "Her brother has stepped up to carry on."

Employees not fond of Matt Gladwell, duly noted. Evie gestured at the display. "Are they scentless? My sister is allergic to fragrance."

"Our fragrances are all natural. Has she shown any reaction to rosemary? We have a marvelous extract. . ." She swayed hips encased in a tight black skirt to the counter containing pink seashell boxes with the contents visible.

What Evie really wanted was Kit-Kat's reactions, but it was difficult tuning into ghostly auras while real people waited for response.

Thank all the heavens, another shopper entered. Evie waved a dismissive hand. "Let me look around and think about it. Help your other customer."

The instant Evie opened her extra sense, her ghostly apparition flared pink and muttered *bitch.*

Tell me how you really feel, Evie thought to herself, then murmured more politely, "You know her?"

Vincent's whore. The aura cycled through anger and confusion and floated behind the counter. Anger flared brighter. *Fake.*

Evie eased in that direction. Apparently the more expensive items were kept in a case behind the counter. The jars and bottles sparkled like crystal, even tempting Evie to touch. The discreetly printed sign named the various products along with long lists of ingredients and their miraculous results.

Evie wondered if her face needed firming or regenerating or if retinol would hide the shadows under her eyes when she didn't clock enough sleep. Somehow, she doubted it, or women wouldn't pay for face lifts.

She thought maybe her ghost believed otherwise. "Is any of this any good?" she whispered. It wasn't as if she knew how to talk face cream.

The aura turned muddy with deception. *Mine was.*

"This isn't your formula?" Evie pulled out her phone and pretended to talk into it. If only she'd had this lovely device when she'd been in school, people wouldn't have laughed at her. But she could never afford one until Loretta came along.

Vincent said mine was too expensive. Then Kit-Kat disappeared behind the curtain that separated the shop from storage.

Maybe she should escape and leave the ghost behind.

"Aren't you Evangeline Carstairs, the ghostbuster?" a nasal voice asked. The emphasis on *ghostbuster* was more sneer than curiosity.

Evie debated ignoring the question. She could abandon Kit-Kat in her place of worship and walk out, but that wouldn't solve her case. Deciding to imitate Pris, she donned an impassive expression, swung around, and raised inquiring eyebrows. She wished she could lift just one. She'd always wanted to look supercilious.

Well, shrimp size and orange hair prohibited that.

Forsaking the peeved sales clerk, Lawless Jane Lawson, columnist and blogger, approached as if smelling something rotten. Apparently dressing like a hobo and having a face on the wrong side of ugly did not shake her confidence as it did Evie's. "I suppose your sick little business is faring well now that another weirdo is running the town."

Sick business? Weirdo? Charming. She'd quit responding to bullies in high school. Evie sauntered toward the door wearing an air of disdain.

Lawson caught her arm. Big bad mistake. Evie spaced out to the aura realm. If she did not mistake, the woman appeared motivated by fear. How did one combat that?

Evie yanked her arm free. "I assume hate works well for you? Are you paid by the click? Or the number of trolls you collect? Unfortunately, ghosts can't buy my services, but anyone of any race or gender can. It's a far broader customer base than bigots." While the reporter stuttered for a response, Evie escaped.

She needed time to cool off before she beat up someone. What was *wrong* with people? Did Lawson's fear warp her thinking so badly that she thought she had to tear down everyone else to lift herself up? Evie winced. That meant the columnist would be attacking Evie instead of Pris next. Oh well.

To improve her humor, she aimed in the direction of Jax's office on the next block. Not wanting to walk in on a client, she texted him as she walked. GOT TIME?

GOT NEWS he texted back.

ALL GOOD I HOPE She walked faster.

TRY INTERESTING

She already had *interesting*. She really wanted *good* for a change.

Rather than contemplate punching sharp noses, she counted her blessings as she hurried down the street. She had a lot more blessings since Loretta and Jax had entered her life.

~

JAX SET DOWN HIS PHONE AS THE WHIRLWIND THAT WAS EVIE FLEW THROUGH HIS outer office. He had time to open his arms to catch her as she landed in his lap and spun his chair around.

"You are my unicorn!" she announced, kissing his cheek.

He demanded more than cheek kisses before returning her to the floor and standing up. "Unicorn? I'm sparkly and horny?"

She laughed happily. That was his Evie. She'd sounded ugly furious on the phone, but she'd apparently recovered. Evie in a temper could be dangerous, so he was glad he'd defused the situation.

"Silver unicorn, defender of justice, mighty hooves raised to trample evil. Look up Jane Lawson sometime and find out why she's so terrified, or I may have Mavis hex her." She took his arm and followed him out. "Where are we going?"

"Ariel's. I want to tell my news only once. Is your fan ghost still hanging around?" He led her into the hall and locked up. One of these days, he'd hire a receptionist to keep the office open when he was out. Today wasn't that day.

"I last saw her at the boutique. That doesn't mean she's not around. She seems to be telling me that the products are fake, although how one can have fake lotion is beyond my knowledge. It's either lotion or it isn't."

"Ingredients list lies? Any value in hiring a chemist?" Jax led her down to his motorcycle.

"Not that I'm aware, although, as I have noted, the lady is not honest and probably wasn't even pleasant when she was alive. There may be myriad folks who would have liked to off her." She climbed on the Harley and hugged him from behind.

When they arrived at his sister's cottage, R&R were already there in their technologically enhanced utility van. They'd helped Jax bring about this outcome, so they deserved to hear his news too.

Ariel emerged from her cave. His neurodivergent sister usually immersed herself in her computers at this hour, but she was learning to adapt. Living with rowdy Roark, adaptation was pretty much a requirement. The Cajun was good for her.

"News!" Evie demanded, climbing off and settling cross-legged on a bench—not easy in a dress and pumps.

Jax tore his gaze from her flouncy skirt and back to Ariel. "The court decided in our favor. Dad's patents and royalties are ours."

R&R hooted and pumped their fists. The women waited—because yes, there were consequences. Winning was not the ultimate goal.

Jax was a lawyer. He knew how to manipulate words. He didn't want to manipulate friends and family, so he kept it simple. "We have been offered a choice. Accountants are calculating the amount DVM Electronics owes us for usurping Dad's patented microchips and circuit board design. DVM is facing mega lawsuits over their fraudulent voting machines. They're in the process of replacing the faulty ones, but it could be years before they see a profit again."

"Ballpark—how much?" Reuben shouted rudely, getting down to the nitty-gritty. It had been his professional engineering report that had convinced the FBI and the courts that DVM and its stockholders were in breach of more laws than Jax wanted to count.

"The company's stock is privately held, so the value is in the assets. We could be looking at thirty to fifty percent of their holdings based on growth over our father's original ownership." Jax gave them time to process and question. No one did. "After the liabilities for all the lawsuits, their net assets would only be in the range of a quarter to half a million dollars. We're not zillionaires."

Roark whistled and glanced at Ariel, who was feeding her pet turtle. Jax wasn't fooled. His sister had the mind of a cash register.

"You're thinking of not taking it?" Roark finally asked, when no one else did.

"With that money, Ariel could buy this cottage from Loretta's trust and do anything she likes. I can actually hire staff and restart my retirement accounts. I can't ignore the cash," Jax warned. The temptation was great to take the money and run.

"Unicorn option!" Evie shouted, watching expectantly.

Everyone else snickered but Jax understood. She knew him too well—or read his aura.

"We take the proceeds in stock, making us a majority owner." He waited. His friends were computer geniuses. DVM was essentially a technology company producing electronic voting machines. They could work it out.

"Losing proposition," Ariel said without expression.

"Probably," Jax agreed. "But until now, profit hasn't been their only motive. They survived the last court battle and kept on making dishonest machines. If we're not involved. . ."

Reuben was the first to whistle in understanding. "*Quality control.* You need someone honest in there making certain they don't pull no more ringers, disrupt no more elections."

Ariel pointed at R&R. Jax nodded. Evie grinned.

"Us?" Roark asked in astonishment. "You'd forget the money, keep the stock, and leave it to *us* to keep the company honest?"

Given what they'd sacrificed trying to keep the military honest, Jax had no doubt they could do it. "Who knows? That stock might be worth millions one day. Except we have to share the board with ambitious, wealthy politicians. We'd be walking a treacherous tightrope."

Evie's big grin disappeared. Watching her expression had given Jax the courage to suggest this mad scheme. Now his antenna for trouble rose. "What?"

"What kind of corporation runs La Bella Gente? Would Kit-Kat have been on the board? Would it be like DVM where major stockholders could demand quality control?"

Shit. Ariel vanished inside. R&R climbed back into their utility van. And Jax kicked himself three ways from Sunday.

Evie had said her ghost had complained of fraud. Motive with a capital M.

Twelve: Pris

Italy

THE TWINS WERE LUCIA'S!

Pris processed that bombshell as Leo led her on a tour of the underground cellars where they stored barrels of oil and crates of bottled wine. Leo informed her that they sent the grapes elsewhere for wine production, but they stored bottles under their own label.

What if the twins weren't Dante's? Maybe that's why he avoided them. Now she really wanted to meet this Lucia. She had so many questions. . .

Retreating to her usual nonchalance, blocking any mental interference, she glanced around at the cavern. High enough for even Dante to stand upright, wide as a warehouse, it was pretty impressive. "Back home, they'd open a rathskellar and have beer parties in here. How far back does it go?"

"The original tunnels were probably dug by the Etruscans." Dante had followed them on his crutch. "There's more than one reason the Romans and our medieval ancestors built fortresses on top of inaccessible hills. Besides the defensive location, the Etruscans had settled there first. They'd already dug wells in the volcanic tuff, dug out the caverns to store their food, keep their cattle, and as shelter against invading barbarians. Entire medieval towns grew out of those ancient farms. This particular hill just wasn't close enough to trading routes to need a fortress."

54

Mansplaining, but interesting. Pris regarded the rough stone walls with new appreciation.

Leo shrugged, unimpressed. "Most of our tunnels collapsed long ago. Since we're not fighting the Visigoths, we've not dug out more than we need for storage." Leo checked the labels on his oil barrels. "This is the new batch. If Lucia doesn't offer a new contract. . ."

"She doesn't ever come home?" Pris had hoped this might be the link they needed to Katherine's elusive half-sister. "Even if her parents are dead, surely she'd want to see the twins? And her farm?"

Dante snorted rudely. "All I've received is their passports and a packet of paperwork signing away her rights, making it clear the twins are solely my responsibility. My mother would probably shoot her if Lucia came within a mile of us."

Looking harassed, Leo ran his hand over his hair. "She's not been back since then. She incorporated her products, started making fortunes, leaving me to deal with her business people these days. I text and email but seldom get a personal reply. She has secretaries." He kicked a barrel.

If it had been Lucia instead of Kit-Kat who'd died, Pris would understand the need to murder. Maybe the two were a lot alike? But no, Kit-Kat had an entourage surrounding her. Lucia apparently preferred hermit-hood. Maybe she lived in a cave.

Now that he was out of the cart, Dante lurched over the uneven ground toward the back of the cavern. "I wonder. . . we'd need a topographical survey. I seem to remember Lucia teasing me with tales of the side tunnels we couldn't excavate. Her father blocked off the back of this section so we couldn't go into them, but it looks like you've expanded. If one might take us down to the lower tunnel. . ."

"Don't you think one of my starving ancestors would have sold any artifacts he found? There's no treasure trove. My luck doesn't run that way." Leo rolled his eyes and headed back out.

Treasure? One more new angle to ponder. Did Italy have pirates?

Never show she cared. . . Digging her hands into her back pockets, Pris swung around to study the high walls and said casually, "Any treasure trove would belong to Lucia, right? It might bring her back here."

Leo scowled. "Then she can pay the expense of digging. I can't."

Dante limped his way back to the entrance. "My students need a project. Give them a chance to follow that lower tunnel. If nothing else, you can turn it into a rathskeller." He threw a defiant glance over his shoulder, almost in her direction.

Pris ignored the flutter in her midsection. "You have students?"

"I work with a local university. They usually have to volunteer in Rome. This gives them something different to explore. The Etruscans were savvy traders, but we've learned they were also accomplished artisans. Centuries before Roman rule they were making exquisite jewelry, pottery, bronze work. . . You name it, they made it."

Leo looked mildly interested. "We plow up pottery shards all the time. Could we sell pottery or bronze? Surely the government wouldn't have any interest in junk. They have more than enough already."

"You can't sell history, no. Although your ancestors may have, and that's why you haven't found anything. You need to go into this in the interest of knowledge, not profit."

Pris didn't even need to open her mind to know what Leo thought about that. But the idea of buried treasure was far more entertaining than hunting poisoners or whatever in heck she was doing here. Instead of following the men out, she walked deeper into the cavern. "What's this huge stone round thing? Did the first cave man invent the wheel here?"

Leo reluctantly turned back. "Victorian oil mill, probably the same essential method as the Etruscans—back breaking labor or mule driven."

She wrinkled her nose. "Looks unsanitary to me, especially if mules were involved." Not concerned with being rude, she wandered deeper into the cave and shuddered. "Is it just me, or is there a cold air current back here?"

Leo grunted skeptically and walked out.

"It's just you. We spent a lot of time chasing drafts when we were kids and found nothing. Let's move on. I want to see what's happening at the other entrance." Instead of leaving, Dante clumped impatiently on her heels, using the rocky wall for balance.

Pris was pretty certain it wasn't just her. "We need Evie to explore. Maybe the ghosts of ancient slaves haunt this place and could tell us where the treasure is." She turned back, keeping her eye open for other tunnel entrances. She didn't know what she could do if she found one, but it didn't hurt to look.

In the dim light, Dante gave her a weird glare, but she was used to that. What she wasn't used to was his mental shiver—one that suggested he might feel the ghosts too.

But he would never admit it. He silently swung his crutch back toward the entrance.

An icy chill ran down Pris's spine as she followed him out.

～

"There's an open tunnel in the back of that cave and Leo knows about it," Witchy Woman announced while parking the car at the steps to his villa.

Dante didn't immediately climb out but frowned at the windshield. "Leo only visited in summers while we were growing up. How would he know more than Lucia?"

"How well did you know Lucia?" she asked acidly, swinging out of the low seat.

Apparently not as well as he'd believed, but they'd been young. He'd gone off to university. She'd stayed on the farm. In those rare times he'd been home, he'd been horny. She'd been willing. She didn't mind being left behind while he roamed—or so he'd thought. He figured they'd marry once he established his career. She hadn't waited.

Devil Woman waited now—impatiently. The silver streaks in her wiry curls practically danced as she tapped her toe.

Dante swung his stiff leg out of the car and glared. "How do you know Leo isn't telling us everything?"

She rolled her dramatic amber eyes. "I will accept that you're a scientist and need proof. You'll have to accept that the only proof I can offer is knowing things I haven't been told. Let's just go with that, okay?"

He didn't want to. It was on the tip of his tongue to say *that's preposterous*. She rubbed him in all the wrong ways, and he wanted her out of the house and out of the life he'd built these last years.

He needed to go back to what he knew best. But despite all attempts to deny it, there was a reason he was better than most at what he did—*and it wasn't normal*.

After today, he had to lift his head from the dirt and take a good long look at why Lucia had done what she'd done. Why hadn't she told him she was pregnant? Why had she left and never reached out to him again? Sure, he'd been a neglectful lover and hadn't exactly promised love, marriage, or even faithfulness. He'd kicked himself for years after she'd dumped the twins on him.

But he'd had years to tamp down his fury. Logic finally prevailed.

If an interfering Malcolm could help him reach Lucia—he should probably call on one of his meddling, too-perceptive cousins, not this veritable stranger.

But Pris was right here at hand and had her own driving reasons to hunt Lucia.

Which meant he had to admit that he knew things he shouldn't know too.

"If I tell you that you might be right about Leo, will you believe me?" He swung ungracefully up the villa's steps. Damn good thing he wasn't attempting to make an impression.

"I'll consider it," she said warily, opening the door. "Why do you doubt him?"

He inhaled and let it all out. "Because someone touched the rocks in the back of the cavern with fear or horror, far more recently than an ancient Etruscan." He left her gaping in the doorway as he swung down the corridor to the kitchen. It felt good to one-up her. Besides, he was starving.

His mother was making grilled cheese sandwiches for the twins. Wordlessly trailing him into the kitchen, Priscilla washed her hands and dived into slicing cheese, bread, and tomatoes. Typical, unlike other women, she didn't immediately ask a thousand questions, but dived into cooking.

"Basil? Oregano?" she inquired, reaching for the garlic cloves hanging by the window.

Emma threw off her apron and hurried out to her beloved garden. Dante figured he should contribute something, but his leg throbbed, and he simply wanted to put it up. He dragged an ice bag out of the freezer. He wanted to be prepared in case her head exploded as she processed what he'd told her.

"Alex, Nan, follow your grandmother and learn which herb is which. Ask if she has spinach." Picking up a knife, he took his usual seat at the table and raised his injured leg on a chair. Might as well clear the room while he was at it. "Give me the garlic. Let me mince."

Pris halted in mid chop to study him, shrugged, and handed it over. "I'm just sprinkling it in the oil. I only need a clove."

He all but rolled his eyes. If she didn't want to question, he would. "Are you going to tell me why you're really here?" he asked, smashing the clove to peel it.

"Because Kit-Kat died, I don't think it was natural, and I want to get ahead of the cops before they accuse me. Obvious, isn't it?" She began assembling her ingredients.

"No. Katherine Gladwell lived in London. She never visited Lucia that I know of. Coming here is not obvious."

"I told you, she *knew* you," Pris insisted, flinging his chopped garlic into her simmering oil. "Her last thought was of you. She was looking at Jax at the time, and maybe she thought she saw you, but she still had to know you to make that connection. And she was *terrified*. My assumption was that you threatened her."

"I never met her that I'm aware of. Now, had that been Lucia. . . That's another matter entirely." He would gladly have twisted Lucia's head off her shoulders for so callously abandoning her children, leaving their upbringing to a footloose father like him.

The twins dashed in carrying garden trugs of herbs and spinach, proudly dumping the leaves all over the counter. His mother followed a little more slowly. She was nearing sixty. She shouldn't have to keep up with five-year-olds.

"Wash your hands," Pris ordered, scooping the leaves into a colander. "Emma, what does everyone drink? Have a seat."

Had she heard him thinking that Emma needed to rest? Or was she just messing with his mind in a good, old-fashioned way? Trying to process how this woman thought might make him insane.

"Bossy, isn't she?" his mother murmured, almost with pleasure. Instead of sitting, she opened the refrigerator for water, wine, and milk.

Dante had no problem with bossy if he got fed and his mother got to sit down —and the twins didn't fling food at him. He still didn't know whether to trust her. He watched as Pris held out the pan so the twins could decorate the tomatoes with chopped herbs.

"Priscilla, do you have children?" His mother asked what he'd been thinking. So maybe women just did that naturally.

"No, just a couple of nieces. But kids this age are simple to understand. Older ones, not so much." She returned the pan to the stove, added the spinach he had requested, and layered on the last of the bread.

Dante sipped his wine and thought about her *understanding* young children. She'd all but said that she read minds. Or vibrations. Or whatever. If the twins were simple—she was understanding that they wanted to be helpful?

To be part of the family, like the adults.

Anyone who paid attention to kids would probably know that, right?

He had spent years pretending they didn't exist. Maybe, if he applied himself. . .

When would he ever have time to do that?

She fed the twins first, adding a few herbs to their plates so they could taste the leaves separately and detect the flavors. Nan didn't care. She gobbled half her sandwich, then climbed down and wandered off. Alex studiously tasted the leaves, wrinkled up his nose, and almost shoved his entire sandwich down so he could follow his sister.

The women didn't correct their manners, so Dante kept his mouth shut and tried to learn—while consuming the plate of sandwiches presented to him. Instead of sitting down, their guest ate while cleaning up.

Then grabbing an apple from the fruit bowl, she headed for the door. "I'm going back to that cave. If I'm not back by dark, tell my family where to find me."

Thirteen: Evie

Afterthought, South Carolina

"Look at this!" Mavis shook a flyer at Evie.

Accustomed to her mother's bursts of wrath over perceived injustices, Evie unhooked Honey, the golden retriever, inside the Psychic Solutions shop, then scratched Psycat's head. The Siamese offered a disdainful snort and returned to watching the world go by from the bay window.

Taking the flyer from her mother, Evie edged Mavis from behind the counter. "Go eat lunch and tell Gertie all about it."

"Read it." Mavis dusted a scattering of dried herbs off her rainbow-hued caftan and marched toward the door. "It applies to you too. I'll have a word or two with Larraine about this."

Since the recount had gone in Larraine's favor, the newly-elected mayor was up to her eye sockets learning her new job, her old one, and the endless supply of journalists cruising Afterthought these days, Evie figured a one-on-one with Larraine wasn't happening soon.

As per habit, she turned on the TV weather and got out the feather duster. Standing still was not in her wheelhouse. She only worked the shop counter to cover Mavis while she ate lunch and ran errands. Beating back the dust and spiders so as not to drive off tourists was a side effect. Her mother wasn't much on noticing grime—probably because she refused to wear glasses.

Leaping down from the window and up to the counter, Psycat meowed a complaint and knocked the flyer to the floor.

"Really? You too?" she asked the cat. Her cousin had attempted to teach the Siamese communication. It had worked a little too well and hadn't exactly led to obedience.

Psy's hiss very much sounded like *yes*.

"I'm being trolled all over the internet. Jax is practically living with his patent lawyers. Everyone is expecting a huge Thanksgiving dinner but Pris isn't here to cook—and you want me to dive into my mother's fights?"

Psy crossed his paws and glared. Cats made lousy conversationalists. Evie swiped the paper off the floor and glanced at the headline.

TOWN COUNCIL TO VOTE ON LICENSING LAW

Licensing, right. She set the paper on the counter and listened to the gloomy weather forecast while she dusted off the collection of crystals and tourist junk on the shelves. It was probably time to give the crystals a good wash. She hadn't done that last spring. She'd been too involved in hunting the villain who'd killed Loretta's parents. At least those ghosts had been more communicative than Kit-Kat.

Her own personal haunt had returned to Evie after la Bella Gente had closed up last night. Speak of the devil—a pale aura developed over the flyer.

"I get it," Evie told the spirit. "You like company. You like parties. Unfortunately, I don't drink and noisy parties put me on sensory overload. And I have work to do."

The ghost's aura of sorrow added a layer of anger. Kit-Kat had a short fuse.

Loretta popped in carrying her lunch bag. "You talking to ghosts again? This one doesn't give off much wiggly air." She settled into the window seat with Psycat.

The kid was trying to see spirits but hadn't quite got the knack yet.

"You decided I was lonely and needed company?" Evie handed her the flyer. "Tell me if I need to rant."

"I need a permission slip to stay after school and work on a math project." Evie's eleven-year-old precocious ward studied the flyer while nibbling her peanut butter apple.

Evie rummaged in Loretta's backpack for the permission slip. "Does that mean you won't be walking home with your friends? Do I need to pick you up?"

"I'm old enough to walk by myself," Loretta argued as she perused the flyer.

"It gets dark early." Loretta knew why she couldn't roam alone. Evie didn't remind her. She signed the permission slip and memorized the day and time she needed to pick her up.

"Huh." Loretta read the paper while digging out her cheese and crackers. "I bet Aunt Mavis doesn't like this."

"Putting it mildly. Pris said something about this earlier. Licenses are just like another tax, right?" Evie returned the flyer to the counter and opened the register to tally the day's take.

"You didn't even read it. Does Jax know about this? Can he fight it?" Loretta opened her phone and punched buttons.

Despite trying to look like her idol, Hermione of Harry Potter fame, Loretta resembled no one but herself. Shoulder length dark hair, large purple-framed glasses for her indigo eyes, and slight build simply said *kid*. Which was far better than the too-adult nerd in private school uniform she'd been last spring.

With a sigh, Evie glanced at the paper again. "It still isn't saying what *licensing* means."

"For one, you have to apply for approval. That means you have to tell them what kind of business you are. And maybe how much money you make?"

Ahhhh. . . Got it. "How did you get so smart?" Evie wrote down the tally for the bank deposit and picked up the paper again. "I'm guessing *psychic* and *solutions* aren't on the approved list of businesses?"

Before Loretta could answer, Jax sauntered in. He might attempt cool and calm, but her lawyer man did uptight anger well. Evie didn't have to read his aura to know he was bristling. He caught the direction of her question immediately.

"It's a control issue." Jax scanned the flyer, then ripped it in two. "The council is furious at having to deal with a mayor with a different agenda than theirs, and they're attempting to reassert their authority."

"So Larraine can veto the stupid law?" Loretta asked, always eager to learn.

Even as disinterested as she was, Evie knew the answer to that. "The council can override her veto. She knew going in that she's fighting an uphill battle."

"The council is used to having its way, with a rubber-stamp mayor. They probably need zoning laws before licensing, but vindictiveness isn't logical." He leaned over the counter to kiss Evie before she could speak. "No hexing the council."

"Probably too late for that. Mavis is on her broomstick. Will you pull obscure laws out of your hat to stop them?" That kiss focused Evie's jumping mental processes.

"I'm not a government lawyer, but I'm looking. In the meantime, your family should explain what the law will mean to everyone they know. Get an audience to the council meeting."

"I'll just say higher taxes." Evie brightened. "I can talk to La Bella Gente's manager and involve him!"

"And hope KK will attach herself to him? Go for it. Meet you back at the house for lunch?" Jax lifted his eyebrows meaningfully.

"We can discuss battle plans." Evie nodded solemnly, for Loretta's sake. "Now take our runaway back to school while I wait for Mavis to crash back to reality. I'll be there in a little bit." A little afternoon delight would brighten the humdrum day. Kit-Kat was turning out to be a useless bore.

Loretta jumped down from the windowsill, hugged Honey, and headed for the door. "Aunt Mavis is just next door. I can walk myself to school."

"Adolescence is going to be a joy." Jax placed his big hand on his ward's slender back and steered her toward his Harley at the curb.

"What do you think, KK?" Evie asked the air, hoping she annoyed the ghost with the abbreviated nickname. "Shall I call and get your good friend and brother Matt on the phone?"

The flyer flew across the shop in a nonexistent breeze.

"You need more practice, KK," Evie called, reaching for the phone.

On the television, the weather report switched to local news.

"The medical examiner's toxicology report concludes that Katherine Glad-well, CEO of La Bella Gente, died of a heart attack, possibly triggered by cyanide poisoning."

~

Returning from his extended lunch with Evie, Jax decided the perks of small-town life exceeded the monetary reward of his prosperous city career. He contentedly settled into his office chair behind a desk with mounting case files. Having a lover willing to adjust her schedule to his was better than money.

His only immediate concern was whether to offer Evie a ring when he proposed. Well, no, he probably needed to rethink proposing half a dozen more times. But his lawyer's mind simply couldn't overrule his illogical need to make a public claim on his eccentric genie.

Proposing *felt* more right than rethinking old arguments. Which was a decidedly Evie argument, but he was coming to appreciate her illogic.

His phone rang, interrupting his useless debate.

"You really need a receptionist or to check voice mail more often." Over the phone line, Larraine's tone held a petulant note she seldom used.

Not having anyone to answer to except himself, and his empty pockets, Jax refused to let the mayor bully him. "Send me cases that pay for a receptionist, and I'm on it."

"I'll send you a receptionist," she replied curtly. "I have a niece with no direction. Motivate her, and we'll call it even. I want you to look into the legality of this licensing law the council is pushing."

"First, you need to look at the corruption laws. Paying me to do city business by giving me your niece is probably right up there. Send your niece over. I'll interview her. If she's worth my time, I'll hire her, and I'll pay her minimum wage. You can provide her with a bonus allowance for keeping a job, if that makes you happy, but keep me at arm's length. And yes, I'd planned on looking into the licensing law, although my gut feeling is that it's perfectly legal and maybe even a good thing, with the right wording."

"Don't make me hate honest lawyers." She hung up.

Imagining the fashion designer furiously shaking whatever wig she wore today, Jax chuckled. Afterthought's inhabitants were far more entertaining than the staid country-club sheep he'd once rubbed elbows with. Who knew he enjoyed colorful? His life certainly hadn't contained much color to appreciate until recently.

His phone pinged with a text from Evie. Picking it up, he read CYANIDE.

Frowning, he started to call, when another text came in from his sister.

BANKRUPT

Evie was normally far more talkative than Ariel, but she disliked typing and usually called. Which meant something was happening. . .

He opened his computer in time to see an email drop in labeled *toxicology report.*

That could not be good. If nothing else, it meant R&R were hacking into the sheriff's files again.

He opened up the report but talk of the short half-life of cyanide requiring toxicological detection within hours of exposure. . . volatility and reactivity leaving measurements highly susceptible to error. . . elevated blood lactate often related to myocardial infarction. . . left him with a headache.

His phone rang with Evie's number, thank heavens. "Give me simple words," he answered.

Understanding his demand, she replied, "Iddy says they waited too long to do tests, and they're guessing based on general observation and a possible trace of almonds in the limoncello glass." Iddy was Evie's veterinarian cousin who knew about a lot more than dogs.

"Almonds?" His brain kicked in and he remembered almonds contained cyanide and the poison often gave off an almond smell. "You can't poison anyone with almonds."

"Probably not, but the almonds KK ate that night would explain any odor on her breath, had anyone detected it. But her boyfriend leapt in to give her CPR, everyone else backed off, so no one reported anything suspicious."

Jax studied the report a little closer. "So they really don't have proof because they waited too late to do testing. Is the sheriff following up?"

"After what Pris told him, he's looking around, but the state cops don't buy mind reading. They won't help unless he comes up with motive, at least. The victim wasn't local, and no one is screaming for justice."

"Except us," Jax added with a sigh. That's how they always got mixed up in these things. People died. No one cared—except Evie, who had a bad habit of listening to ghosts. One had to wonder how many murders went undetected elsewhere. "If nothing else, we have to lay Katherine's spirit to rest and get her out of the house. What's with Ariel's bankruptcy claim?"

"I'll leave that to you. I think she's preparing a report based on hacked bank accounts and worksheets I'm not about to look at, but it has something to do with La Bella Gente and cash flow."

"Okay, but I can't look into licensing laws and cyanide and bankruptcy at the same time. Leave me the licensing laws. You're heading up another unprofitable creek with Katherine, so I'll leave that on you."

"We made money off Granny!" she protested, naming a former client. "Not a lot, maybe, but the feds came through with payment for Rube's reports, and Gump paid our bill. It's more money than I make dog walking."

Her last few Sensible Solutions cases had made a small profit. He wanted her to be happy. "If Ariel is saying La Bella Gente is bankrupt, you might not get paid this time."

"If nothing else, we have to get that nasty reporter off Pris and Larraine. She'll be blowing the cyanide thing totally out of proportion. Is there a legal way to look into Jane Lawson or should I set Reuben and Roark on her?"

"I can look up court records and such. I doubt I'll find much." Jax already had inquiries in. The so-called reporter rubbed him the wrong way, but he preferred staying off her radar.

"I love you!" And she punched off.

Maybe he'd ask her mother if Evie would like a ring. His magic genie never wore jewelry, though, so he was guessing she would prefer a murderer wrapped up in ribbons and bows.

Or a nasty reporter hung out to dry, he thought when the phone rang again and he recognized the number.

Fourteen: Pris

Italy

PRIS SNATCHED UP THE KEYS TO THE FIAT FROM A BASKET NEAR THE DOOR. SHE OUGHT to feel guilty for taking advantage of Dante's pain and hospitality. She didn't. She wasn't sneaking. She'd announced where she was going.

Actually, she was doing him a favor by letting him rest while she ran back to the farm to find a way into that cavern. She'd seen an old road she could take that couldn't be seen from the main buildings.

It wasn't her fault that he swung after her, cursing, as soon as she opened the front door. He was getting too damned coordinated with that crutch.

She hadn't had time to process his declaration that someone had *touched* the rocks in the cavern with *fear or horror*. His admission wasn't as weird as it might sound to most people. She had a male cousin in Savannah who was a psychometrist. Evie trusted his observations. But for a scientist like *Dante* to make that extraordinary claim. . .

He was probably lying to get her attention. Or distract her.

Still, when he insisted on following her out, she grudgingly waited for him to hobble down the stairs and drop into the front seat. His pain pierced her mental blocks for a moment, then cut off. Had he just shut her out?

"You're being ridiculous," she told him, starting the ignition.

"You don't know those caves the way I do. What the hell do you hope to find?"

"I don't know. I just know your friend is evasive. I want leverage to question him more."

"It's more likely that there was some kind of work accident that he doesn't want us to know about. Leo doesn't have the imagination to be more evasive than that. Tell him you can land a lucrative contract in the states, and he'll be butter in your hand." Dante attempted to stretch his long legs, but the car simply wasn't large enough.

"Melted butter, bad image." Pris pondered the possibility of lying to Leo, but she wasn't good at it. She'd simply rather act than talk—a flaw, she knew. But talking never got her anywhere.

"Have you heard anything new from your family? Maybe they've learned that Katherine died naturally."

"It's just noon over there. The time difference sucks. Check the news on your phone, if you want, but it won't change my mind. Katherine died painfully. I don't know what a heart attack feels like, but I don't think it causes seizures." Pris drove past the main farm drive, looking for the lane she'd noticed earlier. She wanted to sneak into the upstairs storage, not drive up and announce her presence.

"Turn right at the curve sign. This car will never be the same if you go down that road, though." He winced as she hit the brake and bumped off the pavement.

"I was planning on walking," she grumbled.

"The entrance is over a mile in, all of it uphill. Just try not to take the bottom off the car with your lunatic driving." He braced himself on the dash as they hit a bump. "I've got a crew in the lower cave. Had I known your plan, I could have had them pick us up."

"I don't work well with others." Grudgingly, she slowed down.

"You're doing better than I am with the twins. You simply don't *want* to work with others. I don't know how you run a business that way."

She parked in a spot between a Jeep and a pick-up. "I cook. My employees serve. Works fine." She slammed out and examined the dirt road leading into what appeared to be an impenetrable hedge of prickly greenery.

A slender young man in a hard hat strolled toward them. He could help Dante out of the car. She hated having the conte touching her. Okay, so she lied to herself all the time.

How did this hidden cave-tunnel connect to the one above? Did it? Could she walk around the hill and up to the storage cave?

"We've almost got the debris field cleared," the cheerful—student?—announced in American English as he helped Dante out of the midget car. "We didn't expect you back so soon."

"He's a masochist," Pris told him. "The professor loves torturing himself. Make sure you kick the crutch out from under him a time or two. Is there a path on the outside leading up to the main cave on top?"

"They built a wall up there to keep anyone from traipsing through the yard." The student didn't seem the least fazed by Pris's grumpiness. "I have the feeling Signor Ugazio doesn't like having us here."

"He doesn't like being told he can't sell the gold cuff he found. He'll like it even less if we find more and it brings more visitors and no money." Dante swung stiffly over the uneven ground.

The man had muscles underneath that blazer. Stupid hormones, getting all excited at the sight of a few masculine muscles. Brains were more important. . . oh wait, he had those too. Dang.

The student loped alongside them. "The tunnel's not large enough for storage, really. Old pigeon holes, so there's probably an air vent or two somewhere. Nothing new or exciting that I can see."

Pigeon holes? Just not asking. "I'm Pris. Do you have a name?" she asked instead.

"Keith." All big white teeth and a few adolescent pimples, the student held out his hand. "The prof never remembers our names."

"The prof doesn't care about our names. To him, people are interchangeable cogs," Pris retorted.

Undaunted and not responding, Dante reached the opening in the hillside and gestured. "There you are. Fetch a hardhat and start crawling."

Crap on a stick. She'd have to *crawl*? Pris shot him a glare. She hadn't intended to explore *tunnels*. Instead, she started up the hillside, to the wall she could see blocking the dirt path. She wanted to explore the big cave above, where she'd felt the chill.

Dante didn't follow. He sat on a boulder and began quizzing his student, leaving her to figure out how to climb a stone wall.

It was easier to climb the tree beside it. Swinging her leg from the branch to the wall, she perched on top to observe. Up on the driveway where they'd parked earlier, men were loading barrels onto a long, open truck, a vehicle like the ones she'd seen them hauling grapes in. She studied the group until she recognized Leo's short sturdiness and cursed under her breath.

Okay, talk, not action. She'd have to hunt ghosts and hidden tunnels another day. She wasn't Evie. Ghosts didn't talk to her. But sometimes, minds did.

Dropping down, she strolled up just as the men were locking the back panel. "Sorry, didn't mean to interrupt. Dante's inspecting his dig and I got bored."

Leo ran his hand through his hair and gestured for the truck to move on. "We're done here anyway. Can I offer you wine or water?"

"Water would be good, thanks. I've been thinking about your Brexit problem and wondering if shipping directly to the US might not solve the situation now that La Bella Gente is opening over there. Maybe they could set up a lotion manufactory in South Carolina. Land and labor are cheap, and the area could use the jobs." Stating facts was easier than lying. She strolled toward a vine-covered gazebo. Inside was a wine-tasting set-up, complete with bar and running water. Apparently grapes and olives were a growth industry here.

"Not my decision." Leo opened a bottle of mineral water he took from a cooler and set out glasses. "But if I ever reach Lucia, I'll suggest it."

Dante had been right—just tell Leo what he wanted to hear, and he'd listen. Now, if only he'd *think*. . . He gave off no interesting vibrations. She had no notion how to direct the conversation to the topics that interested her. "The company is opening bistros as well, selling olive oil along with the food. If you can't talk directly to Lucia, is there anyone else you communicate with?"

"Office staff, mostly. And if Kat is dead. . . I'm thinking I'll go back to selling locally." Gloomily, Leo poured wine for himself.

"Were the Gladwells with Lucia the last time you saw her? Did you say they visit occasionally?" Pris tried to sound nonchalant, as if just gossiping while she rested. She didn't have a lot of practice at casual.

Wrapped up in his own problems, Leo didn't appear to notice her stiffness. "Lucia introduced me to the lot of them that last time she was here, including the models they use for ads. I'd expected blond Englishmen, but her stepfather's family look as Italian as her father. Her mother must have had a thing for Latin men."

"The Katherine I met was blond. Was their mother?" She curled up on the gazebo bench as if making herself at home.

"Yeah, both her daughters resembled her. Katherine was—how do you call it? —a piece of work? Volatile. She bossed everyone around, even her father and Lucia. I assume he's the one with the money though, so maybe I can reach out to him."

"I understand from my family that Matt Gladwell stayed in the US to run the boutiques. Do you think he might have any influence?" Pris had no idea where she was taking this. She simply wanted to keep him talking, see if she could pick up any strong mental vibrations. So far, all she was getting was weariness. Emotion tended to block thinking.

"Let's hope not. He strikes me as a full-time jerk. He's been back here several times with his father. I think they only come by to write off the trip for taxes. They know nothing of oil production."

That brought an angry phrase to his mind, but Pris couldn't translate it. Dang, so much for reading minds if he thought in Italian.

"I wonder if that means Lucia and Katherine were actually running the company? You might be better off selling locally, if so." Finishing her water, Pris stood. "I suppose I better meander back so Dante doesn't leave me behind."

"Driving a stick shift with that leg won't be easy." Lazy amusement crossed Leo's face. "I should drive you home and let him figure out how to get back."

"Doesn't pay to tick off the one who might find treasure, not until he's found it anyway." She strolled toward the wall, hunting for ways to jar his thoughts loose. "What happens if your storage cave is sitting on top of a graveyard?"

An image of bones rose in his mind. Shocked, she grabbed the stones of the wall to steady herself. The image quickly fled. What the heck was Leo thinking about?

"All Italy is a graveyard. We can't stop building if we find bones or we'd all be living in tents." He offered his hand to help her up the stone barricade, apparently unsurprised by her route.

"Pragmatic. I like that." Well, no, she didn't, she decided, but that was better left unsaid. She grabbed a limb and climbed down the tree on the other side.

Leo knew there were bones to be found in his caves. Whose bones? And how old were they?

～

SATISFIED NOW THAT HE'D CHECKED IN WITH HIS STUDENTS, DANTE RETIRED TO THE library fire and his laptop. The villa didn't have anything as modern as a recliner, but the ancient upholstered chair in the library was well-cushioned, and it had a footstool for propping up his leg.

If nothing else, being incapacitated gave him time to finish all the reports he'd been putting off. And he could start work on his next lecture.

Concentrating, he didn't notice the shadows creeping around the edge of the room until one stumbled over a light cord. Lifting his eyes but not his head, he watched as the twins crawled along the bottom of the bookcase. Apparently finding what they wanted, they settled in a corner with a large volume in their laps.

He was pretty sure they couldn't read.

Wondering what they were up to broke his concentration sufficiently to notice the aromas wafting through the drafty halls. Lasagna, perhaps. His stomach rumbled, and he realized it was nearing dinner time—as much as his mother managed a dinner hour anyway.

Distracted by the twins and his hunger, he gave up entirely when he heard male voices descending the stairs. *Che diavolo?*

The instant he set aside his laptop, the twins slid behind the sofa to hide. Prying himself out of the chair with his crutch, he crossed the worn Persian carpet to the shelves, sat on the sofa's arm, and picked up the book they'd been perusing. It fell open to a vivid illustration of naked angels from the Renaissance, many of them children. Right.

He remembered working his way through these shelves when he'd been a lonely child. Unfortunately, he couldn't lean over and haul the miscreants from their hiding place in his current condition. Instead, he pulled down a volume of German fairy tales from over their heads and left it in place of the boring Renaissance paintings. Since they couldn't read, the phantasmagorical illustrations should hold their attention. Quite a few contained children.

Then he stood and worked his way out to the foyer where his unwanted guest waited at the front door, attempting to speak Italian with hand gestures to a couple of what appeared to be workmen from the village. Her gestures were as bad as her Italian. He ought to tie her hands behind her back before she gave them the wrong idea.

A basket that smelled of lasagna ended any confusion. The addition of a couple of bottles of wine still covered in dust from his cellar, and the men beamed in appreciation.

Finally noticing him emerge into the foyer, the workmen lifted their caps, thanked him—in Italian—for hiring them, and departed before Dante could even form a question.

He remembered his mother's childhood tales about brownies who took over the household. He couldn't help the comparison as, garbed in her usual drab, Priscilla vanished the instant he turned his back.

Before he could follow and determine whether she'd just given away his dinner, his mother traipsed down the stairs, her face wreathed in smiles. She was still an attractive woman, more so when smiling. He hadn't realized how long it had been since he'd seen her relaxed instead of frazzled.

She launched into a voluble paean to plumbers who could repair their ancient, intractable plumbing, and Dante finally got the picture. He didn't particularly like it, but he couldn't dampen his mother's delight.

Besides, he was the one who had left the interfering female to her own devices all afternoon. He knew better. Whatever she'd done was on his head. He should have drugged her, stuffed her in a trunk, and shipped her home.

He followed his mother, still chattering in Italian, into the kitchen, where she began throwing in Scots-English in her excitement for Pris's benefit. He hoped the aroma represented his dinner and not just the leftover scent from the one she'd given away, because only a salad sat on the counter.

"I gather you promised itinerant plumbers dinners if they worked on our medieval plumbing?" he asked of Devil Woman, taking a handful of grapes from the fruit bowl to tide him over.

"Priscilla asked if there were any construction jobs in town that required plumbers," his mother explained, while their silent guest whisked up dressing. "So I called around, as she suggested. Maria at the dispensary mentioned some workmen staying out at a worksite who suffered indigestion from their own cooking. One thing led to another. . ."

"And in exchange for dinners, we get working plumbing, I got that. I was simply trying to ascertain how this came about." He finished off the grapes and looked around for something more solid.

With a distracting curl bouncing over her huge—brownie-like—eyes, Priscilla shoved breadsticks at him. She wasn't magic, he reminded himself. It didn't take a mind reader to know he was hungry.

"It's called bartering," his mother explained, obviously quoting the nuisance. "Apparently it's very big in the states. Maybe to avoid taxes?" She wrinkled her brow at that thought.

"Theoretically, we pay taxes on our barters, but there are a lot of loopholes." Priscilla shoved the salad bowl across the counter, poured the dressing into a small pitcher, then turned back to the oven.

Please, let it be lasagna.

Sensing disharmony, his mother wisely went in search of the twins.

"I do not have time to file paperwork on itinerant plumbers who work for food." He transferred the bowl and pitcher to the table, which had already been set.

He could practically hear her think *Not my problem*. Wait a minute. . . He pinched the bridge of his nose. He did not just think what he thought he'd thought.

She produced another lasagna dish, and he relinquished the fight. For now.

His mother bustled in with the twins, shooing them to the sink to wash up. "Pasta dishes are inexpensive and easy. I can make them pizza tomorrow. Perhaps I should set a table up in the front room so their food will stay warm and my dishes don't wander off."

Dante poured a large glass of wine. "A restaurant for workmen, right. We'll have the place fixed up in no time."

Looking decidedly more attractive than she had any right to do, Devil Woman dished out lasagna for the children and a plate for herself. Dante told himself it was hunger and the food in her hand creating that innocent Madonna look.

She dropped a phone on the table instead of plating his food. Gathering up her dinner on a tray, she walked off, abandoning him to his chattering mother and the twins.

No wonder the kids never talked. Their grandmother never shut up.

He tried to push up to follow, but his crutch fell, and she was gone, vanishing like a brownie.

Cursing, he snatched up the phone. She apparently didn't believe in passwords because it opened immediately to the text: KK CYANIDE

With a voluble string of mental curses, Dante grabbed his crutch and shoved up from the table. To hell with starvation. Devil Woman might need to be murdered, but she was incapable of killing anyone or anything except conversations.

Fifteen: Evie

"All right, KK, here comes your favorite shop." Later that afternoon, Evie entered La Bella Gente. Now that she had a goal in mind, she was less intimidated by the posh interior.

Looking bored and filing her fingernails, a different clerk lounged behind the counter. Evie would have been dusting the inventory and rearranging stock, at the very least, but maybe classy clerks didn't do that sort of thing.

Rather than wait to be noticed, she strode up to the glass display case and laid down the council flyer. "I'm from the committee on Afterthought business licensing and need to speak with Matthew Gladwell. Could you tell me how to reach him?"

KK flitted behind the curtains and returned announcing, *in MY office.*

"If you'd like to make an appointment. . ." The clerk reached under the counter for an appointment book.

"This won't take a moment of his time." Pulling out her phone, Evie spoke into it while directing her thought at her uninspired spirit. "Lead on."

KK's pale aura darted behind the curtains again. Evie followed before the clerk knew how to react.

The storage shelves were nearly empty. If Ariel's hacking was correct, La Bella Gente had expanded too fast and was now suffering serious cash flow

74

problems. Lack of inventory ought to prove something, but Evie was after people, not boxes. She recognized one of the tall, dark, square-jawed male model types from the Halloween party. He sat behind a mahogany desk—combing his hair.

Evie was tempted to ask *Hot date tonight?* but managed to restrain herself when Kit-Kat flung all the papers on his desk to the floor. *Way to go, KK!*

"Sorry, I must have let in a draft." As Gladwell belatedly grabbed at his flying papers, Evie placed the flyer on his now empty desk. "I'm Evangeline Carstairs, from Afterthought's licensing committee. We're asking you to join us as we discuss the repercussions of this bill on our businesses. I assume no one told you that you might be subject to a considerable tax and proof of income and assets when you set up this wonderful shop?"

She was learning so much from hanging around people like Jax and his sister! She knew about P&Ls and balance sheets from her days working for a CPA, but she'd not have known how to wield them as scary threats until she heard others do it. Bankrupt businesses, in particular, wouldn't want their financial statements revealed.

Matthew Gladwell sat up straight, looking mildly alarmed as he glanced at the flyer. "That can't be legal, can it? Prihvasie"—*privacy*, Evie assumed—"and all that?"

His British accent was charming. His aura was not. But she'd already known that. She shut her third eye before his pulsating darkness made her too dizzy. "That is what the committee would like to address. We fear this is another example of government overreach. If we could have you and Miss Ugazio sign our petition. . . And it would be delightful if one of you could attend our next meeting. We understand if that might not be possible." She dropped a petition on the desk beside the flyer.

"Lucia never signs anything," he said dismissively, scribbling his name on the dotted line. "And I'm out of town quite a bit. Take my card and let my secretary know of the next meeting." He pushed a business card across the desk with the signed petition.

Never signs, can't sign, never again. . . Kit-Kat sing-songed in her ear. Her aura was practically jumping up and down in fury, but her attempt to knock the monitor off the desk failed. Her ghost didn't have that much energy yet.

"What about Mr. Vincent or Nicolas Gladwell?" Evie suggested, tucking the paper into her capacious purse. "I suppose they've returned to London? We could fax them a petition."

"Nick is waiting in Charleston for the coroner to release Kat's body. I'll give him a call, but he's just marketing and not much on business. Do you have a card? How should I get in touch with you?" He looked her up and down but apparently found her great-aunt's shapeless shirt dress lacking. Or maybe he didn't like short, orange-haired women.

Evie pulled out her fancy new card case with her *Sensible Solutions Agency* business card. "Just a representative's presence would be helpful when we hold our meeting. Thank you. If you'd let us know about Miss Gladwell's funeral arrangements, we'll send flowers. The coroner should be done now, shouldn't he?"

He squirmed a little in his chair. "Still a few more tests. It's all pointless. Nothing will bring her back. Now, if you'll excuse me, I have phone calls. . ." He lifted his phone to his ear and waited pointedly for her to leave.

Unable to think of anything else to ask, Evie departed. Kit-Kat did nothing more than mutter. Of course, listening to one's funeral arrangements might be a trifle disconcerting, even for a ghost.

Back out front, she inquired, "Do you know when the bistro will open? I'd like to buy gift cards for a few friends."

"You can buy cards to be used at any of our operations." The clerk brightened and reached under the counter. She must be paid on commission, poor sucker.

"No, I'd rather wait for this one to open, thank you. My friends don't travel much. Do you know anything about Miss Gladwell's funeral arrangements? The committee would like to send flowers." Kit-Kat's aura prowled the store, not paying attention to Evie's awkward questioning. She hoped the ghost might impart a little more, given time. Or better yet—attach herself to the boutique. Being haunted wasn't all it cracked up to be.

"I believe they're having Lady Katherine cremated and returned to London. It's all so sad, isn't it? She worked all her life to reach the peak of her career, and then her heart gives out."

Cremation, because it was cheaper to ship the remains and the company really was that cash poor? Or to cover up any further evidence?

The clerk pushed a long lock of blond hair behind her ear. "It doesn't say much for working hard, does it?"

"If one enjoys what one works at, it shouldn't be stressful." Evie couldn't resist adding, "And they're saying the heart attack was brought on by poison, so it might say more about whose toes she stomped on her way up the ladder."

The clerk's eyes widened. KK's aura flashed angry enough for Evie to see it without trying. A pyramid of boxes spilled to the floor.

"Oh!" The clerk fled from the counter to fix the display. "These are Lady Katherine's favorite scent. If she was murdered, do you think she's haunting us? That would explain so much. . ."

Evie crouched down to help her. "This town has always been haunted. It's possible. What other things have happened?"

"The inventory keeps disappearing," the clerk whispered while they were both under the table. "We've had complaints about the gift cards, as if a magnetic presence wiped out the balances. Little things that make no sense."

"Phone batteries going dead? I've heard that happens around ghosts." Usually only when Evie was around and channeling them, but everyone's batteries went dead sooner or later. She hoped a little suggestion added encouragement.

"Really?" The clerk straightened to restore her decorative pyramid. "No wonder my battery is always down! Oh, my." She glanced over her shoulder. "I can't tell Mr. Gladwell about a ghost! He'll fire me."

"No point in telling him. There isn't anything he can do." Untroubled that she was scamming the innocent, Evie produced another business card. "Let me know if the problem becomes more troubling. I know people who might help."

Like herself. That wasn't a scam, except KK didn't show any signs of wishing to move on to the next plane. Of course, KK wasn't causing disappearing inventory and empty gift cards either.

The clerk slid the card into her bra. "Thank you! I've invested in this company, and I want to see it work."

Oh, baby, Evie hoped she hadn't invested much. A fool and their money. . . But she couldn't walk away without saying anything. "Have someone knowledgeable check the company's financials before you invest more. And call the number on the card if you have questions. I know people who read the future."

"Nick wouldn't lead me astray," the clerk said confidently. "But I might call if I don't get the raise they promised."

"Nick? Miss Gladwell's cousin?"

The clerk nodded eagerly. "Isn't he gorgeous? I'm hoping he'll stay here in Matt's place."

The pyramid went flying again.

"Oh, dear, I have to go." Evie fled her new best friend, trailing a furious ghost.

Thieves the destructive spirit hissed. *Kill them all.*

～

"Can ghosts kill?" Jax repeated absently that evening as he perused legal websites for information on business licensing while listening to Evie's tale.

So far, he'd learned that the state didn't require a business license. It left licensing to counties and municipalities. Afterthought was the county seat and didn't—yet—have licensing laws on the books and neither did the county. More digging required.

"Maybe, with enough energy." Evie bit her plump bottom lip, diverting Jax from his research.

He forced his gaze back to his laptop to avoid distraction. "Like, when Clancy went berserk and threw stuff across the room and blew out the electricity? If we'd been standing on a cliff, he could have shoved us off?"

Evie just needed a sounding board. It wasn't as if he could help her with ghosts.

"Possibly, but I'm pretty sure ghosts can't locate cyanide and drop it in a glass. They're mostly the energy remains of thoughts and emotions brought on by unfinished business. KK might have the same anger issues as Clancy did, but she was younger and hadn't built up the same level of bitterness and fury, perhaps. It took Loretta's parents months before they generated half of Clancy's energy. I should get rid of Kit-Kat before she grows more destructive, but she refuses to listen."

"Burn sage? Hold a séance?" Jax read ordinances from nearby towns.

"I hate séances. But maybe if we can find out more about her—" Evie leaned over and kissed his cheek. "Thanks for half listening. You've been helpful."

"Anytime." He pulled her closer for a more satisfying kiss. "I'm sorry I can't be more useful."

"You're far more useful doing lawyerly things than listening to my problems. I wonder if Sheriff Troy would take me to the coroner and let KK see her own body?" She pulled away and was gone before Jax fully grasped her question.

He started to jump up, then sat down again. Troy was far too sensible to take Evie anywhere.

Bored with research, he opened an email from Roark, who'd been hacking the sheriff's files for Evie. He'd attached a file labeled *Jane Lawson*.

The first item in the file was a newspaper article detailing how Jane's parents had died from breathing *cyanide* from smoke in a mattress factory fire while Jane was just a teenager. She'd been working part-time at the factory and had escaped the blaze.

Sixteen: Pris

ITALY

EMMA ROSSI BUSTLED INTO THE KITCHEN THE NEXT MORNING, HER BROW FURROWED in worry. "I'm so sorry. I was talking to my sister." She took the plates from Pris and distributed them on the table in front of Dante and the twins.

"Which sister?" the Insensitive Clod politely inquired, while continuing to peruse his morning email on his notepad.

Emma was giving off mental hysteria in two languages. Three, if one considered Gaelic slang derivatives a language. Pris blocked out her alarm and added a stack of toast to a plate. Taking it to the table, she snatched the device from Dante's hands and carried it away, forcing him to pay attention.

Evie often accused her of *rearranging* things. Pris called it doing what needed to be done.

"Your Aunt Margaret, dear." Emma poured a cup of coffee and filled Dante's. "She's in hospital."

Apparently too lazy to gather up his crutch and chase after his computer, the Clod cut toast for the twins. "How serious?"

Refusing to become any more involved in his family's dynamics, Pris sliced up the omelet she'd made and doled it out on the twins' plates, then returned to the stove to start another. She could tell from Emma's anxiety what was coming without reading minds.

79

"Heart surgery. She'll be going in tomorrow. Your Aunt Agnes can take over the bookshop for a while, but someone needs to be at the hospital until your cousins arrive. I think they're in Australia now." Emma sipped her coffee.

"What about Cousin Matilda? Isn't she a nurse?" Dante still sounded unconcerned. He really hadn't comprehended what was happening here.

Pris silently slapped an omelet on his mother's plate and contemplated kicking Dante. How could a man with so much education be such a total idiot?

"Matilda is in Africa. I'm not sure it would even be safe for her to leave the hospital there. There's a plague or something. She'd have to quarantine. Margaret practically raised me. I hate to have her go through this alone." Emma crushed her napkin, then absent-mindedly spread jam on Nan's toast.

"If it were my sister, or even one of my cousins, I'd be on the next plane." Pris knew this was malicious meddling, but sometimes, a big stick wasn't enough.

"You don't have a sister, do you?" Dante finally abandoned his food to look up.

Pris almost heard him making a mental connection before he shut off. Interesting. He had emotional blocks? "Your *mother* has a sister. That's what matters now." She waited expectantly.

"You need to go to Scotland?" he finally asked.

Pris could swear there was terror in his question. She glanced at the twins, but they were busy shoving jam up their noses. Surely he couldn't be afraid of a pair of five-year-olds?

"Oh, I couldn't leave you in the lurch like that," Emma protested. "It's hard enough to keep up with the twins with the use of both legs."

"I'm supposed to be back in the classroom next week. How long would you need to stay?" To give him credit, once he tuned in, he was completely focused. Like most men, though, he was goal-oriented and oblivious to nuance.

"You've been pampered too long, *Conte*." Pris dug into her omelet at the counter. She wasn't sitting anywhere near the testosterone-addled professor, but she'd give him a good shove before Emma tore herself right down the middle. "Your mother has been holding up the fort all your life. You're a grown man now. Suck it up."

Emma clasped her hands and looked panic-stricken, glancing back and forth between her son and Pris. "Would it be too much to ask? If you're staying a few weeks, I can be back quickly. . . ."

Pris raised her eyebrows at Stupid Man. This wasn't her problem. It was his. She could almost hear him swallowing, hard.

"You need to go and stay as long as you like," he reassured her in a tone that almost flashed Big Fat Lie. "I can't travel right now, so I'm here. I'll find someone to help out." Turning to Pris, he actually grimaced as he produced his next words. "If you'll give me a hand until I can find a nanny?"

That had cost him. Good. She shrugged. "I offered earlier, in return for room and board. For a while. I do have to return to keep my business afloat." If there was anything left of it after the cyanide rumors spread—just what she needed, real poisoning to escalate the gossip.

Emma anxiously studied her son. "You can't be running after the children. You need to rest that leg so it will heal. I shouldn't go. We can't ask a guest—"

"I'll tie the bambinos to chairs. Priscilla isn't a guest. She's almost family, right?" He shot her a loaded look daring her to contradict him. When she didn't, he gallantly blazed on. "I'm sure we can entice a nanny or two to do the legwork if Priscilla will do the cooking. We'll be fine. Go, pack. Hug the aunts for me."

When he was good, he was very, very good. She couldn't argue when he was saying what needed to be said.

Emma's frantic mental waves quit beating against the doors of Pris's mind. She almost visibly wilted in relief. "Thank you, thank you both. I'm so worried about Margaret, but the twins. . ." She kissed their curls and slid from the table. "They're so precious. It will be lovely for them to have time with their daddy."

Pris could almost read the evil gleam in their childish minds as they looked up to watch the only mother they'd ever known flee the table. Clueless daddies with crippled legs meant freedom.

"Do either of you know your letters?" she asked the instant Emma left the room.

Wide-eyed, they shook their heads.

"There ya go." She sipped her coffee in satisfaction. "Daddy can start teaching you. Wash up when you're done eating and go find your favorite books."

They scrambled eagerly from their bench, stood on the stool she'd placed at the sink for their benefit, and scrubbed jam off their hands. In instants, they were gone.

"They *are* your kids, aren't they?" Pris asked, possibly spitefully, possibly out of curiosity at Dante's stricken look.

"DNA tested." In disgruntlement, he finished off his omelet. "I would have married her. Dumping them was beyond cruel on so many levels."

"Vicious, actually. Or desperate. And you haven't heard from her since?" Pris mentally composed an email to her ghost-busting Cousin Evie.

"Birthday and Christmas cards so impersonal they probably come from her secretary's mailing list. She's a wealthy woman now. She's not desperate." He drained his cup and looked for his crutch.

Pris refilled the cup because he'd never ask. He flashed her a look that might have been gratitude, although he wouldn't express that either. She could almost appreciate his taciturnity. It wasn't as if she communicated any better. Birds of a feather, flocked together. . .

Flocking wasn't exactly on her mind while he sat there looking handsomely stricken.

"There are many kinds of desperation. Did you ever go to London and hunt her down?" Pris really wished she knew people in London. She'd love to knock on doors. But she had advantages that Dante didn't—unless he really could read emotions on objects. Still, that wasn't as helpful as reading what was in someone's mind as they thought it.

Which she couldn't do most of the time. . . She probably should have practiced more, but most people didn't have thoughts worth the headache of listening.

"I went right after Lucia dumped them. Her business was just starting up, and she didn't have secretaries then. Vincent claimed Lucia was on a business trip to the Netherlands. Katherine refused to talk with me. I left my card on every desk I encountered with a plea for her to call when she returned. She never did. I was too furious to linger. I found one of her business cards on a desk and tried calling the number on it but only got voice mail. Katherine returned my call, said Lucia didn't want to speak with me again."

"I understand Katherine had no children. I wonder if she left a will? May Lucia have inherited her share of the company?" Pris usually left sleuthing to Evie and her weirdo friends, but this was her neck on the line this time. She had to start considering all angles.

Money was the root of all evil, right?

Dante rubbed the back of his neck. "I know nothing about Katherine, but I imagine Lucia has a will. Her father's lawyers would have made her sign something when she inherited all that land. But of course, at the time, she didn't have the twins and didn't like her half-sister very much, so Leo is probably the beneficiary. That might change if Lucia inherits the company. I didn't know Katherine, but a sensible businesswoman should have some plan for incapacitation or death. Someone in the company should have insisted on it."

"You and Leo have good reason to hire a lawyer. Lucia might be a rich woman now. She has a responsibility to the land and to her children. Your lawyer can talk to her lawyers. That's what lawyers are good for."

He grimaced. "I don't want a dime of her money. She relinquished her rights when she abandoned them. I don't need *anything* from her."

The twins raced in carrying armloads of books. Pris raised her eyebrows again.

He wasn't so dumb after all. Pris could tell when he got the message—the *twins* might need the land someday.

She left him to ponder that while she washed up the breakfast dishes.

~

DANTE SETTLED THE TWINS AT THE LIBRARY TABLE. DRAWING THE FIRST LETTERS OF the alphabet for them to copy, he flipped pages on the rest of their book stack while mulling over the conversation with Devil Woman.

He'd been warned Priscilla was a manipulator. One of her cousins had even mentioned that Pris had a habit of *rearranging* things to her satisfaction. She had as much as said herself that she could read minds. Somehow. Sometimes. Maybe. He was starting to suspect that what she did was manipulate thoughts.

She'd certainly twisted his into pretzels.

Lawyers, she wanted him to hire *lawyers* to chase down Lucia. Probably because Priscilla wanted to sic her nosy family on her, but that was understandable if people were being accused of poisoning Katherine. She was also right that he needed to think of someone besides himself.

If anything happened to him. . . It would drop an enormous burden on his mother and the twins. And his fractured leg proved he wasn't invulnerable. He finished off his coffee, couldn't easily stand up to fetch another, and had no one to do it for him.

And now he could see what she was saying when she called him *conte*—he'd been treated like a prince all his damned life. The ancient title meant nothing, but he had land, the villa, and a position that granted him respect. As the only son and heir, he'd never had to ask anyone for anything. It had always been provided. He'd come to expect his life to fall in place—because everyone around him made it so.

No wonder Lucia had left him. She wasn't the type to fall in line easily.

Now, he had to provide his children with what he'd been granted. *His* children. Not just squalling nuisances he had half a mind to give back one day. It wasn't that he disliked infants. He knew nothing about them. He'd been raised an only child in this hill fortress with only adults around him until he was old enough to leave for school. Babies were foreign objects.

But they weren't babies anymore. Holy terrors, maybe, but not babies.

Apparently having scoured the nursery, Pris returned with a box full of alphabet letters: magnetic ones, building blocks, learning toys of every sort.

Dante sorted out the first letters of the alphabet and set them out for the twins to touch. They shoved them off the table and returned to scribbling on the paper he'd provided. Their letters looked less and less like A's and more like boomerangs and bats.

"Your mother has booked a flight at noon," his guest reported. "I'm taking her to the airport. If your children have passports, you'd better hide them. She's likely to panic and take them with her."

He hurriedly checked the table drawer. The passports were still there. He wasn't entirely certain he was relieved. Apparently sensing that, Devil Woman dropped his notebook computer in front of him with a look of disgust and walked out.

He could shout at her about taxis and hired cars, but she was making a point —she wasn't his to order about. He was a fast learner. The twins were his, and he had some catching up to do.

With a sigh, he lifted his aching leg under the table to rest it on the opposite chair, and gestured for the twins to take the chairs on either side of him. "Let's look for all the A words first." He opened their book and let them dive in. It was going to be a long morning.

Only at noon did he understand how damned long a morning could be. Dragging his aching leg to the kitchen, he carried the ingredients for peanut butter sandwiches to the table, along with a carton of milk. The children climbed up to fetch their own plastic cups from the drain board. Sitting down, he realized he'd forgotten a knife. Rather than drag himself back up again, he ordered Nan to fetch one.

Peanut butter was tough to spread on soft bread. By the time he had the twins fed, he realized he was starving and he hated peanut butter.

The twins picked that moment to run out the backdoor without explanation. At that low moment, it hit him—Devil Woman had the car and could go anywhere.

Like back to Leo's storage cave and whatever in hell had happened in there.

That did it. It was noon. People should be up and stirring in Afterthought pretty soon. He texted Jax for all the information he had on Katherine's death. Then he texted Priscilla to tell her the news was bad, and she'd better get back here fast, or he'd call the police.

As far as he was concerned, Pris on the loose was bad news.

He wasn't an expert on manipulation, but he knew how to do it.

When she returned an hour later, white-faced and wide-eyed, Dante immediately regretted his selfishness. Except Alex chose that moment to tumble down the stairs and crack his head in his eagerness to reach her, and they both panicked together.

Seventeen: Evie

"WE HAVEN'T DONE THIS IN A WHILE." EVIE SET A PLATTER OF PIZZA ROLLS ON THE pool table in the cellar where Reuben had taken up residence. Originally her aunt's Victorian coal and storage cellar, it had been converted to a man cave in the 1970s.

Reuben had taken it to space-age levels with more tech equipment than she'd known existed. He'd even had a separate electric line run in. She expected solar panels on the roof any day.

This afternoon, he was running security camera footage from the night of KK's death on a big screen TV while they all found food and seats.

"Not needing a team meeting until now is good, right?" Jax grabbed a beer from the turquoise refrigerator Rube had bought from the thrift store. "It means we're all working and solvent for a change."

"It means we haven't had a juicy case in months." Reuben performed magic and the TV screen split into footage from different cameras.

"I'm thinking one juicy case every few months is all I can take." Evie settled into the plush sofa and studied the half dozen images flashing on the screen. "Kit-Kat has to be the most useless ghost I've ever been saddled with. I can't even figure out what's keeping her here since she doesn't seem to be fully aware that she was murdered."

"Too stupid to move on?" Jax sprawled on the cushion next to her with his laptop and beer. "I'm not a Brit lawyer, but it looks to me like KK and Lucia are personally liable for most of the company's debt. The shares are not publicly held. The top tier of company stock is evenly divided between the officers, but the loan documents are signed personally by KK and Lucia. That's not very bright. Incorporation should shield officers. It's as if the banks refused to recognize the company."

Roark had taken his usual place in one of the computer chairs. He had Jax's sister connected in a corner of his computer screen, but Ariel wasn't paying much attention. She was a numbers person, not a conversationalist. She probably had the sound turned off.

"Lucia's farm is the basic collateral for their growing pyramid of loans, and that's in her name, not the corporation." The big Cajun opened a spread sheet on the computer. "The company buys her farm's olive oil. Then they borrow against the oil to manufacture the lotions and other crap. When sales are good, everyone gets paid. When they're not, they borrow against inventory."

"*People*, folks, I need people," Evie reminded them. "Reuben, slow down those images and help me walk through Kit-Kat's arrival at the party."

He rolled the cameras back to the hour the festivities started. "The Beautiful People all arrived in a block-long limo. I've always wanted to ride in one of those."

"Claustrophobic cave," Jax scoffed.

"And you know this how?" Evie helped herself to popcorn from Reuben's machine.

"Prom night. Bunch of us pooled our life savings. Booze and babes in a dark cave. Never letting Loretta do that."

Evie stifled a giggle and rolled her finger to indicate rolling the video forward. "So, we have Vincent entering with the first store clerk I met, the one KK calls his whore. Does she have a name?"

"Rhonda Tart, if you believe that. Owns some of the bottom tier of stock they're selling to employees." Roark printed out a list, made a paper airplane, and shot it at Evie.

She took another handful of popcorn, ignored the list of stockholders, and watched the rest of the limo party spill into the fashion factory's foyer. "KK and Nick enter together, not looking cozy. Everyone looks angry, don't they? Any background on him?"

"Nicolas Gladwell, Vincent's cousin's youngest troublemaker son. Marketing major, ran up against the law as an adolescent, couldn't land a job until good ol' Cousin Vin took him in. Vincent's family is large and mostly of dubious character," Roark reported. "They own the warehouses where the olive oil and inventory are stored. Been raided a time or two for illegal goods before dey started Bella Gente."

KK's aura rippled in angry, confused colors as she floated around the room, apparently examining Rube's non-existent décor. Evie had to keep half her attention on the ghost for fear she'd destroy delicate equipment.

"All right, so these two big oafs entering with Matt? Related also?" She studied the two men she'd labeled as male models.

"His boyfriends," Rube said, chomping into a pizza roll. "They both live with him and pose for ads in return. Why did I never think of a ménage a trois as a means of keeping a roof over my head?"

Evie flung popcorn at him. "Because brains get you further, faster, and with less drama. Do they own employee stock too?"

"Matt owns prime stock. Tweedle Dee and Dum don't have money to invest. They may actually be bodyguards," Roark suggested. "They have security backgrounds."

Jax whistled with interest and typed notes.

"All right, then here comes the fun part." Evie did her best to focus on the various images scrolling across the screen. "Larraine invites them all back to her private office while us peons begin to fill the lobby and guzzle cheap champagne wearing our silly suits. Do we have footage of that meeting?"

"Nope, uh, no way." Rube enlarged the frame of the limo party strolling down a corridor and entering an office. "Larraine refuses to allow cameras in her office. I've warned her about that."

Evie flung more popcorn at him. "Even gay men are clueless," she concluded. "You really think she wants you to see her removing her wig to scratch her head or adjusting whatever she wears under those tight dresses to create her illusions?"

Rube threw the popcorn back at her. "I've seen it all already. She's just secretive."

Okay, *that* relationship was progressing. Evie ate the popcorn.

"The security cameras in my office are all in reception, even if I can't afford a receptionist," Jax reminded her. "Some business matters are confidential."

"Anyway. . ." Evie rolled her hand again, determined not to ask any more ignorant questions about Rube's relationship with the mayor. "Do we have any idea if refreshments may have been served behind closed doors?"

"Larraine has a bar in there." Rube fast forwarded through the empty hall images to the moments before the La Bella Gente group departed the office.

"Larraine's statement to the police—she offered champagne. They thanked her for the bottles in the limo, all except KK, who said she hates bubbly crap." Jax was apparently reading from the police report. "It was later determined that during the drive from Charleston, both bottles in the limo had been opened and emptied. No traces of suspicious substance found."

"And the bottles in Larraine's office?" Evie asked, just as the screen showed the limo party emerging with open bottles in hand. Crude, really crude.

"They finished off the ones they're carrying at the party. Better quality than what Pris served to the rest of us. Those bottles ended up in the recycle bin with all the others. Due to Pris's efficiency, they were carried off before anyone really started investigating." Jax huffed in disgust.

"Which in small minds keeps both Larraine and Pris on the suspect list— except KK didn't drink champagne. Lame. Lawson only reports what suits her message. We need our own blog to get the whole truth out." Evie sipped from her iced tea and studied the less than merry group in suits.

"Except the sheriff might object to broadcasting what ought to be official reports," Jax reminded her.

She stuck her tongue out at him, and he kissed her. She'd have to do that more often.

Rube stilled the footage so they could examine the group emerging from Larraine's office. "KK has her shot glass already. Not good."

"Larraine's statement says Nick carried it in his inside pocket along with a small bottle of limoncello. The others verified this." Jax flipped through the police reports Roark had hacked. "She started drinking it when the others toasted with champagne. We have no film of who may have touched the glass or bottle in the office."

"Maybe Nick's just KK's accessory, like an overlarge tote bag. What reason would he have to murder her? He's simply a suit with pockets. They don't even act like they're together. She's hanging back in the rear, arguing with the Tart." Evie winced as Reuben resumed motion and KK smacked the other woman hard enough to make her stagger. "Ouch."

They watched in silence as the tall blond clerk stormed off, and KK sullenly led her drunken parade into the foyer.

Rube enlarged another screen. "Rhonda fled to the restroom. No cameras in there either. She doesn't appear with the group again. There's a shot of her later leaving by the front entrance."

"Police records show she took a taxi back to the apartment she rents near the shop. No one admits the incident happened or why. They all had their backs turned." Jax reached down for the plate of pizza rolls he'd left on the floor. "I don't think a slap constitutes motive for murder though."

"Larraine didn't see it?" Evie studied the frame again. Larraine had been leading the parade. KK only stalked up beside her after Rhonda fled in the other direction.

"So, there they all are, looking sullen." Reuben enlarged the frame showing the beautiful people huddling together near the podium while Larraine introduced them.

"And grabbing more champagne. I'd be flat on my face after that much alcohol." Evie watched as Vincent topped off everyone's glasses, except KK's.

"Nick pours her more limoncello." Rube pulled up that frame. "But KK leaves the glass on the table when she goes to the podium to speak."

Evie groaned as people crowded around the podium, obscuring the glass, the table, and the beautiful suits. Rube had the sound off, but Evie had already heard the boring speech. She studied KK up close now. "I wish I could see auras on film. She looks tense and not very happy. Pris said she sensed a lot of anxiety."

"Well, if she'd just learned they were nearly bankrupt, that would take the edge off the excitement, wouldn't it?" Roark filled his mouth with popcorn while watching.

"Actually, she's starting to look a little queasy," Evie decided. "She's staggering as she comes down from the podium. Look, Nick has to catch her arm and help her. Of course, if she's gone through that entire bottle, she ought to be flat out drunk."

"If the poison was in the bottle of limoncello, it's had time to act. Depending on the quantity, cyanide is almost instantaneous." Even Jax watched the video now.

"What happened to the bottle?" Roark asked.

"Watch." Rube scrolled the video slowly forward as the crowd around the podium broke up and returned to food and gossip.

Evie studied the action as Vincent emptied the small limoncello bottle into the shot glass. Matt handed the glass to KK. Nick stuck the bottle into his coat pocket. One of the male models handed KK a bowl from the buffet just before Pris arrived with the caviar.

"Almonds?" they all asked at once as KK swallowed a handful of nuts from the bowl, then swigged her drink.

An instant later, La Bella Gente's CEO bit into Pris's caviar and collapsed on the floor, convulsing. The almonds and the tray of appetizers disappeared beneath a dozen feet as everyone rushed to help—including Pris.

All the cops needed was motive and her cousin was in a deep vat of trouble.

Eighteen: Pris

PRIS FED THE TWINS THE NEXT MORNING, STILL STEWING IN ANGER AND DISAPPOINTMENT at being manipulated into returning to the villa instead of exploring on her own as she'd intended. The damned selfish prince needed... to learn how to handle children.

She dampened her roiling confusion, appreciating the reason for his deception. Dante had gone into total panic over a little blood. If she hadn't been there... At the very least, he needed a nanny before she left him again.

With the twins fed, she sent them off in search of their father and swiped the laptop Dante so carelessly left lying about. Carrying her tea and the computer, she locked herself in her bedroom.

Evie had sent streams of information yesterday. Her ADHD-afflicted cousin hadn't compiled or even read these reports, Pris knew, but she'd somehow mushed all the information into a concise summary.

Limoncello, the most likely source of cyanide. Pris's almonds and caviar to confuse the issue. Opportunity by everyone in Kit-Kat's vicinity, including Pris— if she wasted time poisoning almonds or caviar. Means and opportunity obvious for all. Motivation—*murky.*

She read Reuben's research on cyanide. The poison salts could have been added to the almonds to accelerate death, or the nuts could have been used to obscure any lingering evidence in the shot glass, or both. Whoever had done this had been methodical and planned ahead and knew Kit Kat well.

The cops had kept information to a minimum, but Jane the Lawless Lawson was spreading ludicrous rumors of jealous rivalry to stir up the mindless masses. Because Larraine's sexual predilections were well known, the blogger hinted at Pris's as well. Jane apparently thought all sex was unchristian or illegal. She described seductive glances at the wealthy newcomers and private meetings in closed offices. She produced evidence that Pris had once checked on the space La Bella Gente had rented for their still-unopened bistro—as if she might have resented someone else taking it over.

Pris had evaluated almost every available restaurant space between Charleston and Savannah over the past year. *Of course* she'd investigated her hometown first. The space had been too large and expensive for her needs, so she'd moved on.

The reporter hadn't. Why?

She read the report on Jane's background and adolescent tragedy. Parents dying from cyanide did not explain her hatred of Pris and Larraine. Or of everyone else in the universe who wasn't like her—ahhh, a clue.

Pris wasn't like Jane Lawson. True, she was white and cisgender and not the typical target of most of the reporter's bigotry, but unlike the rest of her family, Pris didn't attend church—as Jane did. As a caterer, Pris worked late on weekends. She liked sleeping on Sundays. That probably wasn't enough to catch Jane's critical eye—but Pris also had a reputation for being *weird.*

Weird was pretty normal for her family, but people accepted reading tarot and talking to ghosts as entertainment, an acceptable means of making a living in Afterthought's cotton fields.

But because it took too much effort to block out morons, Pris wasn't entertaining or sociable. Worse yet, she streaked her hair with dye according to her mood that day and didn't abide by any dress code except her own. *Everyone* thought she was peculiar, including her own family upon occasion. But she had no one to account to but herself.

Apparently, she should have consulted Jane about that.

Childish voices interrupted her reverie before she could list all the ways Jane had probably concluded Pris was a *witch* and a suitable target for the narrowmindedness that drove the columnist's internet popularity.

Furtive knocking followed the whispers.

Well, she had promised Emma she'd look after the kids. Conte Dumquat had probably given up teaching the letter A.

She unlocked the door and the twins tumbled in carrying a stack of Disney DVDs. They pounced on the laptop.

Of course, Dumquat had worked out the best way to occupy the twins was in front of a screen—the one she was using, naturally. Not so dumb after all.

"Give me a minute," she told them, shooting off Evie's emails to Dante's mailbox. She hoped they exploded all his devices.

Then she carried the laptop downstairs to the kitchen where she could keep an eye on the twins as they settled into their movie. Where was Dante and what was he doing now?

The kitchen was chilly, so she fixed hot chocolate for the children, then threw together dough because she needed to pound something after reading all that crap Evie had sent.

As if led by his nose, Dante arrived, appearing underfed. In her anger at being deceived yesterday, she'd heated up Emma's frozen pizza for the twins and the plumbers, leaving her host to his own devices. No telling what he'd fixed for lunch yesterday. This morning, he'd had to fix his own breakfast. It was nearly noon. A healthy hunk required large amounts of sustenance.

He poured himself a mug of thick coffee and rummaged in the refrigerator. At least he'd received the message that she was furious. "Do you have a grocery list?" he asked. "I could send in a delivery order."

Silly question. She *always* kept lists. If nothing else, the plumbers had to be paid with food. She pointed at the notepad in the corner where Emma kept her cookbooks.

He picked up the list and settled at the table with the twins and his phone. Sipping his dreadful coffee, he called in the order. Score one for the man.

Pris lived for silence, but the one building between them now felt uncomfortable. Why?

"I talked to Benvolio, Leo's foreman," he said once the order had been called in.

Ahh, that must be it. She needed him to *help* instead of hinder. She was obviously more worried than she'd realized if she expected him to care about her predicament instead of his. She'd learned to ask for help when her mother had gone gaga over a conman a few months back, but she didn't like it.

Grudgingly, before she covered herself in flour, she produced cheese and crackers for snacking. She left them on the table for him to munch and dole out to the twins as needed and returned to her dough. That was all the encouragement she'd offer.

He seemed to accept this as approval and talked as he sliced cheese. "Ben was there five years ago, on the day Lucia and company arrived. I'm not good at dragging information out of people, but he said Lucia seemed to be happy. He doesn't remember the names of everyone with her."

Pris had no idea what this had to do with anything, but she listened as she pounded the dough into submission.

"The interesting part is that an older man spoke sharply to Lucia and the second woman. Ben doesn't speak much English. He just had the impression that this man was running the show, not the women, even though Lucia owned the farm and the other woman argued with him."

"KK and her father?" Pris suggested.

"That's my guess from his description. Ben said Lucia was showing everyone around, explaining operations, greeting employees the way she always did. Leo was working on a machine and stayed out of it. Ben heard sharp words more than once, but he had his own work to do."

Pris slapped the dough into a ball with impatience. "You're saying this is the last time Leo saw Lucia, but they barely even talked?"

He looked a little startled at that assessment but nodded. "He had no way of knowing it was her last visit. I imagine there was a little bit of tension over being left on his own for months while Lucia was with her mother in London. When Ben left to go into town for parts, the visitors were all in the gazebo, sampling the oil and drinking wine. Ben thought Lucia had finally returned where she belonged and maybe they were celebrating."

"Lucia must have had the twins with her, right?" She covered the dough and set it in the oven to rise, then turned to the refrigerator to decide on lunch.

"Ben hadn't realized the twins were hers. They had a nanny caring for them." Dante's voice contained a hint of bitterness as he chomped his cheese. "Our housekeeper at the time said the woman who brought the twins to the door had brown hair with streaks of gray. I assume that was the nanny."

"Wait a minute—Lucia didn't even bring the twins to the door herself? That's cowardice on a grand scale!"

"Not telling me about my own children was cowardice. Not letting us know she was coming was just par for the course. She knows I travel, and my mother isn't tied to the house." He whacked the cheese a little harder than necessary and caught it before it flew off the table.

"Our housekeeper said a blond woman unpacked the trunk with all the baby supplies," he continued. "But she didn't come to the house. The nanny didn't speak Italian and our housekeeper's English was poor. She was so shocked, that when we finally came home, she was still shouting and gesticulating more than making sense."

"I can imagine," Pris said dryly, remembering how the twins had been dumped on her the first day here. "How long did it take you and Emma to come home?"

Dante covered his face with his hand. "I was in Crete. My mother was in Scotland. The housekeeper quit the minute I returned. She'd had them for a day and night."

Ouch. Pris winced. "Infants, baby formula, diapers—yeah, if I were her, I'd do the same. Mothers just don't *do* that." Pris struck a salami with a small cleaver. And then her mental block parted and she stared at Dante. "Did you touch any of those baby things when you got home?"

He looked at her blankly, then at his hands, grasping what she was asking. "It's not what I normally do."

She got that too. She blocked mental vibrations. He had learned to block any psychometric disturbances. She waited, slicing more salami and starting on a tomato.

"I don't think it would do much good to handle them now. The toys are in tatters, the clothes given away, the carriers well-used. . . and in the attic." Where he couldn't reach them on a crutch. "I can't fathom learning much."

"I'd just really like to know how Lucia felt giving up her children. I simply cannot get past that. I'm not in the least maternal, but even I. . . " Pris looked at the two adorable five-year-olds glued to a laptop screen and singing mermaids or whatever. "Even in utter exhaustion and facing starvation, I don't think I could abandon them."

She set out a loaf of crusty bread and an assortment of vegetables and salami, but her heart wasn't in the food. She must be coming down with something.

"I can tell you how to find the carriers," Dante said hesitantly. "I don't think it will do any good though. It's not something I do well and after all this time. . ."

"Do you get images from ancient artifacts?" she asked, removing her apron.

"Sometimes. There is never a guarantee. The image has to be strong and usually emotional." He looked dubious.

"I can't think of anything more emotional than giving up children. Tell me where to find the carriers."

"Give me the sandwich makings, and I'll start on those," he offered, amazingly. "It will take a while to climb up there and dig around under all the covers my mother uses."

"I can't believe you didn't do this the first time around." She transferred the ingredients to the table.

"I wasn't exactly in a receptive humor, if you can imagine," he said with crisp accents and none of his occasionally lazy Scots burr.

She memorized the directions and left him to lunch while she set out to explore the ancient villa. She was used to hundred-year-old houses. Afterthought was full of them, and her cousin Evie lived in one they all used for storage.

The villa, though, was gorgeous, filled with marvelous antiques and art, elegant plaster ceilings and beautiful wallpapers. She gawked in awe and thought this must be what a museum was like, not that she'd ever been in one unless a trip to see dinosaur bones during school counted.

Even the attic was orderly, as attics go. Evie's was a hodge-podge of boxes and furniture their family had shoved anywhere they could find room. This one was so huge and well curated that Pris could tell each piece had been brought here with the intent to be reused. If she ever learned Italian, she could decorate a restaurant. . .

As if Italy needed another restaurant.

The carriers were found neatly stored in a box in a corner that almost screamed Infant Department. The box was light but awkward as she eased it down the attic steps. Still, she didn't want her impressions anywhere on the plastic handles. The realization that Dante might get nosy and try to read her thoughts on anything she touched made her cringe.

As her mind reading probably made him cringe. Swell.

She carried the box into the kitchen and set it down beside Dante's chair. The twins glanced up in curiosity but returned to watching their movie while chomping sandwiches cut into fist-sized bits. She raised her eyebrows in surprise at his thoughtfulness but said nothing, as always.

While she slapped together ingredients for her own lunch, Dante glared at the box with distaste and reluctance. Pris got that. She didn't like looking into the messy contents of brains either. The unpleasantness of contact had trained her to avoid reaching out.

Dante extended his hand and clutched a handle. His first reaction was a wince. "My mother had a bad day. Maybe a lot of them." Then he lifted the carrier into his lap and ran his hands all over, to places people didn't normally touch.

When he grazed the bottom of the seat, his expression turned to alarm. Pris froze in mid-bite, waiting.

"Terror," he murmured, obviously restraining himself for the sake of the twins. "Fear. Grief. Fury. Hysterical panic. And a fleeting image of the cave."

Pris swallowed hard. "Lucia was terrified?"

"Not the Lucia I knew. I don't know this person."

Nineteen: Evie

EVIE SETTLED ON THE COTTAGE FLOOR WITH ARIEL'S NEW PET, A BLACK-AND-WHITE kitten that deigned to allow her to scratch his head occasionally. Looking around at the dimly lit front room where Ariel and Roark worked their computer magic, she screwed up her nose in distaste. She'd much rather be outside in the sunshine despite the nippy November wind.

"Pris is convinced there's something wrong at Lucia's farm, but she's saddled with the babies, everyone speaks Italian, and she can't do her mental mojo. I need a good excuse to poke around the Beautiful People shop and learn more about olive oil. It's the only place where KK talks." Other than muttering and complaining, anyway. The ghost was a serious downer.

"Don't go unless one of us with you, bébé," Roark warned, not looking up from his screen. "One of dem's a killer. And looks like dey're all crooks."

If she had to tell Jax, she'd never get back in.

"How can selling lotions and creams be crooked? Other than claiming grease in fancy jars can beautify you. That's more like fraud, and we'd need chemical analysis to prove that." The kitten leapt up to chase shadows under the desks. KK had cried fraud. Maybe she was onto something.

"Rube got that done." Roark pointed at his screen. "It needs more work but

96

looks like La Bella's products aren't so bella. Cheapest ingredients on the market and no olive oil."

"That's why KK keeps complaining and knocking over jars!" Evie glanced around for the ghost, but KK didn't like the cottage. She'd disappeared.

Ariel scooped up her pet, rubbed him against her cheek, and dropped him in a box on her desk. "Stolen artifacts," she added. She printed out a list and dropped it near Evie, apparently not into airplane creation like Roark. Evie appreciated that they did paper for her. She didn't tell them she didn't read paper any more than computer screens, not if she could ask questions.

"Artifacts? What do they have to do with lotions? I haven't seen any sign of anything old enough to be an artifact, including the shop staff." Evie studied the list of banks and cash flow and went cross-eyed. "Explanations, please."

"Speculation," Roark contradicted. "We have nothing except Pris's reports."

"And money," Ariel argued.

Evie found the prickly relationship between non-communicative Ariel and boisterous Roark fascinating. She tried to compare it to calm, logical Jax and her instinctive fits and starts, and she had to wonder how anyone ever lasted a lifetime together.

She'd kind of like to have a forever relationship, but she recognized her faults too well. A professional dog walker and ghostbuster had nothing to offer a respectable, soon-to-be wealthy lawyer like Jax.

"What money?" Money, she understood, sort of. She'd never had enough for it to be complicated.

"La Bella Gente pays their most pressing debts from an Italian bank account that isn't on the corporate books," Roark explained. "Our resident bank hacker here has been tracing the money trail."

"Lucia's siphoning the farm funds?" Evie studied the page she'd been given but she was lousy at homework.

"Not the farm. The account owner is an Italian shell company with officers listed from a British shell company. As far as we can determine, the physical address is a plot of dirt in some obscure Umbrian village. We'd need someone to verify that better than Google Earth." Roark's accent disappeared when he was deep into the research.

"Criminal behavior, got it, but that's not enough." Evie watched KK's aura appear, emanating colors of boredom. Given KK's natural aura, she'd have been a better party animal and worse CEO than Evie.

Which meant someone else was probably running the show. KK had been a figurehead. Did that mean elusive Lucia was a criminal mastermind? She'd know about Italian banks and Umbrian dirt lots.

"We don't have much," Roark repeated. "Like I said, speculation. But Dante mentioned finding an Etruscan gold cuff in Lucia's caves which he thought was stolen. The curious thing here is that deposits to the anonymous account halted after Dante put his work crew in there."

"Oh." Evie sat up straight. "KK, are you listening? Did Lucia have a treasure cave?"

"Pffft." Papers all over the room rustled as KK flitted about. "Not worth dying for."

After speaking more words than she'd ever managed, the spirit vanished again.

Not worth dying for? Did KK mean herself?

"You may be on to something." Evie texted Pris with what little they knew. It was evening over there. Presumably, her cousin would be done with dinner and not out trudging caves in the dark.

With the text sent, she dragged herself from the floor "All right, y'all, I guess we'd better start researching any new supply of artifacts hitting the Italian market. If KK knew something, Lucia probably knows more. It's time we figure out where our secretive CEO is hiding. Will she go to KK's funeral?"

"I've got a guy over there waiting for word of time and date," Roark admitted. "Otherwise, all we know is that Lucia and KK share their mother's house, but Vincent owns it."

"Then we need to start shaking a few trees. How about this—I give our clueless blogger a list of deposits on the anonymous account. I'll tell her. . . Heck, is she still hating on Larraine and Pris? Anyone else come under her radar?"

"Why are you asking?" Roark asked in suspicion.

Even Ariel turned to stare.

"Meanness." Evie shrugged. "I'll tell Jane the Lawless that her Target of Today's Bigotry is receiving payments from your mysterious Italian account, and we think it has to do with KK's death. Let her do some real investigative reporting."

"Foolish and not safe," Ariel said, frowning.

"Unless you think Lawless poisoned the almonds, why not try?" Evie checked around for KK but she'd gone to whatever dimension ghosts inhabited. Maybe this time she'd stay there.

"Lawson is meaner than you are, bébé. Feed the info to someone else and let *them* go to our narrow-minded blogger." Roark typed on his phone. "Or have Jax do it."

"I'll hex your phone if you just told Jax that. But using a go-between ties in with another of my tasks. That might work. See you later." With the list of deposits tucked in her tote, Evie took off before they could question.

Ariel's cottage was only a mile or so from home, but with the November weather turning cool, Evie had driven over. She was also learning that responsibility for a kid required being adult enough to reach the school quickly, with adequate transport of said child, if only for doctor appointments.

Checking the time, she drove straight to the school instead of stopping at home. Loretta usually walked or biked, but Evie wanted her safely installed with Mavis before she set out on her vengeance campaign.

"People are saying nasty things about Larraine," Loretta said, climbing into the back. "I want to start a blog. If we had a video camera—"

Evie held up her hand in a stop gesture. "Cameras, not my circus. And putting your face out there is an invitation to trouble. I think Larraine can handle herself, but if you want to practice writing. . . "

"As if I need practice," scoffed the eleven-year-old who had written her own legally-correct guardianship papers. "But she ought to know she has supporters. I'll make the blog anonymous so I can say what I like."

Evie stifled a groan. "Said every half-wit on the internet. You will be *respectful*. The world already has enough uncivilized behavior. Lead by example."

"Boring." But Loretta wasn't sulking as she jumped out at Mavis's Psychic Solutions shop.

Life had been so much simpler before computers. Except Evie really did like her cell phone. She used it to call La Bella Gente and ask for Rhonda Tart, Victor Gladwell's supposed mistress. No point in going further if her victim wasn't present.

"Speaking," said a clipped British voice.

She'd really rather see Rhonda's aura as she spoke, but life was seldom simple.

"Miss Tart, you won't remember me, but we've met. I'd like to see your shop prosper. I have some information that might help. It would probably be better if we're not seen together, however. If you'll be there a while longer, I'll send a messenger."

Rhonda wasn't swift on the uptake. By the time her What's and Who's sputtered a complete question, Evie hung up. With a happy smile, she drove over to Iddy's vet clinic. If Roark thought she should be careful, she could really get into cloak and dagger.

Entering through the back door, she found her cousin in the kennel training the mayor's greyhounds. "Do you still have the German shepherd?"

"Trixie? Yes, she's a sweetie." With her long black hair and sharp features,

Iddy looked more like a classic witch than any of them. She glanced up in curiosity. "You need a guard dog?"

"No, a smart one." Evie removed the list of suspicious Italian bank deposits from her tote and enclosed it an envelope from Iddy's desk. She scribbled Rhonda's name on it. "I need this delivered to La Bella Gente."

"This won't get Trixie poisoned?" Iddy asked warily, accepting the envelope.

"Rewarded, more likely. I just want a messenger who can't be questioned. You've established a connection with Trixie, haven't you?"

Iddy read animal minds, and sometimes, they read hers. Evie didn't know how it worked, but Iddy's animal clients were the best trained in the state. Possibly the world but that was hard to prove.

"Having her deliver an envelope to a specific address is a challenge, but if you walk her past the shop. . . "

Evie shook her head. "I can't enter her doggie mind. The target knows me, and it's best if they make no connection to our family. I'll man the desk here while you walk Trixie over and set her loose out of sight. Let Trix enter when someone opens the shop door."

It took a little more persuasion but Iddy finally caved. While her cousin was gone, Evie used the burner app Reuben had installed on her phone to text Jane the Lawless Blogger Bigot.

ASK DONNA TART ABOUT ANONYMOUS DEPOSITS IN LA BELLA ACCOUNTS. DID KK UNCOVER STEPBROTHERS UNSAVORY SEX LIFE?

Mean, Evie, very, very mean. But someone knew about those deposits. She had no way of reaching out to Nick Gladwell—the man who had carried the limoncello bottle. Vincent wasn't in the country. That left Matt and Rhonda. Well, the male models maybe, but who knew where they were. Security guards didn't access bank accounts anyway.

Setting Rhonda—an ambitious stockholder and Vincent's lover—against Vincent's son, ought to roil a few waters. Evie hoped a clue or two might bubble to the top.

Twenty: Pris

PRIS PUT TOGETHER SUB SANDWICHES WITH FRESHLY MADE BAGUETTES FOR THE plumber, whose feet stuck out from under the kitchen sink. His partner was upstairs replacing ancient fixtures.

Dante was reading a bedtime story to the twins in the library. After she tucked them in upstairs, it would still be early. If she had a flashlight. . .

But dammit, she really needed Dante in that cave. He could find out more touching old stones than she could reading Leo's murky mind. Well, maybe it took both of them.

She hated this. She simply wanted to cook. She didn't want to deal with troubled farmers and overbearing archeologists. She didn't want responsibility for kids.

She did, however, want to find out who killed KK.

Evie's text about the anonymous bank account burned in her pocket. She should tell Dante. In a way, this was his battle too.

And Evie's text about the Italian shell company provided a stronger link between Lucia's farm and La Bella Gente and thus to KK's killer. Sort of. Maybe. She was no sleuth. She'd never even read a Nancy Drew.

With shiny new faucets, working commodes and showers, and a warning to clean out the septic tank, the plumbing duo packed up the bag of dinners she and Emma had prepared. She didn't want them underfoot if the job was done.

She tucked the twins into bed, turned on the baby monitor, and hurried back to the library.

Dante was deep in a video conference. Dang.

Fine then, she'd risk arrest and drive over to this address Evie had sent to see if it was a dirt lot or an actual business. If she used the house wi-fi for directions, she wouldn't need GPS. She was an excellent driver. Reading road signs might be tricky. . .

It felt good to do something instead of sitting around, helpless. She ran up to her room and worked out that the address for the shell company was only ten miles away—shades of fraud, Batman! If Leo was behind this, he didn't go far out of his way to set up a front.

She downloaded the directions to her phone, made sure it was charged, and headed downstairs. Investigate had been what she'd come over to do, after all. Dante owed her nothing.

Except the wretched man heard her coming. He limped to the library door before she could reach the foyer. His conference was going on without him in the background.

"Where are you going at this hour? Are the twins asleep?" When he was tired, he rolled his r's more.

She didn't have an ear for accents. It was hard to tell whether that was Scots or Italian.

"They're asleep. The monitor is hooked up to that device on your desk so you can hear them. I'm going for a short drive. You do remember I can drive?" They'd had a memorable one a few months back where he'd hung on for dear life and cursed her in three or four languages. She understood his wariness of her abilities, but the lack of respect burned.

"It's dark. These roads have no lights. And you can't read the road signs, when there are road signs, which there often aren't. Why can't whatever you're up to wait until morning?" There were pain wrinkles around his eyes.

She wanted to sympathize, but she wasn't that kind of girl. "Go back to your meeting. I'll tell you later. I don't think I can miss an entire town."

"Well, yes, you can. If you're not talking about the village, but any of half a dozen nearby towns, they're not all accessible by vehicle. Again, why can't it wait until morning?"

Not accessible by vehicle? How did one go there, on mule back? She'd figure it out. "You want me to take the twins on my fishing expedition?" she asked in annoyance. "They're asleep now and relatively safe. Tomorrow, they'll run circles around you if I leave them with you. Have you found a nanny yet?"

"Actually, I think I have. Stay. Let me finish this up." He waited for her agreement, then returned to his computer.

Pris gnashed at the bit, but the knowledge that she couldn't just drive into town and look for an address daunted her eagerness just a little bit. She should have known it wasn't easy. She needed to take lessons in Italian. Her Spanish was rusty but she could see a lot of similarities.

He shut down and gestured for her to join him in the amazing library. He was a busy man with an aristocratic lineage and a mansion. She was a caterer with a lineage of witches and frauds. She felt as if she ought to be entering with a tray of drinks and nibbles or at the very least, potions.

Hiding a grimace, she perched on the edge of a worn leather chair. She preferred the kitchen, where she reigned supreme.

"One of my students is looking for work. She has many younger siblings and knows how to deal with little ones. She can come on weekends and Tuesdays and Thursdays. That's a start, isn't it?" He opened a bar built into his bookcase and held up a whiskey glass in her direction.

Pris shook her head at the offer of a drink and waited until he'd poured his and settled into his easy chair before she formed a response. "It's a start, yes, if she has references. Once I leave, what will you do the other days of the week? I understand you travel extensively."

He winced as he set his leg up on a stool. "I won't be traveling much like this. Maybe I can find another student by then."

"Have you heard from your mother? Do you know how long she'll be gone?" Pris gave up and sat back, admitting she wasn't going anywhere this evening.

"Her sister needs care after surgery. I can't ask her to return. As much as I hate to admit it, you're right. I've been behaving like a pampered prince and expecting others to handle everything. The twins are mine, and they deserve my attention. I'm just not sure how to adjust my life to accommodate their needs. A dig isn't any place for children." He frowned into his whiskey.

Or maybe it was Scotch malt. She wasn't much into hard liquor.

"Well, at least you have a good excuse for staying home until you figure it out. But my job here is to find out who killed Katherine Gladwell so I can go back to my business." She handed over her phone with Evie's text. "The connections between her death and Lucia's farm are growing stronger."

He scanned the message. "Did she send the information about the deposits? We can drive over tomorrow and look for this shell company address, but the bank where the deposits are being made is a national one. There are branches all over."

"You're not really getting it, are you? Evie is saying that these deposits *stopped* when you and your students took over Leo's cave. We really have to go back there. And we can't take the twins, not with what you felt on those carriers." Pris didn't mind being reckless for herself, but not when innocents entered the picture.

Fear and horror were powerful emotions. What had driven Lucia and whoever held those carriers to drop the children here and run? Ghosts? Who or what had made them fear for the life of the children?

"I'm not letting you go over to Leo's on your own, especially if he's hiding something. I need to oversee what's been done on the tunnel. If we both go, we can take turns with the twins in the car. I'll talk to the students. Then we'll drive up and you can talk to Leo."

"Take the twins to Lucia's farm where bad guys might hang out? And here I thought you were the cautious one." Pris shoved out of her chair.

"Leo isn't a bad guy," he said with a dismissive gesture. "He's just over-worked and fretting."

Pris kept her opinion to herself. Just because Dante looked like lord of all he surveyed, didn't mean he was people smart. She would do well to remember that. "When can your nanny start?"

He pinched the bridge of his nose. "Next week, sorry."

"Don't apologize to me. You're the one stuck here." She really needed to go home, she decided as she aimed for the door. She was getting too damned comfortable with this man. Manipulating Dante's mind was like pounding her head against a brick wall, so she'd quit trying, but she still understood his pain and frustration. "How long before you can go up those stairs or drive yourself?"

"When I'm not eating pain pills?" He studied his glass as if the answer were there. "I promise I'll do everything within my power to help you with your search for a connection with Katherine's killer, if you'll stay until the nanny arrives. I'll manage after that."

"Yeah, right. I'd better start on tomorrow's meals if we'll be jaunting about the countryside." Besides, she had a powerful lot of energy she needed to work off before she could sleep.

Dante might be a self-centered prick, but he was a damned good looking one. And every so often, when he actually tried to behave like a concerned father. . . He set off her bells and whistles.

Telling herself it was because she'd never really had a father, she returned to the kitchen and mixing dough. Old-fashioned biscuits, she decided, comfort food. No ground sausage for gravy, but she'd improvise.

Then she'd go to her room and look for tickets home.

~

LATE THE NEXT MORNING, DANTE FASTENED ALEX INTO ONE SIDE OF THE BACK SEAT while his enigmatic companion settled Nan into the other. The kids were practically bouncing in excitement, making it hard to check that their booster seats were fastened properly.

Guilt ate at him. He never took them anywhere. He should be taking them to carnivals or whatever it was parents did with children. A zoo. He could take them to a zoo. Sometime.

He'd have to give up his travels and settle down at the local university and teach. He resented the hell out of Lucia for leaving him with all the burden. Maybe what he needed to do was go to London and hunt her down again. This time, she wouldn't be expecting him and wouldn't have time to hide.

He couldn't even go to London until he hired a nanny and his mother returned to hold down the fort.

He was bad company as they drove to the farm, but his guest wasn't much better. Priscilla had informed him this morning that she'd found a good return fare out of Rome for the day after next, but she'd keep looking for next week if the nanny couldn't come sooner. He'd given her his credit card so she could buy a refundable ticket instead and wouldn't have to hunt economy fares. It was the least he could do.

The car bumped down the rocky lane toward the cave, and the twins giggled and laughed at the rough ride.

"Something's wrong," Pris suddenly murmured, jarring him from his thoughts.

Instead of hitting the brake, she stomped the gas pedal and pushed the little Fiat until they practically bounced off the roof.

The damned woman was a speed demon,· but his pulse accelerated. He strained to see what she did, but all he saw was the olive orchard. He'd sent one of his more experienced foremen over to make certain the tunnel was safe for further exploration. He didn't want anyone else hurt by falling rocks—although his students had more sense than Leo. They wouldn't ram hard hats into cracked ceilings.

Dust poured from the entrance as they pulled up. *Shit, shit, shit.* Dante bit off his curses and threw open his door before Pris had the ignition off. "Leave the twins buckled," he ordered.

He pried himself out of the rolling tin can with his crutch, not waiting to see how she took his commands. He could see more hard hats emerging from the narrow entrance, tugging someone or something behind.

"Fred's still in there," one of his students shouted as Dante approached. "The whole ceiling collapsed and a large slab landed on his legs."

Given the type of rock in there, *slabs* didn't make a bit of sense, but he wouldn't argue with the assessment. "Have you called an ambulance? Did you construct the supports as you went? Where's the creeper? Can I fit back in there?"

He shouted questions as he approached the entrance. Red dust poured out, obscuring his vision. He grabbed a hat with a light that someone handed him.

"Dante! You can't go in there with that leg," his foreman argued. "We'll need to jack up the slab so we can pull him out."

"He could lose the leg if we leave him too long." Dante had first-hand knowledge of how bad that could be for an archeological career. "Bring me a jack from the truck and some lumber."

He didn't make promises. He hadn't seen the situation. He simply knew he had twice the experience and more muscle than college kids and a forty-five-year-old desk jockey. His foreman knew *what* to do. He physically *couldn't* do it.

Of course, Dante wasn't fit to crawl either, but he could work around that. The rolling flatbed meant for working under cars helped in tight spaces like this one, even more so with his bad leg. The cart was a piece of junk cast out by some service station, but it held his weight. Lying on his back, kicking with his one good foot, he went in head first, illuminating the ceiling and unable to see ahead. This first part of the tunnel was just as he remembered, perfectly sound bedrock.

He'd assumed it eventually connected with the storage areas above, providing an exit or entrance for the original builders. Those areas had withstood thousands of years of use without a single crack. Why would this one cave-in so easily?

"Federico?" he called. "Can you hear me?"

"Si, signor," the student called with an exasperated sigh. "I cannot turn over to lift the slab."

The tunnel had widened at this section. Dante cautiously rolled over on his stomach so he could see ahead. Odd, the slab that had fallen looked more like concrete than volcanic tuff. He spoke reassuringly in Italian. Fortunately, the student had been on the way out and faced Dante.

"I have a jack," he told the kid. "If I can lift this corner and push the lumber under it, I should be able to lift the whole. I don't know if it's enough. Do you think you can move?"

The edge of the slab appeared to be resting on the student's thigh. If he could pry that edge up. . .

"Si. I am well padded. It is the angle trapping me."

Hampered by his injured leg and the narrow space, it took Dante forever to situate the lumber, the jack, and exert enough pressure to lift the stone even an inch. Federico worked with him, pushing and lifting where he could, sliding the trapped limb slowly as the weight rose off him.

They both gasped in relief as he finally wriggled free.

"Do you think you can push the cart back without using that leg? It needs to be x-rayed." Dante crawled to one side to help his student to the wheels.

He ignored Federico's protests, sending him off so he could examine the fallen ceiling.

No Etruscan had created this space. A more modern entity had widened the original narrow exit with metal tools and attempted to reinforce it with concrete.

Then someone else had deliberately weakened the reinforcement. A rubble of chiseled concrete blocked the rest of the tunnel.

THE TWINS WRIGGLED AND PROTESTED THEIR CAPTIVITY, KEEPING PRIS OCCUPIED WITH their antics. She'd made a lunch basket and produced sandwich squares to settle them down. She needed to be monitoring Dante, his student, and all the worried people crowding the tunnel entrance, but she had only so much mental space. All she managed was to send messages to the heavens.

Finally, after two eternities, she heard the crowd yell in relief. She instantly sought Dante's distinctive mind, but his thoughts were an impenetrable maze. She could tell he was very *not happy,* but he didn't seem to be in too much pain. He was safe, at least.

Act now or regret it forevermore.

Once the ambulance arrived, Pris signaled one of the students. "Look, I need to let the kids out to run about, but it's too dangerous here. I'll take them around to the farmhouse. Can someone run Dante up there when he's ready to leave?"

If the damned man had hurt himself pretending to be Hercules, there were medics on hand. She couldn't help him.

She might want to weep and scream and call him three kinds of fool for risking his life playing superhero with a cracked leg, but logic warned that she couldn't help him.

Fortunately, the student spoke enough English to understand, and being female, she happily agreed. Pris suspected half Dante's classes were there because of him and not the subject.

They were welcome to the insufferable professor who needed no one and nobody except servants.

She eased the Fiat back to the road at a more sedate pace, promising the twins they could get out and look around. She hoped Leo would be gracious enough to offer them the ubiquitous lemonade, and hopefully, bathrooms, but she wouldn't hold her breath. Dante's villa wasn't too far away. She could always take them home.

After she played around with Leo's mind a little more. So yeah, she could be goal-oriented too.

She didn't have to wait long after pulling up the drive and releasing the kids before Leo arrived. It looked as if he might have slicked back his hair and slapped on some pomade for her benefit.

He was seriously not her type, but she smiled in appreciation anyway. At least he noticed her existence. "*Buon giorno*, Signor Ugazio."

He helped her lift the picnic basket from the car floor. "Are you running away from Dante, I hope?" He glanced at the twins, who'd discovered the gazebo. "Are those Lucia's? I haven't seen them since they were in diapers."

"This is Dante learning to take care of them," Pris said dryly. "He got caught in a kerfuffle down below. Five-year-olds can't sit still for long. Do you have water or anything I can offer them?"

She could tell the tunnel collapse fretted at Leo's mind, but she couldn't read his actual thoughts. He relaxed his mental guard at her innocuous question, and she poked a bit as he answered.

"We have water in the cooler and cans of lemonade. Afraid I don't have anyone to make the real stuff these days." He led the way over to the gazebo bar and handed out drinks.

One-track minds were annoyingly just that. Pris could tell he agonized over finances. Even a cave-in and Lucia's children didn't distract him from adding up costs of blocking off the tunnel. Leo was useless.

He handed the twins cans, noted their resemblance to Dante, and forgot about them, much as Dante did, apparently.

Pris attempted directing Leo's mental energy. "Will the tunnel collapsing again be a problem for you?"

She received the distinct impression of relief before he shuttered his thoughts and replied with caution. He wanted the tunnel closed?

"I know Dante hoped we had Etruscan tombs, but the dead should be allowed their privacy, shouldn't they?" He opened a can of soft drink.

"I hadn't given it much thought. Dust to dust is my preference. Grave goods belong with the living. They're just temptation for thieves."

"And archeologists," Leo added with amusement.

But he wasn't really amused. He was seeing bones again. And *money*? Good grief, did everything relate to money? She'd hate to administer a Rorschach test on this man.

"You're not worried that your oil tanks won't someday fall through the floor into the tunnel below?" How did she steer a conversation to bones? She usually avoided her gift for good reason—it made for senseless conversation.

"There is probably a hundred feet of dirt below the tanks." He shrugged in unconcern.

"Or maybe if the floor falls in, you'll find the tombs," she suggested.

She almost caught a glimpse of gold coloring his thoughts. Gold? Then a car rolled up the drive, and he emitted a wave of panic. Pris glanced over her shoulder at a black limo parking in the pull-off beside the Fiat. "Customer?" Although one did not panic over customers.

"Hardly." He strolled away, leaving her to entertain the twins. The name *Gladwell* came through loud and strong, though, and not with pleasure.

Even simple-minded Leo had way too much crammed inside his cranium to read clearly. Sorting out what he knew about Lucia's stepfamily was an impossibility requiring a deep dive into memories she couldn't possibly access.

Of course, if Leo meant to murder anyone, did she really want to know that?

Lingering out of sight in the gazebo, Pris studied the older man exiting the car and slapping Leo on the back. Vincent Gladwell had been right there with KK when she died. He'd lost his only daughter, and instead of planning her funeral, he was on a pleasure trip? That's what Leo had said the Gladwells did when they visited.

His son, Matt, climbed out on the other side. Hadn't Evie said she'd just talked to him back in South Carolina? Maybe they were holding KK's funeral here? Why? She was English.

As the men walked toward Leo's office, she could see the tension as well as sense it. Vincent's mind was a bramble of fury. Matt's seemed to have a single focus—wine. He left Leo and his father and aimed for the tasting room inside.

With her focus on the men, she lost track of the twins. Before she knew it, they darted out of the gazebo in pursuit of a farm cat.

At sight of them, Vincent halted. Pris heard one thought loud and clear —*Damn bastards!*—before a thicket of curses created another impenetrable mental hedge.

Guilt, murderous hatred, and fear seeped through the thorns.

Twenty-One: Evie

EVIE TESTED THE BACK DOOR OF LA BELLA GENTE'S UNOPENED BISTRO. IT WAS unlocked, as Roark had promised. A man with his acute hearing, who could open safes, had no difficulty with this flimsy doorknob lock.

It was still early morning, before the boutique next door opened, but the morning sun hadn't filtered into the bistro's kitchen area. She nearly stumbled over a stack of pallets and a few garbage bags waiting to be hauled to a dumpster. Apparently beautiful people didn't like taking out trash.

She tapped the mic Reuben had given her. "Testing."

"You're good. Camera's on the alley," Reuben reported in her earbud. "I'll let you know when the pest arrives."

She'd sent anonymous messages to both Rhonda Tart and Jane Lawson suggesting this meeting place. She hoped they'd heeded her wise advice, or this was all for nothing.

Of course, given the relative cluelessness of both parties, she was probably just being nosy and accomplishing nothing anyway. Pris was over there with the real villains.

As Evie picked her way past the trash, hunting for a hiding place, KK flitted about in near invisibility. Apparently, she had little interest in the bistro. Did she even realize only a wall separated her from her favorite place, the glittery

111

chrome-and-glass shop? Evie still couldn't pinpoint why KK was clinging to this mortal coil. The ghost appeared purposeless. She'd always thought spirit energy needed a good reason to apply itself to staying in this plane of existence.

The dining room was mostly dusty empty space. No tables or good hiding places, just a serving counter and a. . . Evie studied the dark windows of a cabinet and opened it. Maybe for wine bottles? Although the shelves had never been installed. There were cartons leaning against the sides. She scooted them out of the way and stepped inside—perfect size. The window was a problem though.

She stepped out, set a broomstick and a rag inside as a test, and decided that in this dim light, she could stand against the wall and not be seen. "I'm in and ready," she whispered into her mic.

"Lawson in alley," Rube reported.

"This is almost exciting," she whispered back.

Reuben had insisted a microphone was sufficient for listening in on the blogger and Rhonda and that she needn't risk herself. Evie had to remind him that she needed to physically *see* people talking as well as hear them. Auras didn't show up on equipment.

She leaned against the wall of the cabinet in the best position for observing the empty room and watched the Blogger Bigot ease open the kitchen door. As usual, Jane Lawson's aura was murky, more with fear than anger at the moment. Of course, paranoia seemed to be her permanent state.

Right on time, Rhonda entered through the boutique door. Her aura displayed an unhealthy level of ambition and. . . greed? Hmmm, did that mean Rhonda was only after the money? If she really was Vincent's mistress, she wasn't getting much action with him in England all the time.

Dressed in upwardly-mobile fashion of designer dress and heels, Rhonda stopped halfway across the empty interior, looking a trifle surprised that Lawson in her usual khaki drab was already present. She'd probably expected to have to unlock the back door.

Evie winced. She probably should have locked it behind her.

"You have something for me?" Jane asked tactlessly, searching the shadows as she approached. "I don't see why you couldn't email it. The address is on my website."

Because I wanted to see you in action, Evie thought. Well, and see what KK might do, but the ghost didn't even seem to notice the meeting.

Rhonda crossed her arms. "If you don't like it, I can find someone else."

Evie doubted that, but it shut up Lawless Lawson, who stayed shut up, waiting, glancing around with nervous curiosity. The shaggy-haired blogger was an odd bird, not working hard at earning her information. Evie had the uneasy notion Jane was up to something. Her aura reflected a high level of stress and bitterness to go with a shade of dishonest intentions.

"I only agreed to meet you because a tipster suggested you might be interested. I have no idea what this information means." Rhonda produced the envelope from her jacket pocket.

Finally showing some initiative, Jane reached for it. "Any idea who the tipster might be?"

"Someone who said they wanted the boutique to succeed. There's a bank name on there. I thought it might be a list of Katherine's transfers from the shop account to her own."

Jane studied the paper. "She was sneaky that way?"

Evie could almost see the war between Rhonda's need to dump her grievances and her desire to protect the company she was invested in. The yellowish gold in her third chakra probably didn't reflect the aura of a killer, just someone struggling for control or respect. Still, Evie acknowledged she needed an open mind. She was new at this detecting business.

The ghost's aura brightened, if anger and resentment counted as brighter. KK buzzed about a little faster, but there was little in here a ghost could disturb. Evie really needed to figure out how to communicate with her.

"I didn't know Katherine well," Rhonda admitted. "Those sums are too large for just this shop though."

"But it might explain why this dump never got finished." Jane shoved the list in one of the many pockets of her camouflage vest. "Payoffs to our tacky Mayor Ward, I bet."

"To an Italian bank?" Rhonda's nose tilted upward in disdain.

"Not a big leap for the mayoral toad. Italian fashion and all that. Makes sense to me."

Ah, the bigot will out. Evie rolled her eyes.

"Makes life simpler," Reuben murmured in her earbud, as if reading her thoughts. "Gay. Fashion. Italian. Fascist. Bad."

She almost snorted, except she was afraid Rube was right. Jane wasn't the brightest bulb and simple thought patterns probably appealed.

"Katherine and the Gladwells are British," Rhonda said in a contemptuous tone easy to produce with her rounded vowels and plummy accent. "Only Lucia is Italian."

"Huh. Now there's a clue. Has anyone ever seen Lucia? Do you even know what she looks like?" Nervously pacing, Jane wiped her finger over the filthy counter. "Maybe she's hiding right here in plain sight."

KK vanished into the kitchen. Normally, Evie didn't have difficulty focusing on three things at once, but the conversation seemed more important. She ignored the ghost.

"Lucia is in all the commercials," Rhonda reminded her. "Everyone knows what she looks like. There is no way she could have killed Katherine. She wasn't even in the country."

"But she could be siphoning off funds," the blogger pointed out. "No idea where your tipster got this info?"

"None, whatsoever," Rhonda said stiffly. Evie guessed a controlling personality didn't like admitting not knowing it all.

"Well, you have more access to financial records than I do. Rustle some up, and I'll see what I can do. Otherwise, all I can do is stir the cauldron."

"You want me to turn over confidential records?" Evie thought Rhonda's aura seemed more intrigued than appalled, but that was just her biased interpretation.

She didn't like Rhonda much more than KK did. Darting out of the kitchen, the ghost toppled one of the trash bags near the shop door. Their not-so-friendly spirit had actually become agitated. Huh, another point to ponder.

Jane jerked nervously at the thump of the falling bag and eased toward the back door. Rhonda was still too wound up to pay the trash any attention.

"Nick Gladwell coming up the alley," Reuben whispered in Evie's earbud. "He's not looking happy."

Well, make that all of them. "I'm not learning a thing," she whispered back.

Showing more animation than she ever had, KK flung herself back and forth across the ceiling. Evie wished the damned apparition would speak.

Outside the cabinet, the demented blogger sneered as she eased toward the exit. "If you wanna move on up, you have to get those pretty fingernails grubby. I'll be in touch." Saluting, Jane spun on her army boots and shoved through the swinging door to the kitchen.

KK finally shouted in Evie's head. "Smoke!"

A whiff of pungent air seeped inside the cabinet.

"Oh, crap. Rube, can you see fire?" Evie debated bursting out of her hiding place, but she hated blowing her cover for a ghost's unreliable warning. She waited for Rhonda to leave, but the clerk was tapping into her phone.

"Camera isn't picking up—" A litany of curses followed. "Flames just shot out the back. Get out now!" he shouted in her ear.

Almost in the same moment, Jane rushed from the kitchen. "Fire!" She headed for the boutique door.

Wide-eyed as she finally noticed the smell, Rhonda clattered on her heels ahead of her, grabbing the knob first.

The door didn't open.

Evie watched in horror as the clerk rattled the knob and shoved harder. *Nothing.* Jane shoved her aside. The door wouldn't open. Evie couldn't see flames but the stench grew stronger. If Jane couldn't go out the back and the shop door was locked. . .

Both women and Evie turned to study the front exit—a locked mechanical door protected the glass exterior. Unless they knew how to open it. . .

"It's a trap!" Jane shouted, freaking out and slamming into the shop door as if her scrawny frame might break it down. She bounced off it and hit the floor, where streaks of small flames now crept along the wall toward the bags of trash.

Accelerant, Evie concluded. Someone had poured flammable liquid beneath the door.

Twenty-Two: Pris

There were reasons Pris blocked her mind from the mental aberrations of others. Vincent Gladwell's irrational hatred of the twins was one of them. Did she act on a reaction that was only in her head?

She couldn't take chances with children involved.

As Vincent disappeared into the farm office with Leo, Pris packed up the lunch basket and hastily ushered the twins into the car. Once she had them buckled in, she texted Dante. He didn't answer.

Gladwell's animosity toward the children had shaken her—badly. She'd lived with her insane gift for nearly thirty years, had learned to block bad vibes, and wasn't easily shaken anymore. That Gladwell's hatred was strong enough to penetrate all her barriers was a warning she couldn't ignore.

What could Vincent have against the twins? If she was interpreting his ugly thoughts correctly, he wished two adorable innocents *hadn't been born*. Why?

Was this why Lucia had left her babies with Dante, to protect them?

Personally, she'd like to get up in Gladwell's face and shake a fist and learn what he knew about Kit-Kat. . . but the twins' safety came first.

Dante still hadn't answered by the time she had the children settled and turned the car toward home. She could run back and pick him up if he needed help, but he was a big boy. There were plenty of eager students willing to wait on him hand and foot.

Once back at the villa, she parked the car behind the gate so it couldn't be seen from the drive. The twins thought it all a great game when she steered them in through the back door. She sent them to the bathroom, had them wash their hands, then settled them at the kitchen table with the rest of their lunch and an educational video on Dante's laptop.

Then, she spent forever hunting through the villa for exits and making sure they were all locked. She pushed a heavy cabinet in front of glass French doors. The ancient windows couldn't be secured, leaving her feeling unsafe.

Telling herself she was being paranoid, she munched bread and cheese and settled in the kitchen with her phone and an internet session. She texted Evie and company for more information on Vincent, warning them that he might be more than an incompetent businessman.

In return, she received a flurry of incomprehensible texts about Evie and fire. What the. . . ? Pris counted back hours—it wasn't even mid-morning there. How the blue heavens had Evie got into trouble at this hour?

In a rising state of panic, she Googled Afterthought and found breaking news about a fire in a boutique engulfing a hundred-year-old building. What did *Evie* have to do with this?

Her level of alarm rose as she watched a news video of a bulldozer smashing through the metal door on the building she'd once considered for her catering service, the one La Bella Gente now leased.

Only Jax and his merry madmen would highjack a bulldozer to break through a wall—and that meant Evie was in there. Why? How. . .

Dante texted saying he was going to the hospital with the injured student.

Flinging curses at his oblivious head, Pris texted back that Gladwell was in town, and she thought he was a threat to the twins. She had no idea if that was true. She simply felt it in her bones.

Dante merely texted that he'd be back when he could. He didn't even take the time to call to inquire about her fears. Risking international phone robbery rates, she turned on roaming and punched Dante's number, but it went to his voice mail. He had the ringer off.

In fury, she texted him that her cousin might be trapped in a fire. He didn't respond at all. He'd damned well better be out of reach of cell towers or she'd personally poison him when he returned. She was reaching meltdown mode here. Now that she had roaming on, she tried to call her family, but they were probably either sleeping or hexing the fire.

Seething, she soothed her nerves by whacking ingredients for a meat pie for dinner. She didn't like being out here all alone when she was feeling threatened, and her world was crumbling. She flinched at every odd knock or bang, even knowing the villa was ancient and creaked like an old lady.

She tried to tell herself she was being ridiculous when the doorbell rang. Maybe Dante had forgotten his key? But it was much too soon for him to return. She wanted a security camera.

Leaving the twins at the table, wiping her hands on a towel, she approached the door warily. It had no side windows or even a peep hole for checking the identity of the visitor. Instead of answering, she peered around the drapery to the drive.

A black limo idled there.

Heck, no, she wasn't opening the door for Vincent Gladwell. The bell rang a few more times. The twins crept out in curiosity, but she waved them back to the kitchen. They trotted up to peer over the windowsill. Well, she couldn't really blame them.

She watched as a uniformed chauffeur returned to the limo to report to the occupants hidden by darkened glass. Apparently deciding it was beneath their dignity to peer in windows or check the backyard, whoever was in the back seat directed the chauffeur to drive on. The driver returned to the car, and it rolled away.

Pris shivered. The mental energy she'd received from that car had all been ugly.

She knew absolutely no one to call on for help. She had no way of securing entry. Did Italy have 911?

She checked to see if there was more news from Afterthought but the website hadn't been updated. No one answered her calls, not even her mother.

Time to prepare evacuation plans. She hunted through her contacts for Emma's number.

Twenty-three: Jax

THE METAL SECURITY DOOR CRUMPLED BENEATH THE IMPACT OF THE BULLDOZER. Furious, beyond terrified, Jax backed up and prepared to strike again. Thick smoke boiled from the back of the two-story brick building. Firemen were on the roof and in the alley hitting the flames with cannons of water. He thought some of them may have gone in through the back to attack the kitchen walls, but Evie had texted her location in the wine cabinet in front.

Roark and Reuben placed themselves ready to roll under the steel gate and haul Evie out once the metal and glass crumpled. To Jax's relief, she rolled herself out, shouting.

"Jane ran back in! I can't see her. Rhonda passed out just inside. She's too heavy for me to drag," she shouted at the men, before sprinting directly for Jax.

He jumped down from the dozer, probably to the relief of the contractor and all officialdom. She landed in his arms, stinking of smoke and coughing but strong enough to grab his neck. He swung her up, crushing her close, and covering her sooty face with kisses. "That took half a century off my life, you cretin!"

"I love you too." She kissed him back, snuggling all those blessed, breathing curves into him. "Did you catch Nick Gladwell?"

A medic ran up to administer oxygen but Evie refused to unfasten her grip on Jax's neck.

"I'm telling you nothing until you let the medic take care of you." He unwrapped her hands from his neck and lifted her down.

"No insurance. I have the lungs of an opera star." She darted behind him, using him as shield, and waved the annoyed medic away.

Everyone in town could attest to the power of her lungs, Jax knew.

"I know the routine," Jax told the medic. "I'll keep an eye on her. If she passes out, she's all yours."

Evie stood on her toes and kissed the back of his neck. Not until that minute did he allow himself to feel relief. He swung around and imprisoned her in his arms again. "Evangeline Malcolm Carstairs, I'm this close to turning you over my knee. . ."

She blew a raspberry and cuddled closer again. "Nick? Did they catch Nick?"

"He opened the damned shop door for them! Just because it was blocked from the inside, and he was in the alley earlier, doesn't mean he set fire to his own building." He glanced over her shoulder to watch Roark emerge from under the bent metal, carrying the clerk. Had Reuben gone hunting Jane?

With a huff, Evie turned to watch too. The medics grabbed the unconscious clerk while Nicholas Gladwell in his white shirt and tie emerged from a nearby building and looked on anxiously.

"If Nick didn't set the fire, that's one unlucky family," Evie murmured. "The business is bankrupt. Who gets the insurance money?"

"Larraine. It's her building. The Gladwells may have insurance on contents and improvements and maybe loss of business. Are you wearing a mic? Yell at Rube to get his ass back out here and leave the bigot to the fire fighters." Jax felt his stomach knot as the crowd yelled and the smoke thickened in the alley.

Evie shouted into her mic. Reuben didn't reply.

The throng of sightseers around them parted, allowing a six-foot tower of anguish to shove through. Wearing a reasonably sedate but fashionably slim suit in bright azure, Mayor Larraine frantically searched the throng. Seeing Jax and Evie, she shouted, "Reuben?"

Jax caught the mayor's arm and steadied her on her high heels. "He's still inside, looking for Jane Lawson." Or clues. One never knew with the nerd.

Larraine studied the bulldozer as if contemplating climbing into the driver's seat. Before she could, Roark shouted from the front of the crowd. A fireman joined him to help Roark drag another body from under the crumpled door.

"Jane," Evie whispered as Larraine yanked away and ran for the man rolling out after the unconscious woman. Dressed in camouflage and black sweatshirt, the soot barely noticeable, Rube straightened just in time to catch her. The mayor in her bright blue hugged and kissed him and came away with black all over her front.

"I don't think Rube's used to public displays of affection," Jax said wryly, watching the prof try to hold off the demonstrative mayor.

"Not that I wish Jane ill, but it's a good thing our resident bigot didn't see that hug, or she'd be spewing disgust all over the internet. I think they make a cute couple."

They both glanced at the ambulance where the medics worked over the blogger.

Jane coughed, indicating she lived. That was all Jax needed to see. Reuben could handle himself, although he might be in over his introverted head with the extroverted mayor. "C'mon, let's get you out of here before Loretta runs down to join the fun. Text her, will you?"

Holding Evie's waist, Jax elbowed his way through the crowd while she poked at her phone. Before they reached the first quiet side street, both Reuben and Roark joined them.

"You let Ariel know we're all okay?" Roark demanded.

"Not yet. She's all yours." Jax hadn't spent a lot of time in his past keeping tabs on family, but then, he'd had very little family who cared. Now, he seemed surrounded by people who mattered—because of Evie. He hugged her again, just because he could. And loved the way she hugged back.

Roark snorted and held up his phone so Jax could see. "Ariel is sending information on all the reasons why Evie and Rube oughta go to the hospital and get checked out."

His sister didn't like phone calls so Jax let Roark text her back. Ariel wasn't much used to caring about people either, but she was learning.

"I told Larraine to head for your office," Reuben warned. "She doesn't need to be out there facing off reporters on her own."

"Good thinking. Shall we all repair there? Evie, do I need to order a milk-shake for you?" Jax steered her down an alley as she sent her text.

"Water's good, lots and lots of water. It's way too early for y'all to start drinking, so soft drinks all around. Rube, did you see anyone else in that alley besides Nick?" She continued punching on her phone.

"I had the camera directed at the back door. I saw Jane let herself in. Nick walked past it. If there's a connecting door between the bistro and the shop, he could have used that, I suppose. Maybe it's not arson." Dusting uselessly at his filthy clothes, Reuben broke into a jog as they reached the street where Jax had his office.

Larraine's limo was parked out front.

"It's arson," Evie whispered to Jax. "And someone locked the connecting door."

Twenty-four: Dante

DANTE THANKED HIS DRIVER AND MANEUVERED HIS STIFF LEG UP THE VILLA'S STAIRS. He probably should have gone on to his flat in the city, changed clothes, and got some rest, but for the first time in recent memory, he was eager to be home.

He hadn't left prepared for two days away. He hadn't brought his phone charger. He'd worn the battery out keeping in touch with his student's parents, the hospital, and the crew taking down the dig. He couldn't endanger students for the sake of a tunnel adulterated as badly as Leo's. It appeared as if some drunken Roman engineer had attempted to make a sewer of the Etruscan's tunnel and botched the job. Except Romans didn't use concrete of that ilk.

It was still early evening, but the villa's door was locked. He supposed that was a good idea, even this far out in the country where intruders were rare. His empty stomach rumbled as he located his keys and opened the door. He sniffed eagerly to detect whatever scrumptious meal Pris was preparing. He'd slept at the hospital yesterday and only had a piece of pizza for supper last night. He'd hired a car to see his student home after the hospital released him this morning, then had the driver take him directly back here. He'd not had anything except a roll for breakfast.

No delicious aroma greeted him. Neither did the twins. Not that they regularly ran to him on the rare occasions he came home, but he'd thought lately they were getting used to him. He didn't expect Pris to greet him. She kept a barrier between herself and the world, apparently for good reason.

She hadn't even *known* his students but had picked up on their terror. He didn't think any of his weird relations could do anything similar. He'd spent a lot of the past day pondering how she survived in the real world, but whatever she did was too incomprehensible, possibly more curse than gift, if he was interpreting her correctly.

As he swung his crutch down the hall, the house echoed eerily silent, and a chill coursed down his spine.

The kitchen was dark. Without going farther, he plugged his phone into the charger on the counter and waited for it to boot up.

He had to sit down to read through the flood of messages.

She'd done *what?*

Twenty-five: Evie

EVIE YAWNED, PULLED HER ROBE AROUND HER, AND RUBBED HER BEDHEAD IN THE gray light of dawn. Unshaved and in hastily donned T-shirt and jogging pants, Jax didn't look much better.

"How can anyone so small make so much noise?" Evie whispered, peering around the kitchen door jamb and wincing at the chaos.

"It's not the noise I'm wondering about."

Together, they admired the sight within. Well, *admired* probably wasn't quite the word, but it was indeed an awesome scene.

"Does one jar of jam hold that much?" Jax murmured.

"Extra-large jar. Loretta really likes strawberry. The peanut butter was a pretty good feat though. I didn't think it had been opened." Evie gnawed a broken thumb nail and pondered waking her cousin to help with clean up, but Pris had been beyond wiped after arriving last night.

Dealing with two five-year-olds on a twelve-hour flight in economy seats was bad enough, but Pris had to do it while combating her mental barriers. Apparently, the time change didn't bother the twins in the least. They'd clattered downstairs at daybreak.

"They really are adorable," she whispered. With their backs to the door, the twins kneeled on the banquette of the breakfast nook. Two black heads bent diligently over the table, smearing their concoction over leftover rolls from last night.

Milk dripped off the counter from where they'd apparently climbed up to reach the coffee mugs the men always left scattered there. The gallon jug had proved too heavy for pouring, although how they'd dragged it from the refrigerator was questionable.

"Why didn't Pris take them to her mother?" Jax rubbed his bristly jaw and straightened. "Dante is likely to raise holy hell, and I don't really want to be around when he calls."

Dante might be Jax's distant cousin, but they didn't know each other well. Since he knew so little of his far-flung family, he probably didn't like upsetting them. Evie patted his arm in commiseration.

"Pris's mother lives in an apartment, like Mavis. No room. And I'm guessing Pris wanted a shield of defense for when Dante arrives. Or maybe from whatever caused her to run. Her texts weren't totally coherent." Evie straightened too. "I'll start cleaning up here while you shower. Then you can fix breakfast while I shower."

"Cereal all around." He kissed the top of her head and jogged back up the stairs.

Evie took her time examining the twins' auras, but other than seeing hints of the distinctive Malcolm and Ives hues, she didn't find much more. They were simply too young to have developed strong personalities.

"Good morning, my lovelies, did you enjoy your breakfast?" Evie hoped they spoke English. She grabbed a roll of paper towels to lift the worst of the mess.

Not looking in the least surprised, the twins glanced up with identical chocolate eyes just like their dad's. They nodded happily and returned to coloring rolls with jam and peanut butter. Self-sufficient, nice.

Dressed for school, Loretta bounced down the stairs just as Evie finished scrubbing the vinyl upholstery on the banquette. She'd repositioned the twins on counter stools with bowls of dry cereal so she could clean the nook.

"Why are Pris and Jax arguing?" her ward asked, helping herself to the cereal and a bowl.

"Because that's how they communicate. I'm surprised Pris dragged herself out of bed already." Evie poured milk into the bowl even though Loretta could do it herself. The jug would be empty before everyone ate if she didn't control the flow.

"Her bubble is collapsed. Is she going to live here now too? We'll have to clear out the junk in the guest room." Wise child that she was, Loretta happily settled in with her electronic devices and spooned in cereal between pushing game buttons.

Evie vowed not to worry about Pris's collapsed bubble. They'd yet to discern exactly what Loretta saw when she talked of bubbles.

"That *junk* you want to clear out is antique. We'd have to have a garage sale, after we checked with everyone in the entire family to see if they had anything they wanted to reclaim." Her great-aunt's house had been a catchall for unwanted family heirlooms for decades. Evie kept meaning to do something about them but hadn't had much incentive to do more than clear out the master suite she and Jax shared—which was why all the other bedrooms were full.

Pris had taken Evie's old room. They'd found cots for the twins so they could sleep there too. It wouldn't be satisfactory for long.

The twins clambered down to join Loretta in the booth. Evie grabbed their bowls before they could pull them off the counter. They watched Loretta play her handheld electronic game with such avid interest, that her Indigo Child had to turn it around to show them how it worked.

"They only have tiny bubbles," Loretta said. "Sorta silvery."

"Tiny because they're young. Silvery probably means they're related to us from way back in distant times." Evie cleaned off her hands as she heard Pris and Jax descending the stairs, still arguing.

"It's kidnapping," Jax was insisting.

"He doesn't care. He didn't even attempt to let me know where he was while a killer was running loose! What was I supposed to do?" Her hair in its natural state of brown frizz with a silver streak off her forehead, Pris stomped into the kitchen. She checked that the twins were occupied, then headed for the refrigerator.

"You have proof that Vincent Gladwell is a killer?" Evie asked with interest. "But if he was in Italy, he couldn't have had anything to do with the fire here."

"Minions. He has minions." Pris angrily flung bacon on the counter.

"You have no proof. Why would he kill his own daughter? That makes no sense." Jax stayed out of the way while Pris emptied the refrigerator.

"I didn't say he killed his daughter. He could have, though. He was there when KK died. He aided and abetted the limoncello episode."

"I'll leave y'all to solve the case, shall I? I need to get dressed. Loretta, make the so-called adults keep their voices down so they don't disturb the kiddos." Evie shuffled off upstairs.

Rube apparently hadn't come home last night or he'd have been in the refrigerator by now as well. He hadn't been home the night before either. Maybe he and Larraine had figured out how a flashy fashionista and a professorial nerd could be a couple.

Pondering why people killed before she showered just wasn't happening. She'd much rather contemplate romance.

But if Vincent Gladwell returned to town, she'd sic her family on him and let them figure out what made him tick.

≈

Dante, over the English Channel

Dante's first reaction to Pris's departure with his children had been to book the first seat to the states that he could find.

Then, after reading all the texts and listening to the voice mails he'd missed, he'd taken a step back and called Leo. He'd been too late to catch Vincent and Matt Gladwell. As usual, they'd only been in for a day.

He stretched his stiff leg in the front bulwark row and hooked his phone up to the plane's wi-fi. He had enough frequent flyer miles to go anywhere, anytime, in any fashion he liked, but a flight to the states required that he keep his leg up. That had necessitated a little more juggling and led to another decision. This flight was taking him to London.

While he'd been at the airport, Pris had texted him that she'd arrived in Atlanta, so he knew they were safely with family by now. Before he'd left home, he had checked on the address of the shell company Pris had been concerned about, confirming that yes, the office was a dirt lot. Combining that with the knowledge the Gladwells were in Italy, Dante had made his rash decision to go to London first.

Pris would probably throw that in his face too. But someone had to find Lucia and ask what the hell was going on. He didn't suffer Pris's paranoia about Vincent, but Leo had been evasive and uneasy when Dante had asked questions about the man who bought his oil.

Arriving at Gatwick, he called Pris while looking for the cousin who had promised to pick him up. Managing a crutch and luggage on the tube was too much hassle.

The phone call to Pris went to voice mail.

Despite the aggravation of feeling helpless, he was almost grateful that his snickering cousin teased him by bringing a wheelchair. Once they had his luggage and were in the car, Dante called the rest of his family to let them know he'd arrived. They'd already divided up his list of Lucia's addresses. The plan now was to hit them all at the same time.

There might be more places he didn't know about, but he was making damned sure that every person Lucia had ever known was interrogated before he left the city. If her stepfather really was a danger to their children, he wanted to know why.

Twenty-six: Pris

"No, I don't want to visit a bigot who spouts paranoid conspiracy theories," Pris insisted. "I appreciate you finding room for the twins, but I'm not one of your spooky investigators, and I'm not probing a nasty mind like Jane's."

She threw flour on a wooden board meant for cutting meat and dumped her dough on it. Evie's kitchen was utterly inadequate for anything except the basics, but Pris couldn't stand idle.

And she wasn't letting any more evil into her head or paranoia would become a permanent state of mind.

"Well, Jane's still in the hospital. She can't do much, but I suppose you're right." Evie looked out the back door, checking on the children exploring the yard. "Her aura is mostly murky fear and maliciousness. Even if she knows something, she may not know its importance. For our purposes, she's useless for tracking bank deposits. I just wanted her to stir the cauldron, as she calls it. Although if arson investigators can't determine who set the fire, we'll need to test her truthfulness."

"I doubt I can help." Pris rolled the dough and used a cup to cut out cookie rounds. "The company receiving the deposits is obviously a shell if their office is a dirt lot, as Dante says. I can see Gladwell siphoning funds to avoid taxes, maybe. But why does he hate the twins?"

Evie's Siamese leapt from the refrigerator to the counter and down to the kitchen door, meowing to be let out. Given that Psycat was one of their cousin Iddy's weird minions, Pris heeded the warning. She dusted off her hands and let the cat outside, checking on the kids while she was there. She saw no intruders.

Of course there were no intruders. She had to quit thinking like that. She was home. They were safe. "Maybe it's Dante that Gladwell hates, and he's just transferring his anger to his children."

The instant the cat set foot on the wide porch, Nan and Alex came running. They should be allowed pets. Dante damned well better arrive with a nanny so they could have one.

Evie followed Pris into the chilly November air. "Psycat usually avoids kids. Do they ever talk?"

"Twin talk, mostly." Pris sat on the back steps to show them how the cat preferred to be petted.

"Twin talk? They're not saying anything." Evie studied them. "But they're taking turns without squabbling. Amazing."

Pris shrugged, uncomfortable with explaining. "Scientists have studied twins. There's a mental or empathic connection most siblings don't have. Because these two have been so isolated, theirs may be stronger than most."

Evie glanced at her quizzically. "And you can tell they're not deaf mute how?"

Pris grinned. "I'm psychic."

Evie punched her arm. The twins instantly looked up in concern.

Pris shook her head at them. "Evie is like my sister. We fuss at each other."

They nodded and returned to petting the cat.

"They understood." Evie picked up the long-handled feather duster and swished it across the porch.

The cat leapt at it, startling the twins into giggles. Nan held out her hand for the duster. Evie didn't give it to her.

Pris relaxed against a porch column, letting the game play out. "Their minds are so open and simple that it's a pleasure being around them."

"Unlike adults, who are twisty-minded and blasting ugly thoughts." Evie swished the feathers for the cat to chase.

"Me?" Alex demanded, holding out his hand.

As reward for using his words, Evie surrendered the duster, and twins and cat raced off.

"Yeah, I know. They need to be encouraged to speak. Not my job. I'm just keeping them safe," Pris said. It actually physically hurt to admit that. "Maybe

Gladwell is furious that Lucia gave the twins away. They'd be great in commercials."

"That's stupid. And Lucia giving them up was stupid. We're missing some vital component here. I just fail to see how it connects with KK's death." Evie glanced over her shoulder at a sound in the drive. "A car just pulled up."

Pris grimaced as the familiar fury and confusion reached her. Dante's mind was never quiet, although he acted the part of stoic well. "The twins' father. He's totally pissed."

"Can't say I blame him. Misappropriating his children isn't quite the same as moving flower pots and pets to more appreciative homes the way you did as a kid. I'll try to keep the twins outside until the tempest passes." Evie settled into the cushioned porch swing.

"Someone needs to rattle the man into listening. Why not me?" Pris sauntered into the house as if she weren't shaking in her shoes. She really had pushed him to the edge.

Dante might be politely respectful in public, but he had a temper that probably needed release occasionally before he imploded.

She opened the front door before he'd maneuvered the crutch across the Victorian verandah. A nondescript sedan with an Uber sticker pulled away from the curb.

Leaning against the jamb, Pris watched him unsympathetically. "Took you long enough."

"It's only a result of my upbringing and this damned leg that I don't fling you over my shoulder and cart you to the cops for kidnapping." He shouldered past her, leaving his luggage on the step. "Where are they?"

"Learning to talk to cats in the backyard. You didn't really think I'd harm them, did you? I told you where to find them." With a sigh, Pris followed him down the hall. "You should be grateful."

She left him sputtering while she aimed for the kitchen counter. "What time zone are you in? Coffee, tea, or booze?"

"Coffee." He limped through the kitchen to the back door, even though she could see how much it pained him. After watching through the screen, his broad shoulders finally slumped in what might be relief. "Good morning, Evangeline."

Pris didn't hear Evie's reply. She turned on Jax's coffee machine and poured herself juice, returning to the cookie dough. She didn't intend to explain herself again.

Dante wearily took a stool at the counter. "Lucia isn't in London."

～

132

"WE NEED TO COORDINATE AND GO DEEPER ON THIS," JAX INSISTED OVER THE NEWLY-cleared dinner table.

While he'd been at work, gremlins had mucked out accumulations of—*collections*, Evie had called them. Stacks of vinyl albums, old magazines, fabrics, and assorted whatsits had vanished from the scarred walnut dining table and the mismatched chairs. Stacks of cardboard boxes now lined the walls, but the table was covered in a gawdawful white vinyl cloth so the children could eat with the adults. The battered wooden chairs weren't worth protecting.

The dinnerware was still whatever Evie pulled out of the kitchen cabinets, although Jax was pretty certain that was a complete set of china in the cabinet behind her. Whoever had performed this transformation hadn't attempted anything more elegant than a larger area to congregate, although Loretta and the twins must have confiscated someone's mums and wildflowers for the centerpiece.

A family dinner table. How long had it been since he'd sat at one? Jax almost appreciated the intriguing family the house was accumulating. Almost.

"Coordinate all you like," Pris declared, doling out bread and stew to the twins while shattering any image of peace and harmony. "I'll keep looking after the kids, if Dante wants to play detective, but that's it."

Evie's cousin was an annoying porcupine, but the food situation had taken a turn for the better since her arrival, so Jax grudgingly accepted Pris's eccentricities. Except for breakfast and special occasions, Evie generally forced everyone but Loretta to fend for themselves.

Jax had only met Dante a few months ago. He waited with interest for his Ives cousin's reaction.

"I'm an archeologist, not a detective. I don't know what I can do. But if Priscilla thinks the children are unsafe, I have to listen to the experts." Annoyance definitely tinted Dante's admission, but he dug into his stew without further argument.

Evie raised her eyebrows and Jax almost expected a chortle, but she blessedly kept a lid on her thoughts about Dante and Pris's grumpy relationship. Since when had Pris become an expert with children? Although if he meant an expert on reading minds. . . Jax reserved judgment.

Managing a professional aspect despite his man bun, Dr. Reuben Thompson waved his roll. "None of us are detectives. We find *solutions*. You say your ex, presumptive CEO of La Bella Gente, is not in London. London is a big city. How can you be certain?"

"I have a rather large extended family in the UK, ones who have connections with connections, a veritable network, as you will. Whilst the more mobile of us spread across the city to knock on doors and interrogate anyone associated with Lucia, the other half made phone calls."

Evie interrupted. "Kit-Kat's spirit is having complete conniptions right now. Or tantrums. Unfortunately, she talks about as coherently as the twins, so I don't know what she's trying to tell me, other than that we're stupid. I think you're disturbing her, Dante."

The big archeologist sighed and put down his fork, glancing around as if he might see a ghost. "Katherine? I never met you. Do you know where Lucia is?"

"KK is hovering over the twins and doing her usual cycle of confused emotions. She's still angry. And sad. That's a new one. KK, what makes you sad?" Evie waited expectantly.

Jax sipped his iced tea and refrained from questioning until he was certain Evie hadn't received an answer.

Before he could speak, Pris did. "Séance?"

Evie nodded. "I'll text Mavis about the best time."

Jax shook his head. "That is *not* what I meant by going deeper. We need to set up a storyboard, dig deeper into this shell company and the shoddy products—"

Pris had her phone out, pressing keys. "I'll start the phone tree. I can manage séances, sort of. Let the men take La Bella Gente apart."

"This is *not* a gender issue," Jax protested.

Having finished her text, Evie forked carrots and regarded him innocently. "Ariel will work with Roark, so no, it's not a gender issue. It's a Malcolm-Ives issue. Unless, of course, Dante wants to explore his Malcolm heritage. You're welcome to join us." She gestured at their guest.

"I just want to get back to work," Dante growled. "I'm probably more properly employed exploring the logistics of our London search."

"Did you find anything of Lucia's to touch?" Pris asked, out of the blue.

Jax thought the question odd. Evie, on the other hand, glanced up with interest. Here they went again into la-la land. On the other side of the table, Reuben snorted.

Without explaining, Dante shrugged. "Nothing useful. I just know she hasn't been in that townhouse since shortly after the twins were born." He hesitated, glanced around the table as if to check the level of disbelief, then continued. "I also sensed scenes of violence, so I asked the neighbors. They tell me Vincent was abusive to his wife. Apparently one of the things Lucia accomplished when she first arrived in London was to help Katherine force her father out so their mother could live her last days in peace. I can't tell if he ever hit them."

Jax whistled. Everyone else looked troubled.

Evie broke the momentary silence. "What about the commercials? Rhonda said Lucia performed in the commercials. They had to reach her somehow to do those." Abruptly, she glanced up and hastily scooted her chair back.

A cold whirlwind propelled the paper napkins from the table and rattled the flowers.

"You have to stop bringing your work home with you," Jax told her dryly.

The twins giggled at the mini tempest, then climbed down to chase napkins. Loretta strained to follow Evie's gaze. Jax knew his ward wanted to see ghosts too. He prayed she never did.

"Definitely a séance," Evie said grimly. "Tell us more, Dante. Vincent and the commercials are upsetting KK. I need all the information I can gather going in."

"Evie hates séances," Loretta explained to the table at large.

Dante exchanged glances with Pris, which Jax found as entertaining as Evie apparently did. But he kept his mouth shut and chewed his bread.

Their guest shrugged and continued as if he hadn't been interrupted. "The only people we could find familiar with the commercial shoots hasn't worked with La Bella in years. They say the voiceovers and angles and messages have changed since the early ones, but the images could be any of the shots they took. They filmed a lot of material in that first year."

Pris tore up her bread and crumbled it over her stew. "You think they're photoshopped."

"I know nothing of how one edit's film, but if it's possible, yes, I think Lucia hasn't performed in years." Dante put his fork down. "For all I know, Lucia is as dead as Katherine."

Twenty-seven: Pris

"ALL RIGHT, THEY'RE ASLEEP." PRIS RELUCTANTLY RETURNED TO EVIE'S FRONT PARLOR where the rest of the family had gathered. Well, at least the ones living in Afterthought.

Aunt Mavis sat in the corner by the hearth wielding her tarot. She was the one who always took notes. Pris figured her psychic aunt preferred not to have her mind inhabited by Evie's ghosts.

Pris felt the same way, but Evie couldn't do this alone. Gracie was telekinetic and not too connected to other-worldly apparitions. Iddy, their veterinarian cousin, talked to animals, not ghosts. Iddy's mother, Felicia, and Pris's mother, Ellen, had limited afterworld skills as well.

"Is Loretta joining us?" Pris asked as she took a seat at the card table they'd set up.

"I think she's still too young. What if we access a killer or rapist? She could be traumatized." Evie threw a rainbow-striped cloth over the battered table—not exactly the usual setup for a medium. But Evie liked color.

"I told her she needed to guard the twins, so she's in your room right now with books and games." Gracie took a seat at Evie's right. As a teacher with a daughter, she knew how to handle children better than Pris.

"It's almost time," Mavis warned. "Ellen, Felicia, take your seats if you're joining in."

Mavis was the youngest of the three sisters, but she was a born leader, more like Great-Aunt Val. With age, the sisters were growing more alike, plump, with graying, frizzy hair. Their heights and manner of dress differentiated them, however. Mavis was short and liked caftans and heels. Pris's mother was medium height and favored drab cotton skirts. Iddy's mother, Felicia, was the tallest and preferred leggings and tunics in colors even Evie wouldn't wear. Living with the three Wyrd Malcolm Sisters growing up had been an ordeal, but Pris could appreciate the sheltering circle of family a little better now than she had as an adolescent.

She turned off the lights while Evie lit the candle. Taking a seat between Gracie and Aunt Felicia, Pris held their hands and did her best to block mental energies. If Evie conjured a ghost, Pris wanted to be prepared.

"Katherine Gladwell, Kit-Kat, we know you're here. I give myself over to you to speak."

Pris shivered at Evie's words. Evie hated this part, for good reason. Spirits were often irrational. And the spirits they wanted to reach often got shoved aside by more aggressive ones. Pris only suffered the aftermath of séances, not a direct hit the way Evie did, and still she resisted them.

"Are you here, Katherine?" Aunt Felicia asked, taking charge since Pris refused to do so. "Knock on the table, if you can."

The rickety card table shook. Any of them could have done that, but no one had a point to prove. Evie's ghost was present.

Pris asked one of the questions they'd listed earlier. "Do you know how to find Lucia?"

They were hoping the spirit would speak through Evie, but KK was still reluctant. Or too stupid.

"Knock once if you know where Lucia is," Aunt Felicity suggested.

The table rattled. Now what did they do?

"Knock once if she's in the UK," Pris suggested. No response.

Evie's eyes were scrunched closed. Pris could see she clung tightly to the hands on either side of her. Before anyone could pose another question, Evie's head fell forward, and she spoke in a voice not her own. "Italy. I am in Italy. I wish to see my bambinos. Where are they?"

A wailing wind rushed through the room. The candle blew out, and Evie slumped. Pris suffered the full mental impact of the ghost or Evie or both before the pain had her releasing the hands she held to grab her temples. "The twins," she shouted. "Go to the twins!"

Chairs scraped and Gracie dashed for the stairs.

Pris needed to follow, but she could barely stand. With the aid of her mother, she slumped in the papa-san chair while Evie collapsed on the sofa.

"KK's really agitated," Evie said in a whispery voice. "Lucia makes her sad and angry. And she's. . ." She gestured for everyone to shut their chatter. "KK wants to kill her brother Matt."

Pris thought the more important takeaway was that Lucia was *dead*, unless those were someone else's *bambinos* upstairs.

Worse yet, she'd *heard* Lucia, and the children weren't her only concern. She needed to talk to Dante.

～

"THE WOMEN ARE GOOD, BUT THEY CAN'T DO WHAT WE CAN," JAX ASSERTED, holding a cue at a pool table in the man cave where the men gathered after supper.

Studying the ancient Pac-Man machine as if it were an artifact, Dante was exhausted enough to accept that statement. He wasn't entirely certain he believed it though.

Maneuvering his crutch down cellar stairs had left his leg and shoulder complaining. He hadn't wanted to tell his host that he wasn't supposed to use stairs. Pris had been in one of her moods and probably hadn't even noticed he'd left, or she would have thrown a stink. He hadn't tucked the twins into bed because he was avoiding stairs. And the twins.

She had a right to fling daggers at him. He was a horrible excuse for a father. Well, his father hadn't been much better. Dante had survived the neglect— because he'd had a mother to raise him.

"Ariel is tracing the shell company deposits." The Cajun hacker, Roark, had joined them after dinner. "But they're being transferred from the Italian bank to inaccessible offshore accounts in the same corporate name."

Of course they were. Money wasn't the problem here. The Gladwells had none. Unless the company was making fortunes, they must be stealing from investors. Investigating their shareholders might be more profitable, but Dante wasn't interested in that either.

"Is there any chance that Lucia is siphoning Bella while living on some Caribbean island?" Dante threw that out there just to change the course of the conversation. The Lucia he knew wouldn't do any such thing.

Of course, the Lucia he knew wouldn't have lingered in the bright lights of the city or abandoned her children. Or never call or write anything but generic holiday cards. So what did he know?

But the violence he'd sensed in that household troubled him.

"Anything is possible," Reuben the engineering professor agreed. "*Probable* is a different matter. Why would anyone drain a potentially profitable company is a better question."

"Have arson investigators made any progress?" Jax had abandoned the pool table to study a storyboard on the concrete block wall, but it was light on clues and suspects.

As professional hacker, Roark answered that one. "Fire started in a stack of pallets stored in the kitchen area. They're uncertain how long they smoldered, but there are indicators accelerant was added later, presumably when the fire didn't catch fast enough."

Jax tapped a photo on the wall with his pool cue. "Rhonda Tart, sales clerk, investor, possibly Vincent's mistress, was present and had access to the kitchen." He stretched a string to another photo. "Jane Lawson, previous fire victim, blogger, had access only because Roark picked the lock. But she'd been invited, so she expected Rhonda to let her in at some point."

"Neither has any good motive for starting a fire," Reuben noted.

"Is there any proof the fire and KK's death are related?" Dante asked. "Without physical evidence, what do you have?" He sank into a gaming chair and stretched out his aching leg. He'd been operating nearly forty-eight hours without sleep. That might be a new record for him.

Jax slapped another photo. "Nicholas Gladwell, juvie record for auto theft, had access to the café. He's also an investor, appeared romantically attached to Katherine Gladwell, who was only a kissing cousin at best. He's on the company's board of directors. We have no idea why except he's family and does their marketing."

"Which means he worked with Lucia," Dante reminded them. His tired mind wondered what Evie thought of Nick's aura or if Pris had probed the man's mind. Probably not. He hadn't used his psychometric abilities either, because they were mostly worthless. Or painful. He really wasn't interested in people's dirty secrets—except for the long dead.

"And finally, Matthew Gladwell." Jax tapped the last photo. "KK's brother, Vincent's only son. He might have motive for murder and arson if KK and Lucia stood in the way of his controlling the company. Or if he's siphoning funds and they caught him."

"But he wasn't in the vicinity of the fire," Dante pointed out, sipping warm beer.

"Right." Jax made a note under the photo. "You said he was with Vincent in Italy. But maybe he hired someone."

"Then Matt's not final. We have to add Vincent," Dante corrected. "He could hire minions and is probably in a better position to set up the Italy trip as an alibi."

"And that's still assuming there's some connection between the fire and KK," Roark noted. "You're assuming someone knew the bank deposits had been uncovered and that was the reason for the fire?"

"No assumptions," Reuben argued. "Jane could have just gone bananas. She's on a power trip to drive Larraine out of office. Larraine supported La Bella, hence, La Bella has to die."

"And KK, as figurehead?" Jax suggested.

"In other words, we have nothing," Dante said in exhaustion. "I have Pris's belief that Vincent means harm to my children. I have my own theory that Lucia is out of the picture for reasons unknown. I just want to know if it's safe to take the twins home."

Jax held up his phone. "Séance is over. Evie thinks KK wants to kill Matt, but all she's getting is sadness." He read a new text coming through. His silence was telling.

Paging through his computer, not noticing Jax's sudden stillness, Reuben spoke idly. "Has the ghost finally decided Matt killed her? As far as we can tell, Matthew Gladwell is a gormless turd who does as he's told and parties with male models. Is that enough for KK to want to off him?"

"Perhaps if Vincent favored his son over his daughter?" Dante shoved out of his chair and crossed to where Jax sat. "If you don't mind, it's been a long day. Jax, before I go up, what else did the women say?" he asked quietly, not fooled by his distant cousin's sudden silence.

Jax rubbed his bristly jaw and studied Dante a moment before holding up his phone.

Evie's text read: LUCIAS SPIRIT REACHED OUT TO THE TWINS

Dante almost staggered. Then remembering this was all shadow play, he steeled himself. "I'll think about that better in the morning."

Spirit? Did that mean Lucia was *dead*? Or possibly that Evie was feeding off his fears. How could Lucia have died and no one told him? It was impossible.

As if she'd heard his thoughts, Pris lifted the outside cellar door and called down, "We can throw down an air mattress if you can't climb out, Dr. Ives. I'll send the twins down to join you in the morning, shall I?"

After that text, it would be a relief to bed down here, out of view of the too-perceptive women. He needed time to process. "Do that, Miss Broadhurst," he called back. "Reuben says he has other places to be. Tell me when you've solved the case."

She slammed the door. Unaware of Evie's second text, the other men reached for their beers and belongings and headed out, saluting him as they did so.

"Welcome to the whacky world of women." Jax pounded him sympathetically on the shoulder before heading out. "Where would we be without them?"

Backing up the cellar stairs on his bum, Dante figured. Pris knew damned well what she was doing—tucking him into bed like the twins. She just did it with prickly flare.

That gave him something better to think about besides the twins' mother possibly being dead—which explained why Lucia's hairbrush hadn't been touched since the twins were toddlers and lent new meaning to the violence in her townhouse.

Some days, he hated his eccentric abilities. As a scientist, he didn't trust them—until he had evidence. Talking ghosts weren't any better. Both just led him to visions of horror and not a single fact.

Twenty-eight: Pris

"ONE WAY OR ANOTHER, PLANNED MURDER IS ALL ABOUT THE MONEY," EVIE INSISTED after sending Loretta off to school and Jax off to work the next morning.

"You're forgetting crimes of passion," Pris argued, chopping vegetables while her cousin washed breakfast dishes.

They both stewed over Lucia's unexpected presence last night, except Pris didn't want to expose all her thoughts just yet. If Lucia was dead. . . She had to have been buried without anyone knowing of it. Which meant murder, right? Dante had every reason to murder a woman who hadn't told him about his children until she showed up on his doorstep. Could she believe that he wasn't there when Lucia abandoned the twins?

Actually, she rather could. He was never home.

"Someone else needs to do the statistics, but I'm guessing that men don't risk the death penalty unless they're sociopathically possessive, violently drunk, or know there's life insurance or money. No one was passionate about KK," Evie contended. "And there was no violence."

"As far as we can tell, KK only had stock in nearly bankrupt La Bella. She lived off a generous salary. Do you know if she had life insurance?" Pris checked out the screen door. The twins happily ran around the chilly backyard with her aunt's golden retriever. Psycat had retreated to the warm top of the refrigerator.

Dante was still sleeping. She didn't want to talk about Lucia until she talked to him first.

"I'll text Roark about life insurance. Surely the sheriff knows. Anyway, poison isn't a crime of passion." After texting, Evie returned to her original while she waited for a reply. "It has to be about money."

"Poison is a woman's weapon." Pris returned to beheading Brussels sprout stalks. "Rhonda is the only woman in this scenario. Put her together with the money—"

"But Rhonda wasn't there when KK died. KK smacked her and sent her away, remember?" Evie checked her phone screen.

"You don't have film of what happened in the mayor's office. Rhonda could have poisoned the limoncello while she was there." Pris had barely met any of the suspects, but anyone hanging around Vincent was corrupt in her book. Dante said he sensed violence in Vincent's townhouse, and she had read hatred for the twins on the man's mind. Hate and violence were villainous behavior.

But KK's brother Matthew had lived in that townhouse too. He'd been everywhere KK was. And then there was Nick. . . She couldn't do this.

Evie madly texted, presumably sending all these questions to her team. "But Rhonda could have died in that fire. She wouldn't have lit it herself. Did someone know she was KK's killer and attempted revenge?"

"Someone didn't want her telling what she knew? Or more probably, didn't know she was in there." Pris dumped the sprouts in a bowl and hunted for seasoning.

Evie's phone swooshed. "We don't have enough to give the sheriff. And if we say poison is a woman's crime, the finger points at you. At least Lawless Jane isn't stirring up trouble from her hospital bed."

"Did she burn her fingers?" Pris asked sarcastically.

"Huh, hadn't thought of that. But phones take dictation. Maybe she saw me in the bistro and guessed I was the tipster? I thought I was pretty well hidden. Maybe I won't go online to check if she's back."

"No reporters on the doorstep yet." Pris began dousing her butchered ingredients with oils and potions. Cooking was her witchcraft. "Probably ought to prepare ourselves though."

Evie grimaced. "I'll bring down the gobbler for an early warning system. You check the blog and see if she's posted." She took off her apron.

"You don't still have that awful thing?" Pris called after her. "It can't possibly work."

But Evie had MIT engineers on hand who could make it work. A giant motion-activated turkey that bounced up and down and gave off the world's most awful racket was an embarrassment—but the perfect warning system. Thanksgiving was just around the corner.

And Pris had no jobs lined up. This might be the first holiday since she was sixteen when she wasn't catering someone else's festivities.

Before she could leave the kitchen, Evie's phone pinged. Reading her text, she waved it at Pris. "KK had the kind of life insurance paid for by the corporation. La Bella Gente benefits."

"And Lucia?"

Evie shrugged. "Probably, but since she's not been declared dead, the company is still paying for her insurance."

Pris gave a grunt of disgust and began battering dough with a rolling pin.

Evie's cell rang again as she carried a three-foot stuffed monster turkey down the stairs from the attic. "Get that for me, will you?" she cried while she wrestled the creature into the parlor.

Pris picked up the phone and hit play after the call went to voicemail.

Mayor Larraine Ward's calm drawl covered a lifetime of fury. "Lawson is claiming I burned down my building for the insurance and to cover La Bella Gente's misappropriation of funds. She claims she has evidence. Can Jax smother that woman in her hospital bed?"

DANTE HAD TOSSED AND TURNED ON THE AIR MATTRESS IN THE CELLAR HALF THE night, despite jetlag and exhaustion. Adjusting to the possibility that the woman he'd cursed these past years might have been dead instead of enjoying the nightlife of London. . . didn't come easily.

But by morning his leg had sufficiently rested to climb out of the cellar with only a modicum of difficulty. His fist merely dented the metal crutch bars.

When he entered the yard, the twins raced up, giggling, and a giant hole yawned in his midsection. They might really and truly be motherless, and a worthless father like him might be their sole provider. He almost hated that more than fearing Lucia might come back for them. He apparently still harbored the illusion that she might care about them.

Time to wake up to reality. They were his and his alone. Somehow, he had to show that he could love them twice as much as one person.

He couldn't catch the twins while gripping a crutch. He settled on the porch stairs so they could hurtle into his lap to show him their treasures. That they came to him was an overwhelming experience in itself. When Nan held out an odd-shaped rock and asked "Is this an arrow?" he almost fell over at her interest as much as the fact that she'd *talked*.

"It could have been," he said carefully, trying not to discourage her. "But it isn't chipped enough to work. Arrows are hard to make." How did she even know about arrows?

The screen door opened and Pris stepped out carrying a blessed cup of coffee. "Evie has an arrowhead collection in the attic. You should ask her about it."

The twins instantly scrambled from his lap to run inside. They didn't shout excitedly, but they'd have to say something at some point if they wanted to see arrows.

Dante took the offered mug. "They need people around to force them to communicate, don't they?"

"Yup. Your mother is fabulous, but like any exhausted mother, she lets them entertain themselves. At least it isn't with TV." She leaned against the porch column. "We need to talk. Want to eat first?"

"I'm never going to sleep again, am I?" With a sigh, Dante handed back his mug and pried himself upright.

"If you've been sleeping the sleep of innocence all these years, then I'm guessing you don't have as much to worry about as the Gladwells do." She held the door until he was inside.

She suspected *he* might have murdered Lucia? Of course, she did. At least she wasn't accusing him. . . yet.

"We're almost on the same page then. I didn't kill her." He propped himself on a counter stool and sipped his coffee, heating the morning chill from the inside.

Under the Siamese cat's watchful eye, Pris began removing ingredients from the ancient harvest-gold refrigerator that might qualify as an artifact in a few years. "Yeah, I was kinda counting on you not being a passionate fool."

He would have laughed had the situation not been so serious. Grimly, he swigged his caffeine. "I really can fix my own food. I've just never tried it one-handed. This crutch is like having a broken arm as well as leg."

"That's okay. I talk easier if I'm occupied." She threw bacon on the griddle and dipped bread in a bowl of eggs. "And yeah, I imagine we're on the same page. It never made sense that a healthy mother would abandon her babies except under duress. And with all that land, she wasn't poor or starving."

"I should have investigated then, but I was too furious. And scared. I was working a dig in Crete while finishing my doctorate. I knew nothing of babies. I called lawyers." He sipped his coffee and spoke one of the fears he'd conjured last night. "I should have had Lucia's domestic situation investigated, but I was more concerned with my own."

"You had no way of knowing. We still don't know anything. Until we do, we should refrain from speculation." She flung the egg-laden bread on the griddle.

"I hadn't met the Gladwells back then. I just assumed Lucia had found a more exciting life." He rubbed his scruffy jaw and realized he must look like hell. But they needed to have this discussion now, while it was still raw on their minds.

Pris flipped the bread, then refilled his coffee cup. She'd apparently already showered because she smelled of gardenias, and her hair was slicked back. He liked it better when the curls formed around her face. And he had no right noticing.

"Last night. . . " She hesitated and nervously ran her hand over her hair, as if sensing his interest. Which she might. Dante shut down his thoughts so she could continue. "After Lucia spoke through Evie, she entered *my* head. I heard her speak only to me. No one else. That's never happened. I'm not a medium. I don't talk to ghosts."

"Yeah, right, and I don't see things on hairbrushes either," he countered. "I'm convinced Lucia last touched that brush when the twins were infants screaming bloody murder. I saw the image of the babies and picked up a mix of love and fear and something I can't really name, but it wasn't good."

Her glare dissolved at that admission. "I won't ask how you got into her toiletries, but I really did hear a voice speak. The message I received—and let me be clear, I don't guarantee I didn't just have a brain aneurysm—said to *tell Dante about the artifacts.* That's all I got. I think she went in search of the twins then."

"Artifacts?" He rubbed his temple. "That means nothing to me. Lucia had no interest in archeology. For her, it was all about the farm. What artifacts?"

Pris slid the bacon and French toast on a plate and set it in front of him. "If we want to speculate, which I know you told me not to do, if her life was the farm and the last time she was seen was at the farm. . . What are the chances the artifacts are on the farm?"

Dante almost choked on the bacon.

Leo had found a gold Etruscan cuff on the farm—in the tunnel, the one that had collapsed when he'd tried to explore it.

Twenty-nine: Evie

Shoving her cold hands into the back pockets of her jeans, Evie studied the burned-out bistro. Beside it, the boutique still stood, although the bricks were scorched on this side and the cracked front windows had been boarded up.

A skinny Black woman in a police uniform stopped beside her. "People like that don't belong here anyways."

"People like what? Italians? Beautiful people?" Even old school pals could be bigots, she supposed.

"Both." Philomena Marquette crossed her arms and glared at the blackened buildings. "Foreigners bring trouble. They ain't hiring or selling to locals. Did you see any Black folk in there?"

"Well, I only went in when it was empty, so I can't say." But she had a point. Evie had seen boutiques like this. Their market generally geared toward beautiful—wealthy—white people. Sexism, classism, and racism all rolled into one and called *marketing to a niche audience.*

But it was reverse bigotry to call them foreigners and object to their differences. Her ADHD mind regularly revolved around subjects like this without forming a verdict.

As far as she could determine, KK and Lucia hadn't been wealthy, just white and beautiful. Did British qualify as *foreign*? She preferred that everyone be considered a citizen of the world, but people were still fighting the Civil War. *Different* happened, and that apparently equaled *foreign*.

"You don't think Pris poisoned the owner because of this dump, do you?"

147

Evie asked to avoid a headache and because the rumor annoyed her. "She didn't want the building. It's too big."

"Ain't big now. Bet Larry'll give your cousin a good deal on what's left."

That was insulting to Larraine's chosen name, but the mayor had grown up here as Larry, and it rolled naturally off the tongue. And it wasn't as if Philomena was trying to be PC.

"'Course, if everyone thinks Pris poisoned the owner, she ain't likely to have many clientele, is she?" Philomena cackled.

"Now I remember why I pushed you on the playground." Growing up in a small town wasn't all people helping each other like in Hallmark movies. Small towns and small minds often went together, along with long memories of past transgressions.

"Yeah, well, you were a little snot, and I got you back good, so I reckon we're even. Here comes Larry. I better get goin' or he—she'll—have my ass." Philomena marched across the street and out of sight.

"That Till's little sister you talking to?" the mayor asked. Today, the fashionista wore what was probably an Italian suit of cream silk with gold buttons down the side of the slim, knee-length skirt. Larry looked good in heels.

"Yeah, Phil and I went to school together. But she has a point—why did you buy this building for strangers? You had a whole town full of people who could have rented it."

Larraine swung her little gold purse and studied the ruined building. "I met them at a grand opening of the boutique on Hilton Head. I'm afraid I name dropped and said I'd met Dante, the Conte Armeno here visiting family."

Ah, so that was KK's interest in Afterthought. And how Dante was connected, sort of. "They knew Dante?"

"They said they did, anyway. Of course, that was before I realized that even if their *products* were Italian, Katherine and Matthew were English. Oops. They said they were expanding into small towns in the south. I said Afterthought was a small town just outside Charleston and Savannah, and maybe we could do something with my fashions and their skin care. And they showed up. What else could I do?"

Evie wondered if it was the opportunity offered or Dante's name that had drawn Katherine here. "Why small towns, I wonder? I mean, Hilton Head, yeah, a small rich town might make sense. But most small towns in the south. . ."

"Don't have enough money for more than Walmart, right." Larraine rubbed away a frown between her eyes. "I didn't give it much thought. I wanted to thumb my nose at the bigots and naysayers who said I'd never make mayor. These folk were proper English and all that. It sounded good at the time."

"So you just rented it to them without any financials?"

"They had a big glossy boutique in Hilton Head! Who am I to look a gift horse in the mouth? I had visions of sidewalk cafés and Beverly Hills shops and. . ." Larraine gave an unladylike sigh. "Delusions of grandeur."

"Well, they looked pretty grand there for a while. But it's beginning to sound like they had the world's worst accounting department—or they were running a scam. A pity we can't feed Lawless Jane some really tasty tidbits so she'd quit gnawing on the targets of her prejudice and work on real clues."

"Lawless Jane." Larraine snorted in derision. "I'm agonna sue that bitch's camouflage pants off. I'm talking to Jax next. I want him to tell me what the libel and slander laws are all about. This job is a lesson in lawyering, for sure."

"Don't talk like that in front of your constituents," Evie advised in amusement. "You'll lose your cool cred."

Larraine pointed at her. "If I do nothing else, I'm making all the changes I can before they vote me out two years from now. You need to get your air-headed cousin to start a restaurant and hire all colors of folk and ugly people. We'll start a trend."

"Licensing laws," Evie reminded her. "How will you keep your council from keeping out anyone they don't like?"

Larraine grinned evilly. "Because I know how to dig dirt. We need zoning laws to keep them in line, but that council ain't touching nothing without me." The mayor sauntered off on her high heels before Evie could tell her that Pris hated restaurants and would be a really lousy restaurant owner.

Ugly people? As contrasting to Beautiful People, right. A market of *real* people instead of upscale ones would suit Afterthought. A Citizens of the World Café!

Once that empty lot was cleared of debris. . . it would make a lovely outdoor café and green space to counter the gothic courthouse and Victorian office buildings on the next block.

And the school was right down the street. A bakery, maybe? A bakery school —for *real* kids. Pris could do that.

Not if people thought she had poisoned KK.

Jane the Blogger Bigot needed to be muffled or pulled into the fold. What made her tick? Could Jane have set that fire? Why? It didn't make sense. Of course, none of this made sense.

Evie pulled out her phone and called Pris. "Let Jax handle Larraine's problems. We need to tackle yours. Be ready to go to the hospital when I get back there."

Pris hung up on her, but she'd see the light eventually.

"Miss Lawson hasn't had many visitors. She'll be delighted to see you." The nurse looked Dante up and down, apparently equally delighted to see him, as well she should be. He was wearing his professorial duds of tweed coat, elbow patches and all, and still looked like a hunk out of a fashion magazine.

Pris decided the woman wasn't worth kicking. Any female in her right mind would drool over Italian shoes.

Feeling invisible beside the *conte* and his giant bouquet of mums and carnations, Pris stayed in his shadow as they were led down the hospital corridor. She gave Evie the evil eye as they passed her in the waiting room, but her cousin was spaced out, communing with the dead. Pris shuddered. The hospital was probably full of ghosts.

Stiff and in obvious discomfort, Dante swung along on his crutch, holding the flowers in his free arm. Pris grinned and screened out his mental cursing. She didn't know if he was deliberately thinking obscenities for her sake, or if he wasn't aware that his thoughts escaped when upset. The very proper conte had an expressive vocabulary.

As they approached Jane's door, Evie jumped up and began asking the nurse questions about another patient. Pris wasn't about to inquire how her cousin knew who else was here. Distracting the nurse allowed Dante and Pris to enter Lawson's room without anyone catching the patient's reaction to her visitors.

"For me?" the patient asked in surprise, sounding girlish instead of surly—obviously seeing only Dante.

"A gift from La Bella Gente, signora," Dante said, as coached. He even threw in his best Italian accent for good measure.

"Why?" Jane immediately became suspicious. That's when she spied Pris. "You! Are you here to murder me too?" She reached for her call button.

Setting the vase on the stand, Dante moved the button out of reach. "Miss Broadhurst is innocent. She's here to find the real killer now that you've driven Bella out of town."

Pris waited with interest to see how Jane reacted to being the hero of her own story. She'd been the one to suggest this approach. To her amusement, the blogger's limited mind almost literally froze. She emitted no coherent thoughts, only panic.

"I was right. You disconnected her narrative." Just a little proud of herself, Pris nudged Dante toward a chair. "Let me take it from here. Find a way to put up that foot." She settled on the bed's edge so he wouldn't do the gentlemanly thing and insist that she take the chair.

He narrowed his eyes and growled at her—which she found damned sexy. At the same time, he brushed against every object within Jane's reach, practicing his little used psychometry.

"Evidence," he reminded Pris.

Right. Reading Jane's mind and proving her thoughts were two different things. Pris signaled Evie, who sauntered in while the would-be journalist was still hyperventilating.

"No wonder you blog, Jane," Evie said as she rearranged the flowers and pulled out a bent one. "It must be frustrating to be speechless just when you have so much to say."

Pris bit back a chuckle. "She's getting angry. Keep it up."

Her cousin propped herself on the other side of the bed. "I was there, Jane. I told the sheriff that the fire spread *after* you left through the kitchen. What happened? Did you forget to leave the route to the door clear and had to turn back? The accelerant went the wrong way?"

"You're crazy. You're both crazy," Jane finally sputtered. "Your whole family is crazy."

"Well, as we used to say as kids, it takes one to know one." Pris patted the covers over the patient's legs. The blanket stopped short of her bandaged feet. "Now Dante over there is perfectly sane. Should we let him talk?"

Dante grunted and watched them skeptically as he propped his injured foot on the bed rail. "Miss Lawson, we know your parents died of cyanide poisoning from a mattress company fire that you barely escaped as a teen. We've also seen the fire department's report on the arson that caused that fire. We could ask the sheriff to open your juvenile record from that period. We'd rather not."

Evie chuckled. "Muddy red in her first chakra and a scary yellow in her third. You did well, Dr. Watson. She's both scared *and* angry."

For Dante to have spoken that much—he had to have "seen" something on the objects he touched. Pris's stomach clenched. Jane had accidentally killed her parents. Had she been driven to kill again?

"I was just a kid and didn't know better!" Jane protested. She glanced frantically at the nightstand as if searching for a weapon, but they had her surrounded. "It was cold in that warehouse."

Pris had read the history. Jane's parents had been reported to social services on several occasions for abuse. People damned well ought to be licensed before allowed to have children. After the fire, Jane had ended in foster care and therapy. No one ever proved that the fire she'd started to keep warm had been intentionally set to burn down the factory with her parents inside.

Pris removed the cell phone on the stand and handed it to Evie, then pushed the landline out of reach. "We really aren't interested in your juvenile record, although if you continue slandering me, it may get mentioned to appropriate persons."

They'd only guessed about the cause of the bistro's kitchen fire, but for Dante to use a veiled threat, he must have *seen* enough on some object to confirm her guilt. That still wasn't evidence.

Evie's schoolteacher sister read mysteries and claimed that detectives in stories insisted confession was easier than hunting evidence. Pris could see why. Only she didn't have a persuasive bone in her.

"What has us curious is *why* you would set fire to the bistro." Evie twirled the flower she'd removed from the vase. "You are a person who acts out her anger with words. If, instead, you *burned* out everyone you hated, you'd have done more damage by now than General Sherman."

Good line. Pris admired Evie's glibness, while attempting to focus on Jane's mental reactions. She hated doing this. The bigot's mind was a cluttered labyrinth of fear and negativity. But when it came to herself, Jane was quite clear.

"I didn't do anything," the blogger protested.

"She thinks Rhonda knows more than she's saying," Pris reported.

"About KK's death? The money? The fire?" Evie asked looking like a playful genie with her orange curls brushing the shoulders of her bright yellow sweatshirt.

No one had introduced Evie, but Jane apparently recognized her. She scowled and didn't reply.

"I'm seeing jewelry." Puzzled, Pris tried to work out Jane's convoluted fears.

"That's what I thought I saw," Dante said in surprise. "But it's an ancient pendant, so I thought it was just me." He studied Jane. "If you saw what I'm seeing, and it's genuine, it's worth a fortune on the black market. Are you trading in stolen artifacts? Were you trying to frighten Rhonda?"

The expression of shock on Jane's face made this whole painful exercise worth every second.

"It's okay, Janey," Evie said reassuringly. "All we want is KK's killer. Tell us what you know, and we'll go away, and you'll never see us again."

The police might, but Jane's fear won over common sense.

"All I wanted was an interview with Lady Katherine. I went down to Myrtle Beach when she opened that store." With a sigh, Jane reached for her water glass. Her bandaged fingers made it difficult. Pris held the glass for her to sip at the straw.

Satisfied, Jane pushed the glass aside. "No one would talk to me. My blog and my column in the paper have an enormous audience, but I wasn't *important* enough. At the time, I thought the store was Italian, and I wanted the dirt on the foreigners."

Which proved Kit-Kat might have been smarter than anyone thought—if she kept the columnist out because she recognized her bigotry. But Pris accepted that Jane's version was probably right. With her self-cut hair and camouflage attire, Jane always looked like a frumpy homeless person. KK and company were snobs.

The blogger looked self-righteous as she added, "I found a back door to the boutique."

Pris winced at Dante's mental contempt over breaking and entering.

Unfazed, Evie patted the patient encouragingly. "Good investigative reporting. Did you go through the trash?"

Jane nodded. "And then I heard them arguing about a necklace Lady Katherine was wearing. I didn't know who she was at the time, but it was that stuck-up clerk, Rhonda, who said they needed the cash for inventory, not to go around her neck. That snot *knew* something. I thought I could force her into talking. The door into the boutique shouldn't have been locked."

Excellent reason to start a fire, right. How often had the insane blogger used that technique to make people talk? When Jane grew silent, Pris held out the cup for her to sip again.

"You saw the necklace?" Evie continued as if they were just gossiping, but her eyes seemed to be following an agitated ghost.

Pris wished she knew what KK had to say about all this.

Jane muttered in reply, "The necklace was in a photo of Lady Katherine in the Charleston newspaper. Ugly old thing."

Pris lost patience with Jane's crabby opinions. "So what happened in Myrtle Beach after you heard them argue?"

"Lady Katherine laughed and asked what Rhonda was going to do, tell Daddy? It sounded like a threat, as if she would retaliate."

Evie nodded curtly, possibly conveying KK's agreement.

"Then what happened?" Pris asked cautiously, sensing Jane was reaching a mental breaking point.

Jane scrunched her shoulders. "Vincent Gladwell. He came in the back door, heard everything, and saw me. He shouted awful things. I ran out, but I could hear him hitting Katherine and both women screaming at him."

Thirty: Jax

LaWanda, the mayor's eighteen-year-old niece, glanced around Jax's barren office and sniffed. Not quite as tall as Larraine, considerably skinnier, and bespectacled, she'd be called a nerd in any universe except the fashionista's. Larraine had evidently dressed her for success in the red jumpsuit, power Afro, and purple glasses frames.

"Do I get a computer?" was all she asked.

Roark and Reuben were crawling all over his inner office attaching microphones and cameras in preparation for the potential client and murder suspect due to arrive shortly. Jax just needed a body at the desk. He hadn't figured out what to do with her yet. "Eventually. We're still setting up the office. I need you to learn the phone system and hold visitors out here until I allow them in. We'll work out a routine later."

LaWanda sniffed again. "I handled the principal's phone system. It's not complicated." She settled into the mesh office chair Evie had dug out of the attic and began looking for adjustments.

Given the lack of client list, a receptionist who could handle a phone and a chair was all he required. Jax returned to his office to rein in the spooks eager to apply their trade.

Reuben was fixing a microphone under Jax's desk while Roark checked a totally unauthorized security camera over the door.

"This is overkill, guys," Jax protested. "I hate having cameras in my private office. Client information is confidential."

"Nick Gladwell is not yet your client, and he could be a killer for all we know." Reuben plugged in his earbuds to check the sound.

"La Bella Gente is a client," Jax argued. "He could be representing them."

"We'll remove the equipment and you can throw out the video if he's here on business," Reuben agreed, stepping back to test his earbuds.

"Interrogate, *bon ami*," Roark said. "It's what you do good."

"Yeah, well, it would help if I knew what crime I'm interrogating about." Jax opened the boutique's file on his laptop. "I have no idea why he made this appointment."

"To find out who knows what would be my guess." The lanky Cajun climbed down from the chair he was using and carried it toward the door.

"Out," Jax ordered, watching the camera in the corridor. "He's here."

His friends picked up their equipment and vanished into the file room. Seconds later, Jax's teenage receptionist greeted the client's arrival and paged Jax on the intercom. So she really did know a bit about office equipment.

He would have appreciated the smooth organization his office was finally achieving, except he knew R&R were in it for the money. Insurance had offered rewards for finding KK's killer and the arson at the bistro. Evie's hungry team was looking at major pay-outs.

At his visitor's entrance, Jax stood to shake Nicholas Gladwell's hand. "Good to see you. How are you holding up?"

The other man looked worse for wear. The Bella team had always been bright and shiny when he'd worked with them before the store opening. Nick was the classic stereotype of a slick salesman, Italian shoes and all. Today, a dark shadow of beard marred his square jaw and his eyes had developed bags from lack of sleep.

"I've been better," Nick admitted, settling into the chair in front of the desk. "The insurance company is giving me grief. I'm hoping you can help."

"I'll be happy to try, although I'm not sure what I can do. They've sent inspectors?"

Nick nodded. "The arson charge is holding things up. They want to blame our employees. They're demanding a complete inventory of stock along with receipts. Rhonda is still in shock and refusing to return here. She's gone over to KK's store at Myrtle. Matt is hunkering down at Hilton Head, claiming he's too busy. I'm marketing. I know nothing of the back office."

Jax frowned and tapped his pen. "Matt is back? Why isn't he handling all this?"

"He came back fuming. He wants the London store. He'd leave the boutiques to Rhonda, if he could. But Hilton Head at least has people he'll talk to, so he won't leave."

Neither Matt nor Rhonda wished to return to the scene of the crime? Interesting.

"What about corporate?" Jax asked. "Shouldn't they be in charge? Shouldn't they send someone to handle the financial end? Send new employees?"

Nick settled in the big Morris chair from Evie's attic and crossed an ankle over his knee. "The boutiques were Katherine and Matt's ideas. They each operated their own. Afterthought was Kit-Kat's. No idea why she decided on this place. Corporate has no interest. Kat was supposed to handle it all. I'm only here now because of her."

Jax nodded as if he understood and reached into his grab bag of questions. "I'm really sorry for your loss. Katherine seemed like a dynamic businesswoman. I understand she and Lucia Ugazio developed the lotions using the Ugazio oils, so I suppose it's natural that she wanted to control the sales."

Nick grimaced. "The amount of oil required for the lotions is ridiculously expensive. They gave up on using that a long time ago. We've only been selling Lucia's bottled virgin olive oil in the bistros. KK was furious about that. That doesn't mean losing the inventory still wasn't expensive. The packaging costs nearly as much as the ingredients. If the insurance would come through, I could pay off the outstanding bills and close up the shop."

Jax donned his best lawyer straight face. "Could Miss Ugazio step in? Or was she angry at not using the olive oil in the lotions as well?"

Nick waved a dismissive hand. "I haven't seen Lucia since the year I was hired. I was told she went back to Italy. If I can't get Matt or Rhonda to step up, it's all on me. I hate leaving bills and wages unpaid. I know what it's like to struggle for money. It's obvious the store is a loss. Insurance needs to cough up some cash."

Huh, another one claiming not to have seen Lucia in years. Evie's ghostly encounter seemed more and more likely. Jax held back a shudder at the thought of a long dead woman speaking through the woman he loved.

Concluding Nick really was almost as financially inept as he claimed, Jax poked at his willingness to dump his grievances. "If you'll forward what you have, along with the insurance adjustor's information, I'll see what I can do. Shouldn't the store have had a bank account covering expected expenses?"

Nick shrugged. "I cannot imagine how they were operating. Income didn't match outgo as far as I'm aware. The account was almost empty. I tried asking Matt and Rhonda since they had access, but they shut me down. All I encounter are Matt's bullies now when I ask questions."

"Bullies?" Jax settled back in his chair and waited expectantly.

"His boyfriends. He hired them to keep Vincent and KK off his back. My family is not the world's most functional. I'm thinking of leaving the business and becoming a lion tamer." Nick's sarcasm bled through.

"Matt was threatened by his *sister*? About what?" Jax aimed for idle curiosity.

"Jewelry, apparently. It was a running argument. KK liked old gold and gems. She'd have them shipped in with the oil. Matt liked cash. Vincent had to slam their heads together occasionally. I stayed out of it." Nick pushed up from his chair. "I've bent your ear enough. I'll send you my files, although if the insurance doesn't come through, I don't know how you'll be paid."

"Off the top of any check," Jax assured him with a laugh. He stood and shook hands. "Send me addresses and contact numbers for Matt and Rhonda, as well, would you? Maybe I can intervene and persuade more from them than a family member. Will Vincent be taking charge of his daughter's remains? I understand the coroner is about to release them."

Nick looked unbearably sad. "No. He refuses to return here. As far as I'm aware, he's not even preparing services."

"Grief-stricken, I suppose. I'm sorry the burden falls on you." Jax walked him to the door.

The moment Nick left the office, R&R returned, crowing.

"Italy!" Roark shouted. "Old gold from Italy! Smuggled in oil!"

Reuben was already poking at his phone. "Artifacts," he said the instant someone answered on the other end. "Italian artifacts in the oil shipments."

EVIE CURLED UP ON THE CUSHIONED, WICKER LOVESEAT SWING JAX HAD INSTALLED ON the back porch. She welcomed the arm he curled around her and lay her head on his shoulder to watch Dante's children run around the yard with her mother's golden retriever. "Tell me people are basically good."

"*Most* people are basically good," he said agreeably. "What brought this on?"

"The Gladwells, I think. And maybe Jane, although I think her tragic childhood warped her. She won't confess, but we think she started the fire out of spite and a twisted hope that she could force Rhonda to trust her. She's not precisely rational." She turned to kiss his jaw.

"And where's your unfriendly ghost right now?" He cuddled her closer.

"She's been flickering out and looking grim since our visit to our sociopathic blogger. I'd really like to get KK into the same room with her father."

"You think Vincent is the reason the ghost is lingering? He's not leaving the UK."

Evie shrugged. "After Jane's revelations and Dante's claims. . . I know about domestic violence in an intellectual sort of way, but the Gladwells seem so upper crusty British. . . Stupid of me, of course. But then I look at the twins and think about Lucia."

"She may have rescued them from an unhappy situation?" Jax suggested.

She nodded. The screen door bumped open and Pris emerged with a pan of brownies. Offering the chocolate, her cousin spoke as if she'd been listening. "Dante is watching your office video. He reached explosive at the mention of old gold. We need to unleash his rage."

The twins came running, shutting off any discussion of how one went about uncovering artifact theft, much less murder and arson. Pris held the platter out of the children's reach. "What do you say?"

They looked briefly perplexed, consulted each other with looks, then Alex extended his small palm. "Cookie?"

"Brownie," Pris corrected. "What else do you say when you would like something?"

"I want a brownie." Nan stuck out her little chin.

Evie chuckled. "May I have a brownie, please, Pris?" She held out her hand and was rewarded with chocolaty goodness.

The twins brightened, repeated the magic phrase, and ran off with their reward.

"One needs to be a mind reader to bring up children?" Jax suggested, accepting the decadent dessert.

"Worried?" Pris taunted.

Evie shivered as she considered potential children. Men tended to flee once faced with kids who sometimes knew too much—or acted too weird. She'd like to have kids someday, but she didn't want to lose Jax.

He finished chewing his mouthful of chocolate and shrugged. "Kids are just another challenge."

Evie almost melted like the chocolate.

Dante limped out to join them. "Leo has to be the thief," he declared, taking one of the porch chairs. "The photograph of KK with the necklace doesn't tell me enough. It could be a museum replica. But if Bella is receiving stolen artifacts in their oil shipments, Leo has to be involved."

"Evidence," Evie said at the same time as Jax. They elbowed each other, just like an old married couple, and her already melting insides were reduced to hot bubbling liquid.

Pris set the half empty pan on the porch rail and perched beside it. "Let the police handle it."

"I've set some of my London relations on the Bella warehouses." Dante helped himself to a brownie. "They'll notify the police if they discover anything. I've talked to colleagues familiar with the black market for Italian artifacts, and they're working that end. But Leo—"

"Is your friend and neighbor," Evie commiserated.

"And Lucia's cousin and potential heir if we find evidence that she's no longer alive." Dante looked miserable. "I knew he was hiding something, but I just cannot fathom. . ."

"I looked into it. In Italy, it takes *twenty* years to have someone declared dead, and no one has even reported Lucia missing. As next of kin, Leo would have to make the report. Stay out of it, Dante," Jax advised.

Dante watched his children playing in the twilight and shook his head. "I can't. If there is any chance that Lucia was murdered. . ."

"You still can't do anything," Pris told him. "Let's stick with what we have here first."

Evie reached for another brownie. "R&R dug through the sheriff's records for KK's list of possessions. It includes a necklace. We'll ask Sheriff Troy in the morning if you can see it—and touch it."

"I don't suppose they'd let him touch the limoncello bottle?" Pris asked.

"Troy knows we're weird. If we can give him directions that solve the case, he won't argue." Evie rocked the love seat with her toe. "I'm just now realizing that psychic crime solving means we never have evidence and always need confessions."

Jax squeezed her warningly. "A good interrogator can work with knowledge. Let Troy do his job."

Evie kissed his jaw soothingly. "You are so trusting."

And her family had learned not to be, which was why they resorted to under-handed methods of which Jax did not approve. Usually. Maybe he was coming around?

"We need to question Matt and Rhonda," Pris said. "What will it take to get them in one place?"

"A weapon?" Jax suggested darkly. "Letting a ghost terrorize suspects didn't work so well last time."

Dante looked puzzled.

Evie wrinkled her nose at mention of her last case. "It didn't work as intended because we had the wrong suspects, but we drove the crazy ladies into crawling out of the woodwork anyway. I don't think we have crazies here, unless we count Jane."

Pris shook her head at Dante when he started to question. "Don't ask. I'll tell you later, but you won't like it. Let's stick to here and now. How do we approach Matt and Rhonda?"

"Inventory," Jax said gloomily. "I tell them if they want the insurance money, they need to come here and verify the inventory lists against items on the shelf and sign off on it."

"That will take all of two minutes. The place was practically empty when I saw it." Evie shoved curls out of her eyes.

"Now who's the naïf?" Jax tapped her on the head. "They'll sneak in to fill the shelves with damaged goods or damp boxes or whatever it takes. Just give them enough time to hang themselves—*if* they're the thieves you think."

"Plotting, I love it," Evie cried. "I'll get Dante into the sheriff's office tomorrow. Jax can entice Rhonda and Matthew into insurance fraud. And R&R can film it all!"

"While you're at it, spring Jane so she can burn down the rest of the building," Pris said dryly. "I'm putting the kids to bed before you figure out how to raise Lucia from the dead."

"Sarcasm, lowest form of humor," Evie shouted after her.

"Do not do anything that will return Vincent to these shores," Dante warned. "The man apparently has no conscience."

Thirty-one: Dante

DANTE TRIED NOT TO FEEL LIKE A FOOL FINGERING THE ORNATE MULTI-PENDANT GOLD necklace while hoping for recent impressions of KK. He could at least offer his professional opinion aloud. "It is definitely Etruscan, probably 5th century BC, one of the best pieces I've ever seen. It belongs in a museum."

Little of KK clung to the gold. Dante had the feeling she was too weak to leave her mark on real life and certainly not on a piece this rich in history.

Sheriff Troy nodded with interest. "But as a motive for murder?"

Dante shook his head. "Selling it would require knowing people willing to acquire ancient artifacts under the table. That, I cannot tell you. I do have colleagues making inquiries."

"What about Jane?" Evie asked. "She saw it. She was angry. She might know about gold but not museum pieces. Is that motive enough?"

Dante knew she asked the last for the sheriff's purpose, but she was reminding him to look for impressions from a woman he scarcely knew. Dante shook his head to let her know there was nothing of Jane on it.

"We'll ask the others who were with Katherine at the time of her death. It's all we can do. From all reports, the boutiques were losing money. How could the owner afford priceless jewelry?" The sheriff returned the necklace to its bag and pushed the limoncello bottle across the desk. "The bottle has been fingerprinted. Everyone touched it. Can you differentiate types of limoncello?"

Dante brushed his fingers over the writing, as if inspecting that, just in case this was being filmed or watched. He shook his head again. "This is a fairly common brand, perhaps a little more alcoholic content than others. More sugar than lemon, which may be why she preferred it."

But Vincent's vengeful anger had touched it. There were other impressions as well. Vincent just came through loudest.

Dante rose when Evie did, shaking the sheriff's hand and thanking him for his time.

Evie had one last parting question. "Did y'all look to see how much insurance KK's policy paid to the company? Do they still get paid if she was murdered?"

Troy frowned at her. "Not your business, Evangeline, but Jax will tell you that a murderer can't benefit from his crime."

"But a company can't commit a crime," Evie replied, before sashaying out.

So, if any one of their suspects killed KK, the others would benefit? Because any insurance money sure the hell wasn't paying company bills from everything they'd seen.

"YES, OF COURSE." TALKING TO MATTHEW GLADWELL, JAX TRIED TO SOUND reassuring over the phone. "Nicholas is in town. I assume he can open up the store, but he says he's not competent to create an inventory. The insurance payment has to be based on physical evidence. Videos, receipts, actual counts, all go toward proving the value."

His career in criminal fraud had taught him how to deal with higher end crooks than Rhonda and Matthew. They had the brains of petty smash-and-grab thieves and none of the financial skills that would have set up off-shore accounts, or even set up the company itself. KK and Lucia had probably been the brains there.

Murder didn't take brains. It took luck. Selling artifacts? That had to be Lucia, but if she was dead. . .

Or maybe Lucia was the killer, hiding safely on some Caribbean island. Maybe her spirit didn't need to be dead. He was living the Twilight Zone here.

He only knew he had to clear this up so Dante could go home with his children, R&R could claim their reward, and he could relax knowing Evie was safe and not looking for trouble. Well, that last part was iffy even if he solved all crime everywhere.

Jax got Matt's agreement to meet him tomorrow at the boutique. He repeated the conversation with Rhonda, who refused until reminded her lack of cooperation could be construed as evidence against her should the sheriff decide he had to make arrests in KK's death and/or the arson.

Out of an abundance of caution, he called the hospital to talk to Jane the Blogger. They informed him she'd been released. Jax grimaced and checked online, but the blog hadn't been updated since she'd insulted Larraine.

He spent the rest of the day introducing himself to the board of directors of DVM Electronics, the voting machine manufacturing company whose majority shares he'd just acquired. A few of them even remembered his father. Standing in for the father he'd lost at age twelve had never been his goal, but it felt oddly right to be doing so, especially since it meant he could reward R&R for their loyalty. Monetarily, it might not be much, but in terms of respect. . . They'd have resumes they could employ one day.

By the time Jax got home that evening, he was feeling pretty satisfied with himself. Always a mistake.

As they had the previous night, everyone retired to the back porch after dinner to watch the children run off their energy before bed. Tonight, Pris passed around pumpkin tarts for a preliminary Thanksgiving taste test.

"I need to run around with the kids to work off these things," Evie complained.

"Or use your bike more often, instead of the car." Pris waved one of the tarts. "Where's Loretta? You could follow her around all day."

"She's with Gracie tonight, learning to sew. It's hard to transport sewing baskets on bicycles."

Jax hugged her. "We'll go back to starvation rations after Pris leaves. Eat your tart. Have we made any progress on the artifacts?"

She elbowed him for the starvation remark but took a tart.

Dante spoke up. "My colleagues have dug up a few suspicious offers on the black market. Your team is investigating, but these sorts of transactions are fairly untraceable. We'd have to set up a sting. Since all we have is KK's necklace and Jane's claims, that's not enough to go on."

"The sheriff is poking around, stirring up nests where he can." Evie finished off her bite-sized tart. "Maybe you can pry more out of Matt and Rhonda tomorrow."

"Jane is on the loose. She posted bail on the arson charge and is out of the hospital. As a precaution, I have the fire department on alert for my meeting with the Gladwells." Jax rocked the swing. "R&R will have cameras on us, but I don't expect much. I think Jane simply wanted to make the Gladwells suffer."

"Her aura is unhealthy. She needs serious counseling more than prison." Evie perked up. "Will Troy take video as evidence if Matt or Rhonda say anything incriminating?"

"Court might not, but what are the chances the Gladwells know that? Troy can use it in his interrogations. But admitting murder, or even theft, probably isn't happening." Jax hugged her sympathetically. "We might catch them in inventory fraud at best."

"Did anyone find out who locked Bella's door before Jane's arson?" Pris sat on the porch steps and wrinkled her nose at the tart she was taste-testing.

"That was Nick," Jax acknowledged. "Perfectly innocent. He discovered the door unlocked when he entered the empty shop and thought someone had forgotten to lock it. Since all the other doors were locked, he thought Rhonda hadn't come in yet. He was taking a customer phone call in the back when he smelled smoke. He ran out to the alley to call 911 and had no idea people were inside."

"Are we believing Nick?" Pris asked from the step.

"Unless you're picking up anything otherwise, his aura is pretty solid. He has some iffy bits like any of us. If Jax believes him, I'm good with that." Evie reached for another tart.

Jax thought he ought to preen if someone as perceptive as Evie trusted his instincts, but logic prevailed. "If experience counts, then I'd say he's telling the truth. It's hard to know how deeply he was involved in the operation. He's the only one who appears sad about KK's death."

"Dante, what about Leo? Do you think he was responsible for the cave falling on you? Surely he had to know something?" Pris picked her tart apart, tasting just the crust.

"The tunnel section I saw last appeared to be Victorian construction that simply crumbled. I can't say Leo knew anything one way or another. Anyone digging through the tuff could have disturbed that concrete. Plot later. Kids now. It's dark and they're being too quiet." Dante stood and shouted at the twins to come in.

The twins didn't answer. Instead, Honey, the golden retriever, barked frantically—from the street?

Jax's stomach knotted as Evie jumped up.

"The yard is fenced." She jogged to the weed patch dividing her yard from the neighbor's.

Jax trailed after her, searching the darkness for giggling, hiding imps.

No twins.

He beat at the overgrown shrubbery and shouted, "Nan, Alex."

Dante limped out carrying a flashlight.

"KK," Evie whispered worriedly. "In the back corner."

Dante pointed his light in that direction. "The bushes are bent." The flashlight revealed the extent of the damage and the missing fence boards.

Evie shoved through the narrow child-sized opening while Jax and Dante ripped at the boards to enlarge it. In the street on the other side, Honey wildly raced up and down, barking, as if she'd lost her best friends.

"Limo!" Evie cried frantically. *"KK is saying limo!"*

Thirty-Two: Dante

SEARCHING FOR COOL, CALCULATING LOGIC AND ONLY HEARING THE ROAR OF TERROR in his head and the echoing emptiness in his chest, Dante tapped into his mobile. Beside him, Roark recklessly drove the utility van down a two-lane road toward the interstate, hoping to catch up with a limo. Roark's phone beeped, and Dante grabbed that one too.

"Ariel says stop at the abandoned gas station." He read the message aloud, then returned to checking messages. As far as they'd ascertained so far, the ghost's warning of a large black car in the neighborhood was correct, except no one knew its direction. All they could assume was that whoever had the children would be fleeing for an airport.

Dante's worst nightmare was that the children wouldn't make it that far. What hornet's nest had they stirred? Jax had called Matt and Rhonda. Jane was out of the hospital. Who else?

Why the children?

To get him to do something. What? All he knew were artifacts. They wanted the necklace? He couldn't force the sheriff to release it.

Focused on reaching Atlanta, Roark frowned and slowed the van down. "How she know where we at?"

"Ariel is included in the group text. I don't know how she knows location."

"Tracking calls," Roark shouted excitedly. "My brilliant bébé learned to track the phones!" He swung the van off the road into the cracked concrete pad of an old service station.

Dante wanted to physically shove the van down the road, but it would take him longer to climb out than for the bicyclist he assumed was Ariel to cross the road and unlatch the panel door in back.

Ariel flung in her bike and slammed the door. "Not a plane."

They'd alerted the police about missing children, but not even Sheriff Troy could make the leap of faith from a ghost saying *limo* to some unidentified Gladwell kidnapping Dante's children for reasons unknown. KK hadn't been clear on the occupants of the limo.

Evie had, however, persuaded the sheriff to send an Amber alert and notify the police in three states to watch the airports—after Evie's mother produced a neighbor who'd seen the children being thrown into a limousine.

Dante had a suspicion that Mavis had *seen* that in her crystal ball and twisted a neighbor's arm. Having learned to trust his family's weird instincts, he was grateful any way it worked, although he was pretty certain his mother's family didn't lie to the law.

Dante couldn't figure out *why* anyone would want his children, unless it was Lucia and she was alive. He needed to cling to that insane hope to stay sane, which only proved he'd reached the cliff's edge of hysteria.

"Not a plane, then what, bébé?" Roark asked as the door slammed.

"Marina. Beaufort. Charge on Bella credit card." Ariel began manipulating the assortment of equipment in the back of the van.

Before Roark could swing back to the road, Dante read another text. "Wait. Pris is right behind us."

"Texting?" Roark cried. "The way she drives?"

Glad he wasn't the only one who thought Pris drove like a fiend out of hell, Dante held his breath as a battered dual-cab Ford with a bed cover squealed into the pull-off. Roark muttered a few curses.

Dante's phone rang. Answering, he heard Pris's anxious voice on the other end. "Let Ariel navigate for Roark. If the kidnapper tries to escape through Atlanta, Roark can bring him down. But if the limo is heading for Beaufort, I can beat his dinosaur van. Wanna be my navigator?"

He'd seen Pris drive when she was on a tear and knew he was taking his life in his hands to climb in that vehicle. His children were worth the risk. Blessing her for realizing he needed to be in on this, he trusted her as his best chance of reaching the marina first.

He swung open the van door and eased out. "Text the others with the change of plans," he told Roark while grabbing the cane Evie had given him. "Keep the lines open."

"Rather you than me, *bon ami*," Roark shouted after him.

Dante hauled himself into the pickup cab and buckled in. "Why a marina?"

Pris slammed the engine into gear and peeled off, leaving rubber on the cracked concrete. "Use your imagination."

He'd rather not. He was a scientist. He wanted facts.

To take his mind off the nightmare of his imagination, he glanced at an incoming group text from Ariel. As instructed, he opened her email. Jax's sister might not communicate much in person, but she knew how to disseminate information. The email contained lists of all the charges made recently on a Bella credit card. Those charges included first-class tickets to Atlanta from *London* and a rented limousine.

Vincent. The only Gladwell left in London. But why? Nick had said Vincent had vowed never to return. But who else could it be? Lucia? As far as he was aware, everyone else was here.

What had set Vincent off, if he was the ticket holder? The inventory Jax planned? Their visit to the sheriff?

The recollection of the violence on the limoncello bottle kicked Dante's terror up ten notches. "If Matt is already in Hilton Head, then this plane ticket looks like Vincent Gladwell may be meeting his son."

The whistle Pris emitted was not one of joy. "Beaufort isn't far from here. . . or from Hilton Head. Either of them could have booked that boat. But why?"

"Exactly what I'm asking myself. What did we do to stir the sleeping beast? He can't possibly know that we suspect Lucia is dead, can he?" He followed the rapid fire texts that followed but no one had any idea.

"The necklace," Pris said with a question in her voice. "If he heard you visited the sheriff. . . And maybe KK had warned them of you. She thought of you just before she died, remember? Was she afraid you'd recognize the necklace? Lucia may have told her that you knew artifacts. . ."

"And her family must know that necklace is worth a fortune. . . " Dante shook his head in disbelief. "I cannot think like a thief. It may be possible that Vincent has discovered my contacts are making inquiries on the black market."

"And he's running scared? Can Ariel follow any other credit cards?" Pris maneuvered the truck around a semi on a blind hill.

"She's in the back of the van playing magic computer." Following the text on his phone, Dante blocked out Pris's terrifying driving.

"Where's Reuben? That's usually his job."

"He's with the mayor and the cops, feeding them everything he dares. Given the probable illegality of some of this data, that's a job in itself." Dante read through the scrolling messages. "Reuben says Jax is on the way to Savannah on his Harley and can be diverted to Beaufort. Evie is heading for the Charleston airport. That's apparently not far either?"

"They're both aimed for the coast but not as direct as the route we're taking. Tell Rube to send them to the marina. At this hour, no one is catching a commercial flight to anywhere except Atlanta, and Roark will be talking to security there. But if Ariel isn't finding credit charges for a plane, the boat is it. We just don't know what they plan to do with it." She hit the gas and passed a sedate sedan tooling along only a few miles over the limit.

As she accelerated, Dante gritted his teeth and found the GPS map on his mobile so he could follow their route. Rather than picture his innocent children, terrified and on a boat heading into the Atlantic, he distracted himself with curiosity. "How did you learn to drive like a bat out of hell?"

"Father's a stock-car driver. He taught us all. You know anything about stock car racing?"

"Not a whit. Not certain I want to know. Where is your father now?"

Twilight had turned to a wintery dark. The two lane made a T with a slightly larger road. Barely slowing down to watch for oncoming headlights, Pris swung east and floored it. "Let us just say Dad was a better driver than a mechanic. At race speeds, engine failure is not optimal."

"And the mechanic for this rusted piece of junk?" Dante focused on the phone so he didn't have to watch her whizz past traffic. But he was utterly aware of the fearless driver in the seat beside him. The devil woman really needed a red streak in her hair.

"Understand that South Carolina probably has more mechanics than peach trees, and if I say I have the best in the business, that means you'll find none better anywhere. Worry about human failure. I want to commit murder."

"I know the feeling." Voices screamed in his head. He could almost believe KK and Lucia were here, blasting him with their cries. He didn't even have to understand their words. He felt them in his gut.

Children weren't kidnapped for any good reason, and he knew without any doubt that his children had not left of their own accord. They might have poked through the fence to explore, but they would have been found by now if that had been the case. Evie's neighbors and her dog trainer cousin were canvassing the streets, flashlights and tracking animals in hand. The dogs had found no scent.

"You're mentally blocking me." Pris gunned the truck through an intersection as the light turned red. "I don't know what that means. Most people can't do that."

"I don't know what it means either. I simply go inside my own head when outside influences are too distracting. I learned it whilst staying with my mother's family. They're as intrusive as you and yours."

"I do that too. Maybe we all learn to do that. People talk too much as it is. Tapping into their thoughts only increases the noise factor, so I don't usually bother. But you're an enigma, so I get curious." Apparently spotting a police car, she slowed down through a small town, then floored it once outside of city limits.

"Is this the road a limo would take?" he asked, not wanting to question her curiosity, because he'd have to admit his own about her. And as welcome as the distraction would be, he wanted to concentrate on his children, as if thinking about them would keep them safe. Were they sleeping? Crying? Scared?

"Right now we're on the main highway, such as it is, but it doesn't go straight in the direction we want. The truck is geared for off-road. I'm taking the hypotenuse. Prepare yourself."

He recited the Lord's Prayer in Latin out loud as she careened off the highway down a rugged gravel road.

"That's good. I like the Latin. It's soothing, like a monk's chant. Keep it up." She skidded through a muddy creek and out the other side.

Chickens scattered. Or maybe they were turkeys. He didn't know his farm fowl.

"You know where this marina is?" he asked, hanging onto the door grip as she swerved around a farm truck parked in the lane. They were fortunate it was after dinnertime and everyone must be home, watching their televisions.

"Beaufort isn't that big. Find the marina address, plug it in. We see boats, we check the name on the sign. I'm betting Vincent doesn't know the low-end places so it's just a matter of finding the right turn-off."

"I just don't understand *why*." Dante fielded more texts. Reuben apparently was keeping track of everyone's location by some mysterious means. Roark was a long way out from Atlanta, but the others had diverted their paths and were converging on Beaufort.

No reports of the children or the limo.

"I refuse to speculate, or I could go to a dark place pretty quickly," Pris admitted. "Let's assume Vincent wants you to do something, and they're his leverage, okay? And we really don't know that it's him just because we sense his violence. I mean, I think about hating and murdering people all the time. If I could be convicted for my thoughts. . ."

"Understood, but I can't let it go. If I had some notion. . . I could be preparing. But I can't even drive a damned car." He pounded his cane against the floorboard.

"I like the walking stick," she said. "From Great-Granddaddy's collection?"

"No idea. Evie handed it to me. It's pretty sturdy. Might be easier to maneuver for short distances. I was hoping it might contain a weapon, but I've not found a release." He ran his hand over the curve of the carved oak.

"He used it mostly for walloping, but I'd be careful about that. Great-granddaddy had a reputation." She steered back to a normal highway and flew past a semi.

"A reputation for what?" Dante said another prayer and was grateful for flat land. Oncoming headlights warned them to pull over as she passed traffic at improbable speeds—providing all vehicles had their lights on.

"His enemies often ran into pointed objects. No one ever charged him, though, so we have no proof that he wasn't just lucky. Hold onto your hat."

He wasn't wearing one. Dante gripped the door handle tighter as she drove off the road and through a log barrier, skidding in the gravel as she hit the gas again.

"We're going around the town," she reported. "No one out here at this hour. Maybe a few gators."

"Gators? Isn't it too cold for them?"

"Probably, but climate change and all that. This is swamp." To prove her point, she splashed through a stream and out before the truck bed could skid.

They hit a normal—if nearly invisible—road not long after that. Her speed increased. He zoomed in on the GPS map and read the names of local restaurants and hotels—on a road that wasn't this one. Dante squinted and tried to read unlit signs. He couldn't even catch glimpses of water at this hour.

"Beaufort isn't on the ocean. We're skipping the river and heading straight for the island. We're not near any marinas yet," Pris warned.

His mobile binged with an address, and he punched it into the GPS. "Take the next turn."

They slewed off onto a shell road leaving a trail of dust.

Thirty-three: Evie

EVIE WISHED SHE HAD JAX WITH HER. HER SUBARU MIGHT BE A FOUR-WHEEL DRIVE, but it was too low slung to drive off-road. The highway to Beaufort from Charleston was a lonely place at night, and her fretful thoughts resembled the swirling, directionless ball of color floating around the car's interior that was KK.

Evie's thoughts were as grim as the black T-shirt and jeans she wore, the only colorless ones she owned. If she meant to blend in with the shadows on more nighttime expeditions, she might have to acquire new attire.

Feeling useless because she couldn't persuade a stupid swirling rainbow to talk, she gave up watching the ghost and debated whether detective work require that she buy depressing outfits.

The phone rang, and she let it connect with her audio system. She was so high-tech these days.

"Pris and Dante have reached the marina. Limo's not there yet." Reuben's voice reported. "How far out are you?"

"Highway 21 ahead. I'm pushing twenty miles over the limit, but once I hit Beaufort, I'll have to slow down. Can't say. How about Jax?"

"He knows the Georgia back roads, so he's moving. He's about as far out though. If the limo is actually going that way, it can't be far ahead of you on 21." Rube hung up.

Pulse racing, Evie prayed they were correct about the limo's direction. And that Mavis was right about seeing the twins in it. And that the limo driver had taken the highway route at normal speed to avoid detection. That was asking a *lot*.

She concentrated on gratitude for her family's extra abilities and pushed the fear deep down inside. Those children were too precious to be harmed.

She and Jax had to reach the marina from the north and south. The goddesses only knew what route Pris had taken to get out in front of the limo. Afterthought wasn't on a highway to anywhere.

Evie told her phone to call Pris. Her cousin answered with a surly *What?*

"Is there any chance you can pick up any mental vibrations from the twins as the limo approaches the marina?"

Hesitation, which meant Pris was being forced to think instead of react for a change.

"Possibly, but not too far out. It's quiet here. Dante knows how to shut himself down, so there's just me and the gulls. But I'm more likely to pick up the vibrations of the driver or whoever is with them. Kids need sleep."

Evie prayed they were just sleeping. "All right. KK is still with me but she's not connecting. We should be there in less than half an hour. How's Dante holding up?"

"Not well. He's out limping up and down the marina. I assume he's hoping he'll recognize whatever it is he feels when he touches things, but it's not as if he knows Matt or Rhonda or any of them well enough to recognize their vibrations or whatever."

"All right. Don't let him do anything foolish until we're there to fish him out of the water." Evie punched off and turned onto the highway leading through town and to the island.

She couldn't call Jax on his motorcycle. Not hearing his calm logic made the drive lonely and just a little scary. Which gave her too much time to build up her terror of what could be happening with those poor babies. She refused to play the blame game, but if even she felt guilty for not keeping a closer eye on the kids. . . Pris and Dante had to be writhing in abject misery.

Because of some murderous bastard who thought two innocents might stand between him and what? It was always money. Children were more about control than passion, normally—unless Lucia was behind this. Evie had good reason to be certain she wasn't—and a dead Lucia had to be the clue to it all.

Please, let the twins be sleeping and not afraid.

The streets were quiet as she rolled into town. Breaking the speed limit only meant catching more red lights, so she paced herself on the green. . . and was rewarded with the sight of a large black car with a long band of shiny taillights stopped at the next intersection. She hit the phone and notified Rube so he could ping everyone else.

She didn't know if the police would respond. Stopping fancy cars not breaking any law was probably iffy. It wasn't as if they had a license plate or even a model for the kidnap vehicle.

The road was empty enough that she could stay a quarter mile behind, allowing work trucks and evening revelers to slip in and out between her little Subaru and the limo. Not until they were out of town and on the way through the silent island did she feel conspicuous.

A Harley roared up behind her, then sped past. Evie almost dissolved in relief. With a wave, Jax raced the bike ahead of the limo. He knew the routes to all the marinas. His adoptive father had owned a yacht.

Reuben phoned in again. "Pris reporting a BMW parking in the lot. I ran the plates, but it's a rental. I'll dig into the rental records next, but you may have company."

"Matt and Rhonda aren't that far away. They had plenty of time to drive here if Vincent called them." Evie's stomach ground in anxiety. "For all I know, Nick Gladwell is here too."

"It's out of Troy's district, but the sheriff is calling in favors, trying to get people out there. Try not to hassle any cops if they show up." With his usual lack of farewell, Rube hung up.

The anarchic engineer actually working with the authorities. . . Not a complete stretch. Unlike Roark, Reuben had a proper middle class upbringing. Joining the military may have paid for his education, but it had been a bad fit for a gay Black intellectual. With a little respect and normalcy, he might turn into an upright citizen again.

The limo rolled into the gravel-and-shell marina parking lot. Turning off her headlights, Evie drove down a side street, turned around, and parked where she could hit the main road running. Climbing out, pulse racing, she tried not to crunch shells as she pretended to be a shadow. If KK was with her, she couldn't tell.

Evie was pretty certain that was Jax approaching from the other direction. He waited and caught her hand, squeezing it reassuringly as they watched the limo.

"Pris's truck under the oak in far corner," he murmured.

The limo blinked its headlights and turned them off. The dark BMW did the same.

"There are times when guns might be useful," she said with a sigh. "And if you're carrying, I don't want to know. Weapons are too dangerous with kids around. They're unpredictable."

He squeezed her hand again. "I'm not a cop. I can only use a weapon in self-defense. I'm going to cover the BMW. Dante is almost at the limo. Try not to let KK get the better of you. I'm counting on you to stay safe."

Despite her terror, Evie felt the warmth of his acknowledgment that she had spirit energy for her weapon. She didn't know if that was true, but they were about to find out.

In the light of a dim parking lot security lamp, she watched the limo driver step out at the same time as a man left the passenger seat and a woman out of the back. Two men climbed out of the BMW. She saw no children.

Not liking this, Evie thought as she approached the limo from behind. She couldn't see Dante anywhere.

From the shadows, a sturdy figure in clothes that blended with the night strode directly for the limo's back door. That had to be Pris. The limo's occupants, the Gladwells, if that's who they were, had left the car to approach the BMW and had their backs toward Pris and Evie.

Where were the twins—and their father? Jax had said Dante was aiming for the limo. With his crippled leg and size, he should be noticeable.

Evie waited for the female passenger to follow the men, but she held back, lingering near the hood.

Accepting a mental shove from Pris, Evie slipped up to the driver side back door at the same time as her cousin took the passenger side. Together, they opened up the back seat.

The twins were just starting to stir.

The wave of relief rolling over her briefly blinded Evie to the woman at the front of the car, until she cried a warning. *Damn.*

"Go with Pris," Evie whispered, shoving one little body toward the far door.

She didn't linger to see if they obeyed. The woman shouting was considerably taller and heavier than Evie, but that's why she had taken martial arts training as a teen. She hated being bullied.

As the woman hurried to stop her, Evie slammed the back door. Finally able to release her mounting rage, she waited for her opponent to reach her—*Rhonda*. Evie let her close the gap before she kicked high with all the fury in her, connecting hard with a soft belly. With a gasp, Vincent's mistress dropped to the ground, probably more in shock than pain. In an instant, she was scrambling to her hands and knees, cursing.

Along with her extra six inches and thirty pounds, Rhonda came loaded with spike heels that could do serious damage. Fearing Pris and those babes depended on her ancient training, Evie went for the less dramatic move this time. While Rhonda tried to push up, Evie stomped the clerk's fingers into the gravel.

Once she had her pinned, she released her wrath in a swift chop to the back of Rhonda's neck. It hurt like crazy, but Rhonda flattened.

In Evie's head, KK screamed a war cry.

The men finally noticed the commotion. Shouting, the shorter, stouter passenger Evie assumed was Vincent turned and hurried back.

Just as he reached the front of the limo, he jerked abruptly, flailed, and smacked face first into the car's hood.

In colors of fury and revenge, KK swirled around him, creating a tornado of rocks and shells. He howled and slid sideways along the polished surface.

From his hiding place on the far side of the limo, Dante pushed up on the cane he must have used to cause Vincent's stumble. Smart man. With only one stable leg, swinging a fist might have unbalanced him. But now that Vincent was staggering, Dante could steady himself on the hood and plow a massive blow into the other man's jaw. Despite the hurricane of flying debris, the punch was powerful enough to send KK's father flying backward and skidding through the gravel.

When the older man tried to struggle to his feet, Dante whacked him with the cane. The cane inexplicably clicked, and Vincent shrieked.

The overhead security light glinted on a bit of silver. A blade? Dante had figured out granddaddy's sword cane!

Figuring he had his enemy in hand, Evie kept her foot on Rhonda and glanced over at the driver. He smartly held up his hands and backed away.

The tornado of shell and gravel that was KK didn't go after him. Instead, she swooped back to batter Rhonda. Evie had to stomp Rhonda's other hand to prevent her from fleeing. A quick glance verified that Pris and the twins were safely out of sight in the truck. Amazed that her cousin wasn't peeling out of the lot, Evie assumed she was putting her mental whammies on Vincent and Rhonda, because they stayed down. Or maybe Vincent feared Dante would cut his throat.

At Jax's shout, Evie returned her wandering attention to the BMW. He had one of the men in a wrestling hold—but the other appeared to be escaping for the car.

Stop the murdering bastard KK clearly cried, at least in Evie's head. Having no idea who the murdering bastard was, Evie abandoned Rhonda to rush toward Jax.

Before she could reach him, he easily flipped the square-jawed bodyguard to the ground. Evie was prepared to attack the limo driver if he tried to interfere, but keeping his hands raised, he seemed to be shaking his head in as much confusion as she felt.

"Matthew, get out of here!" Vincent shouted from beneath Dante's wicked cane. "Nick, stop them instead of standing there like a blithering idiot!"

In an attitude of defiance, the driver returned his hands to his side and shoved them into his pockets. "Not my circus, Vincent. I'm not seeing Lucia here looking for her kids."

"Nick, if that's you," Jax cried, leaving the bodyguard on the ground to lunge after Matthew, "Stop Rhonda from stealing the limo."

Oops, she'd been heading for Jax and the BMW. Evie glanced back. Rhonda was in the limo's driver's seat, looking frantic.

Standing in the parking lot between the two vehicles, Nick jingled a key ring. Rhonda couldn't get far.

KK's tornado of wrath slammed into the escaping Matthew before Jax reached him. Caught by the inexplicable hurricane force, Vincent's son shrieked, spun, and slammed into the side of the car.

He killed her the ghost screamed.

He killed her and left her bones to rot!

Oh dear. KK was finally speaking. Evie turned to Dante, still holding Vincent at cane point and watching in disbelief as Matthew writhed under an invisible force. "KK is telling me that Matt killed *her*, not *me*. I'm guessing that doesn't mean he killed KK but *Lucia?*"

"I did nothing," Matt screamed as he ducked and hunkered against the car, attempting to evade the tornado's fury.

Unmoving, Jax kept an eye on the fallen bodyguard, while Evie hovered, not knowing how to stop a ghost from whaling the tar out of a killer.

"She fell. I swear, she fell!" Matt shouted as a particularly large rock bounced off his skull.

"Don't say anything, son," Vincent shouted as both a security van and a police SUV squealed into the parking lot. "Don't say anything!"

Evie sighed in relief. Backup wouldn't help with a furious ghost, but they could protect the twins.

At Matt's admission, Dante abandoned Vincent. Unfazed by the whirlwind and the arrival of authority, he advanced on the target of KK's rage. Jax took a seat on the BMW's hood, occasionally kicking the security guard to keep him down, leaving the arena open for his cousin.

Having a good idea what would happen next and that it might be better if the cops didn't watch, Evie signaled Pris and left KK and Dante to their fight. While Rhonda grappled with Nick for the keys and Vincent staggered toward his son, Pris carried a sleepy Nan and Alex toward the officialdom climbing out of their cars.

"They kidnapped the twins," Evie shouted, running toward the burly security guard and distracting him as Matthew screamed in agony in the background.

"The babies, save the babies," Pris cried, holding a sleepy child in each arm and practically falling under their weight. "Thank heaven you're here, officer. Those men tried to murder us!"

Still holding his handgun, the police officer radioed for backup instead of taking a child.

"They're kidnappers and thieves. They *killed* the lady who owned the fancy boutique," Evie added excitedly, loading the truth with words that made people listen. "And possibly her poor sister."

The security guard grabbed his phone and called for support.

In the background, Matt's screams died to a sullen silence. Evie figured it was safe to leave the guard and help herself to one of the curly mops in Pris's arms. She bounced the heavy child and swung around, hoping to see that Jax and Dante had hidden any weapons. There hadn't been any gunshots, but she hadn't expected any. She just hadn't wanted Matt and Vincent escaping unscathed.

Dante had his foot on Matt's spine and his cane on the back of his neck as the boutique owner blubbered into the dirt. Jax stood over the bodyguard, who simply sat where he'd fallen. Nick was on the ground, groaning. The keys! Where were Donna and Vincent. . .

Vincent hadn't stayed down.

"Watch out," Evie screamed. "They're trying to get away!"

Jax abandoned the security guard to race across the lot.

Rhonda was already in the passenger seat. Vincent had the driver's side door open, trying to lower his battered body behind the wheel.

Before Jax could reach them, KK's roiling tornado slammed the door into Vincent's back, catching his neck and hands between the roof and the door's edge. Vincent screamed in agony.

I know you did it, KK shouted. *I tried to tell the truth and you killed me! My own father killed me!*

When Vincent tried to push the door off his neck, she slammed it again. *I should have called the police on you years ago. I should have called them when you pushed Mom down the stairs.*

Not hearing what Evie was hearing, Vincent merely shrieked and fought with the imprisoning door. Donna screamed from the other side of the limo. Jax folded his arms and watched in interest.

Apparently deciding no one was armed, the police officer jogged up to extricate Vincent from the invisible door slammer.

Still holding down a squirming Matt, Dante glanced in Evie's direction. "That's KK getting even?"

"Yeah, so you don't have to. Both of you, try not to get arrested and let these nice men handle this." Evie gestured at the police cars with blaring sirens roaring into the lot. There was no way she could explain to anyone all the crimes KK was accusing her father of. Once KK got rolling, she'd found her tongue, in a manner of speaking.

Ignoring the commotion, Jax crossed the lot to take the heavy twin from Evie's arms. "Kids look good on you," he murmured, bending to kiss her. "Can you send KK on now, please?"

Oh yeah, peace and quiet again. It wasn't as if a ghost could sit on the witness stand. Evie opened herself to suck the exhausted spirit from the fight.

Satisfied now that she'd done what she'd left unfinished, KK departed willingly.

Thirty-four: Pris

AFTER DEALING WITH THE TWINS CRAWLING ALL OVER EVERYONE AND EVERYTHING AT the station, the cops let Pris leave first so she could put them to bed in the early hours before dawn.

She buckled them into the booster seats she'd brought from Italy, and wrapped them with the blankets she used in transporting food. Alex leaned against her as she fought with the buckle.

"Bad men," he said as succinctly as his father.

"Don't go," Nan echoed her twin's worries.

"I've got you, babes," Pris told them, her nonexistent heart breaking just a little. "And your daddy will be with you soon. No more bad men."

They didn't argue or say more—so very not Malcolms. But then, their mother was normal, and Dante was an Ives, so they were their own selves and adorable —and apparently unscathed by their adventure. The innocence of their protected childhood had apparently allowed them to sleep through most of their ride.

She'd had to leave before she punched someone after she heard Matthew claiming he didn't know why his father wanted a yacht. Unlike Nick, KK's brother *knew* Lucia wasn't waiting on the ship. He couldn't be stupid enough to believe his father simply wanted to take kids on a midnight joy ride.

Pris couldn't suppress that much rage or it would give her headaches for a year—or she'd learn to mentally attack evil minds and become as immoral as Vincent. Walking out was safest.

She'd left Evie blithely claiming that Matt had confessed to killing Lucia, and

Vincent to killing KK. Her cousin had a habit of spinning heads until everyone probably believed the words of a ghost.

At Evie's house, Pris took the children into bed with her so they couldn't escape again without her knowledge. Dante woke her by climbing in on the other side a little later. The twins woke enough to seek body heat and one curled up in each of their arms and fell asleep again.

Unable to reach over and kiss the unshaven, weary man in her bed, Pris kissed Nan's curly head instead. "Everything all right?" she whispered.

"For us, fine." He sounded exhausted and disgusted and just a little bit triumphant. "I don't think it will go well for Matt and Vincent, who are confusing their conflicting stories so badly that the truth may never emerge. The Italian police are closing in on Lucia's farm as we speak. Not sure about Leo yet, but stolen artifacts are involved, and he's the likely source. Go back to sleep." He tucked Alex under him.

With a greater reach than hers, he leaned over to kiss Pris's forehead much as she'd kissed his daughter's. She wanted to believe it meant more than gratefulness.

They both needed the reassurance of normality and safety right now. The morning would be soon enough to work out everything else.

But watching the crippled professor tear apart kidnappers and murderers had been a mind-bending experience. And a heart-rending one. She'd have to go back to calling him Indiana Jones just to keep her perspective. She badly needed to more than kiss him. Damned good thing the kids were between them.

They might have slept through Loretta clattering down the stairs on her way to school, but the twins didn't. The instant both squiggly little bodies departed the bed, Pris woke to find Dante watching her hungrily through drowsy eyes. Lust heated her insides. Thank the goddesses, they were fully clothed.

"Go back to sleep," he murmured. "I will go after them."

"You climbed the stairs." Stupid thing to say, but her brain had gone south.

"I had to be certain everyone was safe. I will never take that for granted again." Looking abashed by this admission, he sat up, easing his leg off the bed.

"We shouldn't have to live expecting the worst." She'd never go back to sleep now. "Use my shower. I'll go down and check on the kids. I'll bring your duffle up."

"I don't want you to wait on me," he protested. "You have done so much already."

"Next time I break a leg, you can wait on me." *Next time.* She'd just said *next time*, as if there would be such a thing. Shutting down the knifing pain she didn't understand, Pris escaped.

Downstairs, she found the usual confusion. For reasons only known to them, R&R were parked at the kitchen island instead of in their own homes, although Rube still half-lived in the cellar with his computer equipment. From what she could tell, they were devouring sausages and eggs and debating how to hack the Italian police. She sent Reuben upstairs with Dante's gear from the guest room off the kitchen.

Evie nibbled at a donut while washing up Loretta's cereal bowl and filling in Mavis, the usual bearer of donuts, on the evening's events.

Evie's eleven-year-old ward swallowed half a fritter and eyed Pris with interest. "Your bubble is growing."

Pris hoped that was a good thing because she felt lousier than lousy.

Across from Loretta, Alex and Nan kneeled on the banquette in the breakfast nook with milk smeared under their noses and toast soldiers in their fists. They waved their buttery treats and showed her a book—plasticized, thankfully. "Read, Pissy, read!"

Evie almost doubled over suppressing hoots of laughter. Reuben returned in time to hear, and he and Roark pounded the island with their fists, repeating, "Pissy Prissy, pissy Prissy!"

Ignoring the dolts, Pris kissed the twins, promised them she'd read later, and opened the refrigerator.

By the time Dante limped in, using the cane instead of a crutch, she had an omelet ready for the pan and biscuits baking. Evie had whispered *Pissy* at her a few times before taking Loretta off to school. Her cousin probably wouldn't let her ward out of her sight until high school after last night.

"Just the man we need to see," Roark crowed as Dante eased into the booth with his children. "The Italian police aren't telling us anything, and we don't speak the lingo."

Well, that explained their presence.

Once he'd settled in with his coffee, Pris slid the omelet in front of Dante and provided cut-up bits for the twins to pick at. "Careful. They'll have you hacking police files," she warned.

"We're just *reading* them," Reuben protested. "They sent a report to the sheriff who's trying to use Google translate with pretty weird results."

Aunt Mavis, the all-knowing crystal ball reader, had taken the remaining donuts and departed with Evie. Pris set the biscuits on the counter and pointed her fork accusingly. "And you *hacked* that report from Troy. He didn't just give it to you."

"We're helping. It's all good, bébé. We need to know if we should be looking for more Bella shipments. They were using deliveries to the stores here to conceal the artifacts. The US market isn't watched so much, and they could sell them easier, probably for higher prices." Roark helped himself to one of the biscuits.

"If we can stop the artifacts from being sold, send me the file." Ignoring her concerns, Dante didn't look up from his eggs or the book the twins were perusing. He had them reading the letters aloud.

Pris sighed at the unmistakable ding of an incoming message.

Dante slipped his phone from his pocket and apparently clicked the link they'd sent. When he began rubbing his head, as if he had a headache, Pris sent the children to the sink to wash their hands. Staying busy was better than fretting over what he was reading about his friend.

"There's a lot of technical detail about the farm and the caves under it," Dante finally said. "I'll summarize for brevity."

He glanced at Lucia's children in concern—this was about their mother.

Pris shook her head. "They don't care enough to understand. Give me a second to set them up with a game. Don't say anything until I'm back."

Now that the dining table had been cleared off, she sat them where she could keep watch. Then she dug a couple of old handheld games out of storage boxes stacked on the wall. They could figure the games out on their own.

Back in the kitchen, she boldly slid into the booth beside Dante. He didn't push her away. If these were her last days with him, she'd take all the proximity she could steal. She didn't generally like intimacy, but Indiana Jones had plucked a previously untouched chord. She told herself she simply wanted to learn about this opposites-attract thing, since Evie and Jax seemed to make it work.

"Understand that Leo is a farmer, nothing more. He knows his crops, knows their worth, knows how to sell them. He's been keeping that farm alive where Lucia barely scraped by. The *polizia* did not find his fingerprints or any evidence that he knew of anything beyond his storage tanks, which he feared my digging might disrupt. He's afraid of change." Dante looked up, apparently wanting their agreement.

R&R slid in across from them and waited expectantly.

Dante returned to translating the material on his screen. "I am gathering from this that when the *polizia* came to interview him and told him Vincent and Matthew were under arrest for murder, Leo told them all he knew—all the things he concealed from me."

Dante looked up to be certain they paid attention. "For background: when we were all young, and I wanted to explore the caves, Lucia told us her father had blocked the tunnels in the storage area." He tapped the file on the phone. "Leo did *not* tell me that when Lucia took over after her father's death, she wanted to expand and opened them again."

Dante scrolled through the Italian text, looking for exact words. "Leo says that after she opened the tunnels, workers discovered ancient tombs with bones. For fear I would bring in experts who would prevent using the storage caves—which I would have done, so he was not incorrect—he wanted her to close them back up."

Pris picked up enough of his troubled vibrations to squeeze his arm. "Lucia refused to close them because she *wanted* you to see them. She didn't care about profit but you."

He nodded. "So Leo says anyway. But I didn't come home, and Lucia's mother in London became ill, and she went away. Rather than spend money or argue with Lucia, Leo set storage shelves with those massive barrels in front of the opening. He really didn't want me disrupting his operations."

Evie returned to the kitchen without Loretta. At seeing their solemn faces, she filled the tea kettle and settled on a counter stool to listen. Jax came downstairs, freshly shaved and ready for the office despite little sleep. Raising his eyebrows, he poured coffee and settled on another stool.

Dante continued translating. "Leo says when Lucia returned with her Gladwell relations, she showed them the storage area and had workmen moving the shelves away from the tunnel. They argued, he gave up, and went back to work in the orchard. When he returned that evening, only Vincent and Matt were there. They'd only partially pushed the shelves back. He was told that Lucia and Katherine had taken the babies and the nanny and left."

He skimmed to find the details. "Leo claims Lucia left a contract behind for the oil that was better than anything he'd been able to obtain on his own. He thought she'd found some way of cheating her rich London relations, so he signed it. Vincent and Matthew left after that, and he never saw Lucia again."

"Have the police gone into the tunnel yet?" Jax asked, smearing a cold biscuit with jam.

Dante nodded. Pris wanted to hug him but didn't dare. He took the matter in his own hands, circled her shoulders, and squeezed. More than lust heated her, but she wasn't about to examine that. She thought he might need the connection as much as she did. This was his girlfriend and the mother of his children they were talking about.

She liked it a little too well that, in this moment, he took his strength from her. Having a partner to shore her up when she was down. . . She'd never thought possible. Dante made it seem so.

After taking a breath to regain his formidable control, he continued. "I've texted one of my colleagues to hie himself over there or the police will be trampling centuries of history. They are waiting on a forensics team, but they're fairly certain the bones wearing silk at the bottom of an old well are not Etruscan. They've seen evidence of recent digging."

A pall of sorrow hung over the room. Hard evidence at last—Lucia was undoubtedly dead, as KK had said.

Breaking the silence, his voice only a little rough, Dante spoke to R&R. "You might want to sift through your files and look for dates of those deposits in the shell company accounts, compare them to Vincent's visits to the farm and shipments to the US. Leo may not know, but my suspicion is that those annual visits to the tunnel produced artifacts that Matt and Vincent hid in Leo's oil shipments to their UK warehouse. Once the European market got too hot, they may have opened the US boutiques so they could ship the stolen goods here. My contacts have reported recent unauthorized sales of artifacts on the American market. They've set Interpol to investigate."

Pris could read his fear. "You think with all the attention you recently applied to the black market, Vincent realized his lucrative business might crash on his head. *That's* why he came after the children. He wanted you to call off the police?"

Dante shook his head. "Can't say. But I think we can assume that Lucia would have been the driving force behind Bella. Once she was gone, KK didn't have the smarts. Vincent and Matt seized the opportunity Lucia had inadvertently shown them, stole artifacts, and used the company to launder the money."

Evie looked sad. "KK thought she was selling elegant beauty products that would make her famous. Since she complained of fraud, she must have eventually discovered the substitutes of cheap ingredients."

"And told them she'd reveal what she knew about Lucia unless they straightened up?" Jax suggested.

"And got killed for her efforts to do what was right for a change." Pris shuddered.

"Did you ask about the reward for catching KK's killer?" Reuben asked, scooting out of the booth.

Evie flung toast at him before Pris could kick the insensitive lout.

~

WHEN NICK SHOWED UP IN JAX'S OFFICE BEFORE NOON, LOOKING EVEN MORE disheveled and haggard than the last time, Jax handed him a strong cup of coffee and offered a flask.

Nick shook his head. "Do you know how to reach Dante Rossi? I need to talk to him before they let Matthew and Rhonda out on bail."

Jax kept his lawyer face on, hiding his shock. "After last night, I don't know if Dante can be separated from his children. What if I set up a call on speaker?"

"I want this off my chest before Matt decides I'm a hazard to his father's health." Nick looked bleak. "This country has lawyer confidentiality, does it not? Will you do this as my lawyer?"

"Currently, Bella is my client. If Bella is defunct, shove a dollar my way, and you can take their place." He hit Dante's number as Nick dug for his wallet and produced a five.

Jax spoke into the phone. "If you can find a quiet place in that madhouse—I recommend the library where no one ever goes—I have a client who would like to speak with you. You're on speaker now."

Dante snorted. In the background, childish voices sing-songed the alphabet, along with an amazingly discordant piano. As far as Jax was aware, Evie didn't own a piano or a TV. It must be a recording.

"Give me a moment to disentangle myself. Do you know what this is about?" the Italian asked.

"Not a clue." Jax looked at Nick, who said nothing. "I'm going to guess Lucia."

"Without the police?" The background noise faded.

"Not yet." Jax gestured at Nick, then to the phone. "You know Dante doesn't have to keep your confidence?"

Nick nodded. "If he wants to call the police, that's his call. I don't want you to feel obligated to do so."

"All right, I am in this bookless library, and the door is closed." A chair squeaked as Dante found a seat.

"Nicholas Gladwell is with me. He's a distant relation of Vincent's and marketing manager of La Bella Gente." With the phone on speaker, Jax sipped his coffee and left Nick and Dante to talk.

Stoic Dante, as usual, said nothing.

Nick squirmed, then leaned toward the phone. "I only met Lucia that one summer in London, when she was doing the commercials. She was excited about having her lotions produced. After she left for Italy, I dealt only with Katherine."

"Lucia must have been pregnant that summer," Dante said. "Did she mention her plans at all?"

"No, but we didn't have personal conversations. She and Kit-Kat were close, sharing the townhouse with their mother. That's what I wanted to tell you. A few years after Kit-Kat took over the operations, we became casual lovers." Nick rubbed his unshaven jaw and sipped his coffee.

On the other end, Dante said nothing encouraging. Jax offered the flask again.

Nick shook his head. "Katherine told me that Vincent was abusive, and that he'd sent her mother to the hospital on several occasions. When they learned their mother had cancer, she and Lucia threw Vincent out, but Kat feared he may have somehow hastened her death. He inherited everything. It wasn't riches, but it gave him control of her mother's bank accounts, the townhouse, and Bella."

Jax started taking notes. Dante merely listened.

Nick took a deep breath. "Kat told me Vincent destroyed the letters Lucia sent to you. I didn't want to be part of the family dynamics, didn't really know the background, and stupidly didn't ask why Lucia didn't just call."

"Lucia always wrote. She considered phones an expensive nuisance, refused to play phone tag, and knew I was always traveling or out of cell range." Dante finally broke his silence, sounding immensely sad. "I think she lacked confidence that I would listen or even answer. And the worst thing is, she was probably right. If she hoped I'd go looking for her in some grand romantic gesture—I didn't."

"Without those letters, you didn't know she was pregnant," Jax reminded him. "You weren't even engaged. As far as you were concerned, she took off for a fancy new life. Any other expectation on her part was unrealistic. It's on her, not you. She could have called, texted, or sat on your doorstep."

Nick waved a dismissive hand. "Whatever. The thing is, Kat said *Lucia kept a journal*. Although she didn't reveal anything back then, Kat had to have known when she told me this that Lucia was never coming back."

The knowledge that Katherine had concealed her sister's death was chilling, but with a monster for a father and brother. . . The whole family lacked a conscience.

When Dante said nothing, Jax had to clarify for his own understanding. "Do you have any evidence that Katherine was there when Matt killed Lucia?" That's what Evie had claimed the ghost said, but they lacked proof.

Nick looked bleak. "I only know what Kat told me. Just before she died, she complained that Vincent was making a mockery of Lucia's dream, and that she wouldn't be blackmailed anymore. That she meant to go to the police, and that if anything happened to her, I was to find Lucia's journal under the floorboards beneath her bed. It sounds melodramatic, but that was Kit-Kat. This must have been well over a year ago, and it was so ridiculous that I forgot about it—until now. And even now, I cannot see how it would help." Nick sat back and breathed deeply, as if a ten-ton burden had been lifted from his chest.

"A journal under the floorboards? She gave no explanation?" Jax asked.

"None. I thought she'd watched some daft movie and wanted attention I didn't give her. She never struck me as being terrified of Vincent so much as needing him because he had control of Bella. The whole family fought worse than cats and dogs. I almost sympathized with Matt for keeping bodyguards. I avoided being in the same room with any two of them at a time. Kit-Kat and I were friends with benefits, no more, and I needed the employment." He looked ashamed at that admission.

"Lucia always kept journals, if just to track crop production. I'll have one of my cousins contact the London police." Dante gave no clue as to his reaction to this bombshell. "This may be something of their mother the twins will treasure when they're older. Thank you for telling me. Shall I keep your name out? My family is well connected."

"If the police let Matthew out, he'll kill me on general principles. If he doesn't, I need to work. I'd appreciate not having my name dragged into the case, if possible, although I'm aware if they put Vincent on trial, I'll have to testify." Nick sat up a little straighter.

"Matt isn't getting out anytime soon. If they have enough evidence, Vincent could be charged for Katherine's death as well as kidnapping. He will be tried in an American court. If you're returning to London, your name probably won't be prominent in the UK news stories," Jax said reassuringly. Although he wasn't a criminal defense lawyer or a journalist and didn't know this for certain. The poor guy just needed time to regroup.

"Vincent will be the news. As accessories, Matt and Rhonda will take second place," Dante agreed. "You won't matter at all to the UK reports."

Nick shook his head wearily. "The public defender says Matt and Rhonda claim to be innocent of any knowledge of Vincent's plans, just as I was. They're planning on letting them out on bond."

Outraged, Jax leaned over the desk to object. "They're *kidnappers,* and at the very least, accessory to murder. They can't do that."

Nick slumped in his chair. "I just came from the police station. Vincent had motive, opportunity and means for Kit-Kat's murder and for kidnapping the children. They've already charged him. He bought the cyanide online, thinking he could hide the purchase. He opened the limoncello bottle—even Matt admits that. I only carried it after Kat began drinking from it. Vincent's fingerprints are all over the bottle, under mine and hers. And Vincent arranged the limo and yacht for the kidnapping. None of the rest of us had a clue. Rhonda and I actually believed that he was taking Lucia's children away from a neglectful dad. We didn't know Lucia was dead."

Rubbing his temples, Jax summed it up. "You may all have had means and opportunity, but Vincent is the only one with motive for murder—Katherine was about to implicate him in multiple crimes. But if Lucia is truly dead, his kidnapping the children still doesn't make sense."

Jax had relied on Pris and Evie's talents when they swore Nick was innocent. Their testimony had allowed Nick out on bail. He'd thought they had enough to keep Matt and Rhonda behind bars.

Dante cut into his thoughts. "From the sounds of it, the police are holding only Vincent for KK's murder and the kidnapping. They can't prove Matt and Rhonda knew about the kidnapping or that Lucia's death wasn't an accident. Although. . ." He hesitated. "Is there any chance *Katherine* also kept a journal, one that might give evidence on how Lucia died?"

Jax sat up straighter. "Call your family," he urged. "If there's any chance that Matthew is a killer like his father, let's keep the bastard off the streets."

Thirty-five: Dante

Leaning against the kitchen counter so as not to strain his leg, Dante held an enormous bowl of rust-colored mush over a pie pan so Pris could scrape the bowl's bottom. Preparations had begun for the Thanksgiving holiday, and she smelled of cinnamon and spice. He tried not to inhale too obviously, but just standing close had him slavering for far more than pie.

He told himself he'd get over it. He was just feeling particularly. . . vulnerable. . . at the moment.

"They think Matt will be out on bond?" she whispered in horror.

He glanced at the twins drawing turkeys around their fingers as Evie had taught them. "Jax called the sheriff, and I talked to the public defender. They both agree there is no evidence that Matt knew about the kidnapping. His bodyguard boyfriend supports that. And a ghost's word that he shoved Lucia into a well won't exactly hold up in court. His lawyer is asking the judge to let him bond out once his funds arrive. Since Rhonda attempted to help Vincent escape when we tried to stop the kidnapping, her bond is higher."

"What about the stolen artifacts and money laundering?" She took the bowl and set it in the sink, sounding as appalled as he felt.

He wanted to hug her and say everything would be fine, but he would only be reassuring himself. And he might not stop at hugging. These last days had left him feeling as if he were walking across hot coals from a volcano in an earthquake, with Pris his only safe harbor. He was grateful she wasn't inclined to hysteria or dramatics—although if she cooked any more food, they'd have to invite the entire town to dinner.

Her frustration might be as strong as his own, and it wasn't just frustration with the crime. There were too damned many people around all the time. He had a hunch—should he ever be able to get her alone—that her kisses wouldn't be as prickly as her attitude but as fiery as the red and orange streaks in her hair today.

"Stolen artifacts and international money laundering require the cooperation of police in three countries. They don't have enough evidence to charge anyone yet." Irritated by his inability to control events, Dante desperately needed to do *something*, but without a podium or a shovel, he was out of his element.

As if reading his mind—which she might possibly be doing—Pris handed him a rolling pin. "You've called your family and your colleagues and set Interpol or whatever in search of Etruscan artifacts for sale. All you can do is wait. Like your mother did. And Lucia. And your children. Start learning domesticity and roll the dough."

Waiting reeked. Which was why Lucia had left. Got it. Didn't like it. Needed to learn how to do it—while shutting down his mind so Pris couldn't read his lusty thoughts. Setting his jaw, he checked that the twins were still happily occupied. Then he retrieved a bowl of dough and slapped it onto the floured board. He'd seen his mother do this a thousand times. He could learn.

The instant he rolled the pin over the dough, Alex climbed on the counter stool to watch. Nan showed no interest whatsoever.

"Role model," Pris murmured wickedly, setting her pie in the oven.

Right. He could teach Alex that domesticity was not a bad thing. Life didn't require airplanes and mobiles every minute. Maybe running 24/7 was an addiction.

Or an escape from his otherwise meaningless existence. *Damn.*

Sitting in the booth across from Nan, Evie manned three mobiles while painting cookies with orange icing and chocolate chips. Dante thought he might die of sugar poisoning before he saw home again.

The idea of that echoingly empty villa was daunting. His mother had called to say he could leave the twins with her in Scotland if he had to return to work. Once upon a time, he would have done it without a second thought. Now, he didn't think he could.

One of the phones rang and Evie answered with crisp efficiency. "Dante Rossi's office."

She'd been fielding his calls all morning, weeding out the nosy journalists and colleagues who only wanted to leave messages of concern. Voice mail would have done the same, but the urgency of the situation required instant response to the right callers.

Evie handed him the phone. "He claims to be the Earl of Ives."

That was one of the callers he needed to speak with immediately. Reaching his busy cousin later wouldn't happen.

Aware that Pris snorted her disdain at his family's titles, Dante wiped off his hands and claimed the mobile. "Gerry, thanks. What did they find?"

"I sent my secretary over." Gerald, Earl of Ives, was obviously on speaker phone. Papers rustled and voices spoke in the background. "There was only one guard at Gladwell's townhouse. My card got her inside. She found the journal under the floorboards and scanned the pages. The images should be coming through as we speak. We've not read them all, but there appears to be two different styles of handwriting. How are the twins holding up?"

Dante tried not to crush the phone in his fist. The question about the children eased some of his tension. "I owe you, Gerry. The twins are preparing for an American Thanksgiving. I don't want to hide them in Scotland unless I have to. They're having fun."

"Right-o. Maybe you'll make it in for Christmas. We'd all love to meet them. Stay in touch." His lordly cousin dropped out.

"You had an *earl* hunting Lucia's journal?" Pris asked, taking up the rolling pin he'd abandoned.

"Gerald is a second or third cousin of some sort. I just called my uncle, and he took it from there." Dante shrugged off the question as he watched the scanned images arriving. "I'll share the pages to your phones."

Alex continued rolling a piece of dough with his small rolling pin. Dante took a seat beside Nan and her industrious coloring. Punching buttons, he shared journal pages with Evie and Pris as they arrived. He sent them to Jax as well.

Abandoning the dough, Pris hovered over the table to study the small screen, apparently reluctant to touch her phone with her floury hands. "Email this stuff to Rube and let him enlarge."

"On it." Evie was typing faster than Dante could read.

"This last date is KK's entry, not Lucia's!" Pris wiped her hands on her apron, grabbed her own phone, and enlarged the page. "Wow, she laid it *all* out. Vincent is going down big time."

"I think we better give these to your sheriff." Sickened at what he'd read so far, Dante struggled with KK's hurried scrawl.

"KK was a dramatic flake and could have made all this up," Evie warned. "She's gone. I can't ask her, and she wouldn't have answered anyway."

"And the sheriff won't listen if you try to reach Lucia's spirit to verify it," Pris added. "Call Jax. See if he thinks this is enough to keep Matt behind bars."

One of the phones rang and Evie clicked on answer, then put it on speaker.

"Do not send this to Troy," Jax said without preamble. "You've interfered with the chain of evidence. I'll get Nick's permission to call the sheriff and tell him about the journal. Then the London police can hunt it properly. I hope whoever scanned these kept off their fingerprints."

"Given Gerry's pursuits, I'm wagering his secretary is an experienced operative who wore gloves and will have replaced the dust if necessary," Dante said dryly.

"But the point is to *prevent* Matt's release," Pris cried. "How can we do that if we have to wait on officialdom? They can't hold him forever."

"His lawyer is already screaming it's a holiday, and he shouldn't be held longer. I'll call Troy, tell him about the journal, and that Evie and Mavis had brain waves about Matt's involvement," Jax said. "The sheriff is good. He'll come up with a charge to hold Matt longer. Just don't tell *anyone* what we have."

Brain waves. Dante tried to imagine a sheriff who would listen to women who had *brain waves*. Afterthought was an interesting place, in a proverbial Chinese way, perhaps.

After Jax signed off, the kitchen fell silent while everyone attempted to read the tiny pages. Dante strained his eyes on Lucia's precise handwriting. Pris gave up and returned to rolling her dough, mumbling under her breath. Dante hoped they weren't incantations or he wasn't eating whatever she was making.

Never a reader, Evie gathered up the twins and led them out. The Malcolm women had a way of adopting everyone as family.

Dante wanted that for himself and his children, but he didn't know how to get it.

"Read me the relevant passages," Pris commanded. "I need to finish these pies today."

"KK only has a few entries, and they're mostly angry ranting," he warned. "One of her last entries says she won't tolerate Matt's interference. She wants the American stores for herself. It sounds as if she thought they were an escape from her London life or maybe her abusive father."

"But Vincent needed Matt here to sell artifacts. KK might not have known about them. I hope they fry both Gladwells. Lucia was fortunate she grew up with her father on the farm instead of in her mother's toxic household." Pris slipped the dough into a pan and crimped the edges.

Dante didn't reply. In shock, he studied a scanned page in Lucia's handwriting on company letterhead—a letter, not a journal entry. "KK apparently

193

saved one of Lucia's letters to me. Her entry says she found it in Vincent's drawer when she was trying to find where he was hiding the cash."

Pris dropped what she was doing, wiped her hands, and sat beside him. He was grateful for her presence but wasn't certain he wanted the world to see Lucia's private conversation with him.

Pris instantly understood. "Tell your cousin to pull that letter before the police find it. I'll tell the others to delete the image." She began typing on her mobile.

Having someone who understood what he didn't know how to say was. . . scary. . . but a relief in this case. With everyone finally out of the way, he hugged her close and claimed her mouth.

She responded with hungry alacrity. The noise of the twins' laughter in the other room jarred them back to reality. Dante took a deep breath, relieved that he wasn't alone in this dangerous attraction.

He forced his mind back to his mobile and scanning the tiny words on the screen. "Lucia's letter is telling me she waited too late to get rid of the babies. Her business required travel, and she couldn't take care of them."

Dante could almost hear Lucia yelling at him to come home and help her. She'd shouted about his absences often enough. "This must have been her last letter. She says London wasn't safe for babies."

"In that violent household, she had to have been terrified," Pris murmured. "Motherhood is not for everyone, even if we're often stuck with it, but at least she recognized that kids shouldn't be raised in that environment, which is more than her mother understood."

Dante struggled to read the fine script. "Lucia begs me to take the twins. If I didn't, she meant to give them up for adoption so they'd have a happy home."

Appalled, he couldn't even begin to register the possibility of never knowing his children, never having known of their existence, if Vincent had had his way. Thank all the heavens that Lucia had at least given him a chance to make things right, even if he'd never responded to her letters.

"She didn't *want* to give them to strangers," Pris reminded him. "I bet she was scared and heartbroken when she wrote that letter, especially since she had no reason to believe that you would take the children."

Feeling sick, he nodded and closed the phone. "I don't think I want to read more now. I need to change into the kind of father the twins need. I just don't know how."

Pris wisely slid out of the booth. "In our branch of Malcolms, family always comes first. It's some kind of unwritten law. That usually means some of us take over the people duties while others take over the monetary, and no one ever gets rich. It works best when we all share responsibility. You have a large family. If you have to work, then you have to put someone in charge of the twins. Your mother is good, but not enough."

Was she saying she wouldn't go with him? Of course, she was. "A nanny isn't enough either." Using the cane, Dante pried himself up. "I'll be in the library."

Leaving the twins to the women. He knew better. Pris had already stolen them once—proving a point he hadn't learned the first time. He knew it now.

How the hell did a man think and take care of children at the same time?

His work was intellectually stimulating, but what was the purpose of all his education if he couldn't apply it to make life better for his children?

Or for a wife and maybe even himself? He needed time to plan. . .

Thirty-six: Evie

THANKSGIVING

"SOUP TUREEN ON THE DINING ROOM TABLE WITH THE BOWLS," PRIS SHOUTED OVER the chaos of a dozen voices. "Rolls beside it. Evie, where do you keep your serving spoons?"

Evie snorted and stacked every plate in the house in the center of the dining table, along with the bowls. "At your apartment and Gracie's house and Aunt Val's mansion and. . ." She didn't waste her breath listing the entirety of people who borrowed from the Victorian's kitchen. That's why the house existed.

Wearing her purple glasses and a sparkly black dress, Loretta grinned at Pris's shriek and laid out the ancient tableware she'd just washed. "Mom always had Thanksgiving catered. This is like watching a holiday movie of everything that can go wrong, going even more wrong."

With an apron still covering her gold, vintage, mini-dress, Evie swatted her ward with a linen napkin. "Don't say that. Don't even *think* that. This is not wrong. This is totally normal. They know to return the tableware. It happens every year. Aunt Ellen will trot along momentarily with all of it gathered. She knows where we hide our door keys."

Small towns had their pros and cons. She'd learned to accept the intrusiveness. Pris, not so much.

"We're here, lovies, we're here!" The mayor's voice cried from the front door. "Where do we put the sweet potatoes?"

"With all the others on the chafing dishes." Mavis passed the dining room on the way to greet Larraine, wiping her hands on her apron and admiring the mayor's offering. "No marshmallows, thank you! My diet thanks you."

Loretta snickered and glanced at the other three bowls of sweet potatoes on the sideboard. "I like marshmallows."

"You aren't a vegetarian like Iddy or on a diet like Mom. Good job, kid. I hereby express my thanksgiving for your assistance and dismiss you to keep an eye on the twins and Aster. I think they're in your old room upstairs. Send Gracie down. We need all hands on deck in the kitchen before Pris starts swinging knives."

Loretta raced into the hall, greeted Larraine and Reuben, who'd apparently arrived together, and made wild horses sound quiet in her dash up the stairs. Loretta loved bossing the youngers around.

"I have the tables set up in the parlor," Evie's cousin Iddy called. "Do we need to set any in the library?"

Evie grabbed a couple of the small flower arrangements Mavis had contributed and carried them to the parlor tables. She shook her head at her veterinarian cousin, who was soothing her pet raven's feathers while Psycat sprawled on the sofa back, watching through narrowed eyes. "Shhh. Jax's sister is in the library. Roark refused to come unless Ariel did. And I think she really wants to be here, so we rashly promised her a quiet place."

Iddy set the raven on his perch on the mantel. "With all these men you've collected this past year, I'm amazed we're not all hiding under the beds. I always thought this house too huge until today."

"Victorians had large families. And Jax collects the men, not me. He and Roark and Reuben are setting up a security company to travel around, inspecting the machines his father's company is producing. They want to put their heads together after dinner."

"Why not before?" Iddy opened a folding chair to fit in an empty spot at one of the tables.

"They're all out back bonding over football and working up a hunger."

"Pris threw them out, did she?" Iddy shoved two more chairs under the last table.

"To be fair, she gave them all knives this morning and let them hack veggies. It's only after the discussion turned into a food fight that she flung them out. Let's see how many helpers we can squeeze into the kitchen. I'm starving." Evie checked that every table had a jar of assorted utensils. Looked like they had enough forks, at least.

"Appetizers! Pris said she made enough to hold us until the turkey is ready." Iddy stopped to answer the front door and let in one of the neighbors, who carried a green bean casserole and wanted to talk about her cat. Iddy handed the casserole to Evie and gestured for her to go on without her.

Balancing the bowl on one arm, Evie snatched a crab puff hors d'oeuvre off a narrow table in the hall. Munching, she passed through the kitchen with all the chatting women mixing and filling bowls, set down the casserole, and continued on out to the yard.

"Good thing y'all aren't dressed fancy for dinner," she called at the men chasing a ball under a bright blue sky.

Reuben already had Roark in a head lock, which seemed to have nothing to do with the ball Dante and Jax were flinging. Jax had invited Nick Gladwell to join them since his client couldn't go home until the authorities were done with him. But the Brit in his tweedy jacket and luscious sweater only looked confused by the action, rightfully so.

"Everyone here yet?" Jax called, letting the ball fly past him toward the distant fence. He and Dante had repaired the missing slats and added crossbars all the way around to make the yard more secure.

"Far as I know. Clean up and grab some appetizers. One of you might want to take nibbles up to the kids. They're being very well behaved." Evie hugged Jax as he reached the porch. "Where's your jacket?"

"In Dante's room," he whispered, before nibbling her ear. "We've got the kids covered. You just magic that food onto the table."

"Buffet. We're doing buffet. Wash up." Reveling in the closeness, loving the buzzy feeling his attention offered, she kissed his smooth jaw. Then she returned to the kitchen as Pris removed the bird from the oven and set the tofu roast inside.

"Half an hour," Pris called. "Iced tea glasses out? Wine for those who want it?"

Even Mayor Larraine had been pressed into service taking glasses out of cabinets, apparently because she was challenging Pris's recalcitrance. "Girl, if you don't open that café, I'll have to kill you."

"Zoning, licensing," Mavis shouted over the racket, adding wine bottles to the glasses stacked in the breakfast nook. "No one's starting anything until you fix the council."

"Ah, honey, that's all done." The mayor poured wine and helped herself to an appetizer. "After I let them zone out their competition, they let me set the licensing rules. It's like negotiating contracts with a school of fish, you gotta cast a wide net."

"So the Bella building will be zoned for a restaurant?" Evie asked through an appetizer adorned with curls of carrot. "And I won't be charged for running my business here?"

"Knock wood and the creek don't rise, whole downtown block will be zoned for small retail and restaurants," Larraine confirmed. "We need shopping, not more offices. And your business is grandfathered in. We're not touching residential zoning either."

"I can do anything I want with the garage? Cool." Not that she wanted to do anything. . . yet.

Pris carried an enormous porcelain dish of cornbread dressing to the dining room without comment.

Evie followed, directing her to the last hot plate on the sideboard. Any more electric burners and she figured the ancient wiring would melt. "Cooking school for kids," she murmured as she helped settle the dish in place. "Does that qualify as a small business?"

"Not retail or restaurant," Pris said curtly. "Still not ready. No money."

"Small business loan?" Reading her cousin's aura, Evie had a feeling Pris was hoping a certain studly Italian would find a way to stay here before she committed.

They both knew that wasn't happening.

The doorbell gave its cranky squeak, followed by pounding on the knocker.

"I've got it," Jax shouted. He was pulling on his sports jacket as he traversed the wide hall.

Evie could see Roark carrying a plate of appetizers to the library for Ariel, which made her heart glow. The angry madman she'd first met was mellowing, if only a little. Instead of shaving his tangled black curls, he'd tamed them, concealing his skull tats, and he'd left out most of his metal. Without the attitude, he was one handsome hunk.

Who knew that Jax's neurodivergent sister could make such a difference in a few short months? Without speaking more than two words at a time, probably. Love was a marvelous thing.

Drinking in the scents of turkey and dressing, the happy excitement of friends and family, she was slow to notice the raven's cry of warning or Jax's silence at the front door until Psycat prowled through the doorway, snarling.

Pris looked up, as if receiving a mental alert. "Are we expecting anyone else?"

"We invited Sheriff Troy, but he was going out of town to visit his daughter."

If the sheriff wasn't in town. . . Uninvited guests could be hazardous to the health.

Alarmed, Evie eased toward the passage into the hall. She peered around the corner and saw Jax blocking the entrance, his stance decidedly that of military alert.

She gestured at Pris. "Find an army to guard the stairs and send the men around front." She hated playing paranoid games but Jax's aura screamed *danger*.

If Troy wasn't in the sheriff's office to prevent Matthew from bonding out. . .

She knew precisely who was at the door. The question was *why*?

Heart pounding, she started to station herself behind the armoire they used for coats, but Pris grabbed her shoulder. "You guard the stairs. This one is mine."

Spooky Pris knew something Evie didn't. Giving her cousin a quick look, Evie dashed to the kitchen to gather her troops. And Loretta thought missing spoons constituted how things could go wrong!

Pris heard Matthew Gladwell shouting, ""Where's Nick? I was told he's here."

Arms crossed, Jax blocked the front doorway with his quarter-back frame. Picking up the appetizer tray in the hall, she elbowed him to one side so she could step out on the porch.

Glamorpuss Matthew wore several days' beard, dark shadows under his eyes, and a rumpled suit that looked as if he'd slept in it. He didn't even give Pris a second glance, although she'd removed her apron, wore her very best brown velveteen dress, and had dyed her gray streak red and orange for the occasion.

Out of spite, she held out the appetizer tray. "Take a chance?" she taunted.

Apparently startled out of his panic, Matthew finally looked at her and blanched. "What are *you* doing here?"

"Poisoning intruders? Getting even with the man who ruined my business?" She waved the goodies under his nose. "Ooooo, maybe witch that I am, I'm channeling Lucia, who wants to punch you in the face, then cut your throat."

Behind her, Jax snorted. Pris invaded Matthew's personal space with the tray, forcing him to back up. Over his shoulder, she could see Roark and Reuben positioning themselves behind the overgrown azaleas at the bottom of the front steps. She prayed Dante had gone to his children. This was the man who'd ruined her business with his lies. The battle was hers.

Matthew looked decidedly more nervous but held his ground, as if he really didn't understand what the rumors he'd spread had done to her. "I just need to see Nick, then I'll leave."

He should be very, very afraid, but Pris merely tilted her head and studied Lucia's killer. "You hit her, didn't you? I can see it in your mind." Well, she had KK's journal to verify her guesses, but he didn't need to know that. A good con meant keeping the victim on an emotional precipice. "You had Lucia on the edge of that well, and you smacked her, just as your father did you and Katherine. Except he was smart enough not to do it near a dangerous hole."

"You're b-being ridiculous," he stammered nervously. "I don't know what you're talking about. If Nick isn't here, just tell me."

Pris bit into an olive-adorned chip and set the tray down on the porch rail so she could gesture. "We all know what you did. *You killed Lucia*. Like the ghoul you are, you've been stealing artifacts over her crumbling bones. What I want to know is why you want to kill Lucia's children? They're babies! Even if they'd seen their mother murdered, what could they possibly do to you?"

"I don't want to kill babies," he shouted. "You're crazy. I still think you poisoned Kat!"

She shrugged. "Kat says otherwise. Witch, remember? We have proof that your father poisoned your sister. We know almost everything else, and the police will soon. But that one tiny thing really bothers me. Your father hates Lucia's children, why?"

Wide-eyed and frightened, Matt backed up again. He glanced behind him and spotted Reuben and Roark looking massive and pissed and blocking his exit. He tried to look over Jax's shoulder, but that wasn't happening. Jax was built like a brass door.

"Nick!" Male-model shouted above Pris's head. "I just need the keys to my office! They told me you have them."

"All your stores and offices are off limits," Jax reminded him. "The police are still examining them for evidence. Did they give you back your passport? I think not."

"He has a fake," Nick called from the hallway behind Jax. "And there's probably cash in the safe. He's about to scarper."

"Nick, you dick, you're fired!" Matthew screamed.

"From what?" Nick called back. "Or are you planning on climbing over Lucia's bones some more and starting up again? I'll give Vincent some credit—he at least knew how to hide the money. What have you got?"

Pris pressed her fingers to her temples in an age-old, meaningless, gesture for psychics that she saved for idiots. "Oooo, I can see it in his head now. Matthew is planning on retiring to the Caribbean on the money he and dear old dad stashed away. And now I think I'm seeing a little more. . . "

Matt's thoughts were so panicked, she figured everyone in the house could hear them, but a little abracadabra always impressed. "I see a *will*. You've seen it too, Matthew, haven't you? Lucia's will?"

"I witnessed it, didn't I? I didn't get a shilling off her!" He appeared to be debating escaping through Jax.

"And neither did Vincent, since he was only her stepdad," Pris crowed happily. She gestured at Jax and the audience gathering behind him. "*That's* what has Vincent furious. Lucia left everything to her children! He needed Lucia alive so they could keep using her farm, stealing her gold."

Pris heard the clump of Dante's cane before his broad shoulders appeared behind the crowd. She'd wanted to drag a confession out of the boutique owner, but Matthew wasn't cooperating. It was time to stand aside and let Dante do his thing. Towering over Jax by nearly a head, her noble Indiana Jones wore a form-fitting Italian jacket and an open-necked white shirt instead of the movie explorer's khaki. The fury on his normally equable features would send any sensible creature fleeing.

Matthew lacked sense. Surrounded by an angry mob, he still admitted nothing.

"You killed Lucia," Dante stated ominously. "And then the three of you left her body in that well so you could pretend *she still owned the farm*?" Fury overcame his normal composure.

"It's not as if babies could run it!" Matthew protested.

Motive for kidnapping, with a capital M. Pris hoped Evie's security cameras had microphones, but they had plenty of witnesses. Behind Dante, Jax was already holding up his cell.

"Until the twins came of age, Leo would still run the farm. You could have kept walking all over him," Dante shouted. "But you left their mother *in a well*! Did you know she was dead? Did you even attempt to find help?" Fury formed cracks in his rock solid mental façade. Like an Italian volcano, he'd emit steam soon.

Pris didn't do reassurance well and had no idea how to calm him as Evie did Jax. When Dante pushed past Jax to get at Matt, she caught his arm to remind him that others were present. A man who swung pickaxes for a living had a lot of muscle.

Firmly shutting her out from his enraged thoughts, Dante covered her hand and squeezed. To her relief, he set aside the temptation of the sword cane and used Pris for support.

"Lucia was *dead*," Matthew said grimly. "Skull crushed, neck broken, dead. It was an accident. She'd just showed us the crap she'd carted up for you to look at. We needed cash, but she refused to even sell the gold until you could see it. But she fell and ruined everything!"

"Kinda ruined it for Lucia anyway," Pris acknowledged dryly. "But it wasn't just a fall. You *hit* her when she refused to sell the artifacts," she added, seeing the scene clearly.

Dante's grip nearly crushed her bones, but he didn't reach out and strangle the selfish twit standing on the edge of the stairs. One good push. . . Pris resisted.

A silent police car rolled to the curb behind the massive gardenia bush by the sidewalk.

"Who did Lucia appoint as executor of her estate?" Jax asked.

Leave it to the lawyer to strip the question to its legal bones.

From Matthew's angry glance at Dante, the answer was plain—Lucia had left the farm to her children and named their father as executor.

Glamorpuss finally whirled around to start down the stairs. The sight of two policemen walking toward him caused him to reach for his pocket.

Reuben and Roark placed themselves in his path. Abandoning his grip on Pris, Dante grabbed both Matt's arms behind his back before he could produce a weapon. His victim screamed as he yanked harder.

"He just confessed to manslaughter, at the very least," he shouted in his plummy accent at the approaching officers. "Plus theft and interfering with human remains or whatever one calls abandoning a body. He also has an illegal passport, so skipping bail might be added."

A policeman patted Matt down and removed a pistol from his pocket. "We could add threatening a police officer and illegal carry. I think that's enough to hold him for a while."

As Matthew was handcuffed and led away, Pris melted against her hero. "The twins?"

Once more using her shoulders for support, Dante lifted his chin to indicate upwards. "Evie has them in the attic with Loretta. They've closed the portcullis, and I think they're planning on piling boiling oil on the gate. They have an entire pumpkin pie and the soup spoons."

"Dessert first, of course. We should all do dessert first. Apple or pumpkin? Or maybe some spice cake with brandy sauce and whipped cream to start?"

The others poured back into the house at her suggestion. Pris couldn't move from Dante's arms. The pressure inside them verged on explosive. He cursed, whether mentally or not she was incapable of telling as his arms tightened around her.

His kiss, when it came, was richer and deeper and more passionate than she had ever dared dream. They were both panting when they came up for air as the shouts inside the house increased. If she didn't get back in there to serve dessert soon. . .

"I need you," Dante whispered urgently. "If you don't return with me, I swear, I will move in here and never leave again."

"Reuben won't like it if you try to excavate bones beneath his man cave," she whispered back, leading him into the house while dodging an aunt, and dragging him into the library. She shut the door and leaned against it.

"A villa *and* a farm," he muttered. "I can't do it. I know nothing of farming. I'm an archeologist! A teacher!"

"A wealthy man," a low contralto said from behind one of the wing chairs.

Ariel. They'd forgotten Ariel. So much for more kisses.

Jax's sister held a notebook computer over the back of the chair.

Pris prevented Dante from reaching for it. "Wealth doesn't matter. *I need to cook.* It's who I am. I am not a caretaker or nanny or any of those warm cuddly things men expect. Italy has more restaurants than people. I'm not needed there."

"Cooking schools. They have cooking schools. You can learn while you feed whatever people need feeding. People always need feeding. Remember the plumbers. You can fix the villa with food, and I'll pay for your school." He reached over and snatched the computer from Ariel.

He studied the website the computer genius had uncovered. "These are the contents of Gladwell's offshore account? It's a bloody fortune, but it's not mine."

"Lucia's," Ariel said succinctly.

"Her farm. Her lotions. Her company. Remember, her name was on everything? Stepdaddy planned to leave her with all the debt while he siphoned the cash into his pockets. And then there's KK's and Lucia's insurance after the dust clears. That's all legit and should cover the company debts at the very least." With a sigh, Pris looked around Dante's muscled arm to study the rather large numbers. Maybe they were in lira. Except Italy did euros these days.

"Stolen artifacts," he added in disgust. "Ill-gotten gains."

"When you find the artifacts, you can buy them back. In the meantime, that's the twin's education right there. You're not really rich when you have kids." Shrugging to hide her spinning emotions, Pris stepped back. "If Lucia's farm has Etruscan artifacts, you'll have your own dig in her backyard."

His whole entire expression and body language brightened as if she'd handed him gold. He returned the device to Ariel. "I can stay home. The twins will go to school *and* have a nanny. Leo can have his orchard. Pris, you can go to school, run a school, come back here, teach kids to run a bakery, or anything you like. If I am my own employer, we can come with you," he added triumphantly.

Scarcely able to tear her gaze from his happiness, Pris settled on studying the tan V of his chest revealed by the open shirt. That didn't help her brain much better. Her heart pounded ferociously while her head tried to deal with all his cascading hopes. "You need a household manager?"

Dante swept her up in his arms again. "I need *you*. I don't care how or why or what you call yourself. I just need you. We'll work out details together."

She nodded against his silky shirt. "That might work."

From the other side of the chair, Ariel snorted.

Thirty-seven: Jax

By midnight, the old Victorian had descended into the usual board-creaking silence as the various inhabitants collapsed in exhaustion from the holiday excess.

Jax knew Evie was still wired and eager in the bed beside him. But this latest encounter with the danger that came with their search for justice had opened emotional channels he wasn't accustomed to exploring. Freaking out didn't come close.

He turned on his side and leaned over to stroke her silky hair to gather the courage to admit, "Sometimes, you and your family terrify me."

In the winter moonlight streaming through the turret windows, she looked briefly panicked. But as she usually did, she spaced out, then rubbed his chest, reading him better than he read himself. "I was afraid today had made you realize you want normal. Instead, you're terrified in the same way you scare me. It's not easy thinking of others beside yourself, is it?"

He breathed a little easier. "It's not just that, although yes, it's a new experience. But you make me feel. . ." He didn't have the words. He unclenched the fist holding him up and produced the crude object he'd been holding. "*Love* just isn't enough to say. Words aren't enough. I use words all the time, but they don't express. . ."

She pushed up on her elbows and covered his face with kisses. "I don't need words. I see auras, remember? Actions work best for me. And I've seen you working hard to adapt to our ways while trying to protect us in your way. That

206

you keep trying instead of giving up says a lot more than words. You were brilliant today. You could have taken Matt down in seconds. You could have had R&R beat him to the pulp he deserved. But you let Pris have her way, and it worked perfectly."

"I would have felt better planting a fist in his face," he grumbled. "So yeah, we're both adjusting. I notice you didn't kick him where it hurts either."

She chuckled and ran her hands over his abs. "Pretty boy wasn't a threat. I think Pris may be a Rainbow child like Loretta and Ariel, hard to understand but a light on the world. It's a good thing we have Sensible Solutions to collect any reward for catching killers so it can be shared. What we do takes a team. It's you who is worrying me. What's on your mind?"

Now or never. . . Jax held out the ugly object in his palm. "I wanted to do this properly, but I couldn't figure out what was proper. You never wear jewelry. Your entire life is a spectacle I can't compete with. I'm a lawyer who likes playing by the rules, whereas I have the feeling you run from anything official. But I'm ready for the next step, and instead of fireworks and beaches and flashy diamonds, this is the only proposal I can think of. Will you please, please marry me so I don't have to gnaw my nails to the nub worrying that you'll run away with the circus?"

Her huge blue eyes widened even more. She studied him first, before studying the embarrassment he held in his palm. "I'm more likely to run *from* this circus than with one." She picked up the silver adorning his palm. "A spoon ring?"

"Pris said someone used the utensil for something other than food and broke the handle off. It's good silver. I just filed the edge and twisted it." He shifted uncomfortably. "The history of spoon rings seemed to sort of fit into your family's culture."

She laughed quietly and held out her left hand. "Servants who stole flatware because they couldn't afford real rings? I think you hit just the right note."

"Without stealing anything," he reminded her, sliding the awkward piece over her finger and squeezing until it fit. "Pris said it was okay to use it. I'll happily buy any ring you want. I just need to give you something *real*. . . Does this mean you accept?"

She reached around his neck and drew him down to her. "It means babies," she warned. "Even if we try not to have them, they will come. It's tradition."

"I'm good with that, especially if it slows you down." Jax kissed her to prevent the protest.

Moonlight glinted off the silver and wrapped them in its glow.

"The spirits are gathering," Evie whispered as he covered her. "Maybe a Christmas wedding?"

At this point, he'd agree to a Martian wedding. He nipped her ear and accepted that his life would never be normal again. As long as he had Evie's arms around him, he could face whatever the future had in store.

MALCOLM FAMILY

Evangeline (Evie) Serena Malcolm Carstairs—sends spirits to light, reads auras
Mavis Malcolm Carstairs—Evie's mother; reads crystal ball
Gracie— Mavis's elder telekinetic daughter
Aster—age 6, Gracie's daughter
Idonea (Iddy)—Evie's cousin, veterinarian who talks to animals
Priscilla Broadhurst—Evie's cousin; telepathic
Loretta Aurora Post—eleven-year-old heiress; sees souls
Aunt Felicia—Mavis's sister; Iddy's mother
Aunt Ellen— Mavis's sister; Pris's mother
Great Aunt Evangeline Valerie Malcolm Brindle—Aunt Val, Civil War re-enactor

BOOK FOUR:

Damon Ives Jackson (Jax)— fraud and family lawyer; Evie's significant other
Ariel Jackson—Jax's sister
Roark LeBlanc—hacker friend, MIT graduate, and former military intelligence

Reuben Thompson, PhD—Roark's partner; engineering degrees from MIT and Duke
Dante Alfonso Ives Rossi—distant Italian cousin of Jax
Emma Malcolm Rossi—Dante's mother
Alessandro (Alex) Gerard Ives Rossi—Dante's 5 year-old son
Arianna (Nan) Iona Malcolm Rossi—Dante's 5 year-old daughter
Lucia Ugazio—Dante's former girlfriend; mother of twins; owner La Bella Gente
Leonardo (Leo) Ugazio—cousin of Lucia; manages her olive oil farm
Katherine (Kit-Kat, KK) Gladwell—Lucia's half-sister; Vincent's daughter; owner La Bella Gente
Vincent Gladwell—Katherine's father
Nicolas Gladwell—Katherine's distant cousin; does marketing for La Bella Gente
Matthew Gladwell—Katherine's brother; officer in La Bella Gente
Rhonda Tart—Vincent's mistress; stockholder in La Bella Gente
Jane Lawson—blogger and reporter
Aunt Margaret—Emma Rossi's ill sister

TOWNSPEOPLE

Mayor Arthur Block—resigned office over land fraud
Sheriff Troy—unmarried, older sheriff of Afterthought
Hank Williams—hardware store owner; town council member; mayoral candidate
Larraine Ward—local fashion designer; mayoral candidate
Philomena Marquette—cop, went to school with Evie
LaWanda—the mayor's eighteen-year-old niece; Jax's new receptionist

The Rainbow Recipe
Patricia Rice

Copyright © 2022 Patricia Rice
Cover design © 2021 Killion Group
First digital edition Book View Café 2022
ISBN: ebook 978-1-63632-078-6
ISBN: print 978-1-63632-079-3

This is a work of fiction. Any references to historical events, real people, or real locales are used fictitiously. Other names, characters, places, and incidents are the product of the author's imagination, and any resemblance to actual events or locales or persons, living or dead, is entirely coincidental.

Published by Rice Enterprises, Dana Point, CA, an affiliate of Book View Café Publishing Cooperative

Book View Café
304 S. Jones Blvd. Suite #2906
Las Vegas NV 89107

About the Author

With several million books in print and *New York Times* and *USA Today's* bestseller lists under her belt, former CPA Patricia Rice is one of romance's hottest authors. Her emotionally-charged contemporary and historical romances have won numerous awards, including the *RT Book Reviews* Reviewers Choice and Career Achievement Awards. Her books have been honored as Romance Writers of America RITA® finalists in the historical, regency and contemporary categories.

A firm believer in happily-ever-after, Patricia Rice is married to her high school sweetheart and has two children. A native of Kentucky and New York, a past resident of North Carolina and Missouri, she currently resides in Southern California, and now does accounting only for herself.

Also by Patricia Rice

THE WEDDING QUESTION

THE WEDDING SURPRISE

School of Magic

LESSONS IN ENCHANTMENT

A BEWITCHING GOVERNESS

AN ILLUSION OF LOVE

THE LIBRARIAN'S SPELL

ENTRANCING THE EARL

CAPTIVATING THE COUNTESS

Psychic Solutions

THE INDIGO SOLUTION

THE GOLDEN PLAN

THE CRYSTAL KEY

THE RAINBOW RECIPE

THE AURA ANSWER

Historical Romance:

American Dream Series

MOON DREAMS

REBEL DREAMS

The Rebellious Sons

WICKED WYCKERLY

DEVILISH MONTAGUE

NOTORIOUS ATHERTON

FORMIDABLE LORD QUENTIN

The Regency Nobles Series

THE GENUINE ARTICLE

THE MARQUESS

ENGLISH HEIRESS

IRISH DUCHESS

Regency Love and Laughter Series

CROSSED IN LOVE

MAD MARIA'S DAUGHTER

ARTFUL DECEPTIONS

ALL A WOMAN WANTS

Rogues & Desperadoes Series

LORD ROGUE

MOONLIGHT AND MEMORIES

SHELTER FROM THE STORM

WAYWARD ANGEL

DENIM AND LACE

CHEYENNES LADY

Dark Lords and Dangerous Ladies Series

LOVE FOREVER AFTER

SILVER ENCHANTRESS

DEVIL'S LADY

DASH OF ENCHANTMENT

INDIGO MOON

Too Hard to Handle

TEXAS LILY

TEXAS ROSE

TEXAS TIGER

TEXAS MOON

Mystic Isle Series

MYSTIC ISLE

MYSTIC GUARDIAN

MYSTIC RIDER

MYSTIC WARRIOR

Mysteries:

Family Genius Series

EVIL GENIUS

UNDERCOVER GENIUS

CYBER GENIUS

TWIN GENIUS

TWISTED GENIUS

About Book View Café

Book View Café Publishing Cooperative (BVC) is an author-owned cooperative of professional writers, publishing in a variety of genres including fantasy, romance, mystery, and science fiction — with 90% of the proceeds going to the authors. Since its debut in 2008, BVC has gained a reputation for producing high-quality ebooks. BVC's ebooks are DRM-free and are distributed around the world. The cooperative is now bringing that same quality to its print editions.

BVC authors include New York Times and USA Today bestsellers as well as winners and nominees of many prestigious awards.

Made in the USA
Las Vegas, NV
03 November 2022

58697688R00125